WINTER DUET

ANNE BARWELL

ECHOES RISING, BOOK 2

A game of cat and mouse across war-torn Europe.

Cover design: © 2020 T.L. Bland
Publishing logo © 2019 T.L. Bland
http://www.thruterryseyes.com/
Cover art is for illustrative purposes only and any person depicted on the cover is a model

Editing: Desi Chapman
Blue Ink Editing, LLC
https://blueinkediting.com/

ISBN: 978-0-9951466-0-0 (epub)

ISBN: 978-0-9951466-1-7 (mobi)
ISBN: 978-0-9951466-2-4 (print)

First Edition published by Dreamspinner Press, 2014
Second Edition published by DSP Publications 2016

AUTHOR'S NOTE:

This is the third edition of Winter Duet. The first and second editions were released by another publishing house. This story has been re-edited, and uses UK spelling to reflect its setting.

Although this story is a world of fiction, it is set against a backdrop of actual places and events. While many of the locations used are real, some liberties have been taken for the sake of a good story.

To my mother who passed away the day after the 3rd edition of book 1 in this series was released. Gone, but never forgotten.

ACKNOWLEDGMENTS

To Susanne for beta reading, all her help with German, and loaning me a fantastic wall map of German that hung from my bookshelf for the month I was working on this story; Reesha for coming on board as beta reader at short notice, and her love for Leo; Lou for beta reading and support; Sharon for always commenting on each new bit as I wrote; and Ann and Elizabeth for beta reading.

To Andreas, thank you for all your help with information about what it would have been like in Germany during that time. To Angela for all her support, encouragement, and the discussion we've shared for so many years—you've been there since the very beginning of this story.

To my writing and reading communities for your support and friendship, in particular RWNZ, and my Facebook groups Anne's Books and Brews, and Kiwi Authors Rainbow Readers. A special thanks to the New Zealand Rainbow Romance Writers group—you guys rock.

Gillian and Emma for all their support, friendship, and awesome accountability.

T.L. Bland for her wonderful cover art.
Desi for editing.
To my family. Love you
And last, but in no way least my friends at Upper Hutt Science Fiction Club and Hutt City Libraries.

Clara Lehrer twisted the loose cotton thread from the hem of her skirt around her finger clockwise and then anticlockwise. The motion was simple enough, but she'd clung to it since the cell door slammed behind her, trapping her in darkness.

She had no idea how much time had passed since she'd been taken into custody. Her captors supplied her with food and water at irregular intervals, and a guard stayed with her while she consumed her meal by the light of a small candle. Clara hadn't bothered trying to make conversation and, to be honest, was quite relieved when none had been forthcoming. She had heard stories from friends in the Resistance about what happened to prisoners of the Gestapo and had seen enough of it firsthand when she'd treated those who escaped.

Her incarceration would be a temporary measure while Herr SS Standartenführer Holm planned his next move. Clara wasn't a valuable prisoner because of her known association with the Resistance, but merely a pawn in a much larger game of chess. Holm wanted Clara's younger brother,

Kristopher, in custody. As soon as Holm had Kristopher or decided she was of no further use, she would be quickly shipped out to a detention camp and probably never seen again.

"Kit, please be safe," she whispered under her breath. If he had any sense, he'd be out of Berlin by now. Kit's world had turned upside down since he made the decision not to allow his work to fall into the wrong hands. While a brilliant scientist, he was sadly naive about how far things had deteriorated as this war progressed.

Clara closed her eyes, remembering the last time she'd seen him. Michel, the undercover Resistance agent, had brought Kit to her, seeking medical attention for the bullet wound in her brother's shoulder. She hadn't missed the way they'd reacted to each other. Kit had strong feelings for Michel, and if she wasn't mistaken, it was mutual. When she'd told Michel to keep an eye on her brother, she hadn't expected that to happen.

She smiled. It wouldn't be only the need to keep his work out of Nazi hands that would motivate Kit to survive this war, but his desire to keep Michel safe.

She shook her head. Unfortunately, knowing Kit, that desire could also work against him. He had a tendency to put himself at risk to protect those he cared about. Although Michel was very capable, he and Kit would need all the help they could get.

The door to Clara's cell swung open. She blinked against the sudden light. To her surprise, Margarete Huber stood framed in the doorway. Her arm was bandaged and in a sling, no doubt from injuries sustained in the recent Allied bombing of the area. The original premises used by the project had been so badly damaged that Holm had relocated with his men to Gestapo Headquarters.

"Fräulein Dr Lehrer." Margarete inclined her head in greeting. She held out her hand. "Allow me to express my apology for the way you've been treated. I can assure you I had no idea you'd been left here."

I'm sure you didn't. Clara took Margarete's hand and allowed herself to be led from the cell. "I hope the man who was brought in with me was not left forgotten," The young Allied soldier had a gunshot wound to his leg. Clara had been assured he would be taken somewhere where he would receive medical treatment.

"Of course not!" Margarete seemed surprised. "He is recovering from surgery and then will be transported to a suitable location." She shook her head. "Our families have known each other since we were children. I am shocked you would think such a thing."

"My apologies," Clara said in the same tone Margarete had used. "These are trying times, and we all find ourselves reacting to things to which we are not accustomed."

Margarete smiled again. Clara suppressed a shiver. She'd never liked Margarete or the way she'd hovered around Kristopher over the past few years despite his continued rejection of her advances.

"Exactly," agreed Margarete. "Herr SS Standarten-führer Holm has asked me to speak with you, as he is busy for the moment." She sighed. "Sadly, we haven't received any word about the whereabouts of your brother or the traitor with him. Finding Herr Dr Lehrer and the information he carries is our priority. We are concerned for his safety."

"All we can do is to continue to hope he *is* safe." Clara wasn't about to confirm or deny whether he and Michel were travelling together.

"Neither is there any word about the escaped prisoners." Margarete led Clara into what appeared to be some kind of office. Two heavily armed SS soldiers stood on duty outside the door. They nodded at Margarete as both women entered. The door remained open behind them. The room had no other exit. "I don't suppose you have any information that could help us find them? Their associate was not particularly forthcoming despite SS Obersturmführer Reiniger's best efforts to ask nicely."

Reiniger was a bully who enjoyed inflicting pain. Clara hoped Palmer hadn't suffered too much.

"No, I don't," Clara replied. Margarete could be asking for one of two reasons. Either Reiniger still hadn't located Matthew Bryant and his men, or they were already in custody and the question was a test of Clara's loyalty to the Third Reich.

"That's a shame," Margarete said softly. She poured a glass of water from the pitcher on the table and handed it to Clara. "It would make things go so much easier for you if you cooperated."

Clara took the glass. "If the reason for your civility is to persuade me to give up my brother, Fräulein Huber, you're wasting your time." Her hand shook, although her voice remained steady. "I have no idea where he is or if he is still alive."

CHAPTER ONE

Kristopher Lehrer peered at himself in the small oval mirror Michel handed him. Although the face looking back at him was his, it gave him a shock to see himself with darker hair. For a moment, he thought he'd seen something of his father in his reflection, but pushed that thought aside. The news of his father's death still hurt, although it hadn't changed the fact they would have never agreed about the decisions Kristopher made before he'd left Berlin.

"It's... different," he said finally.

"That's the idea." Michel Faber ran his fingers through Kristopher's now dark-brown hair and picked up the scissors. "I did like you as a blond, mon cher."

"It will grow out, but hopefully not too soon." Kristopher placed the mirror on his lap and pulled the old towel around him. "Do you think it will be enough? I still look like me."

"The Gestapo are looking for a blond scientist." Michel began cutting Kristopher's hair, altering the length and style into something more appropriate for a man in the German Army. "People see what they expect. Once you're wearing your uniform, and if you don't draw too much attention to yourself, hopefully luck will stay on our side."

"What about you?" Kristopher twisted around to look at Michel when his hand stilled. "You haven't changed your appearance, and Holm and his men know what you look like." Michel's hair was dark blond, and he had striking brown eyes with a hint of green. Kristopher loved Michel's eye colour, especially the way the green seemed to deepen when they made love.

"You're their target, Kit, not me." Michel shook his head. "The files they have on record are for the original Obergefreiter Schmitz. I suspect it is one of the reasons my cover was compromised. Holm was already suspicious, and my identity papers, while good, would not have stood up to scrutiny once he compared them to Schmitz's. We did not look anything alike, and he was a lot younger than me." He shrugged. "We worked with what we had at the time because we had no choice."

"We don't have much of a choice with this either." Kristopher turned around again so Michel could finish the task at hand. "When you're done, I'll trim your hair for you too. It's grown somewhat since we arrived at St. Gertrud's."

They'd been hiding in the attic for over two months, only venturing outside at night, and then not going any further than the pond at the back of the convent. The trip from Alexanderdorf to Switzerland was a long one, fraught with danger. It would be foolish to attempt it before Kristopher's wound was fully healed. They had escaped one close call, shortly after they'd arrived, when SS Obersturmführer Reiniger had searched the convent. In his nightmares, Kristopher saw Michel tortured and heard himself screaming for Reiniger to stop, that he'd tell Holm anything he wanted. He couldn't let that happen.

One life for thousands.

Could he sacrifice the man he loved to save others? He might have to, although he wasn't sure he could. He'd take a bullet himself first, but if he was killed, then Michel's life would also be forfeit. Michel was useful as leverage, as a hostage to ensure Kristopher's cooperation. Nothing more.

Kristopher had always known the weapon potential of the energy source he'd helped design. When he'd joined the project, it hadn't been a priority. After the war began, most believed Germany would soon achieve victory. That and the fact the uranium enrichment was going slower than planned would have made it impossible to get a bomb ready in time to be used. Kristopher still remembered his relief upon that discovery. When had everything changed? Dr Kluge had led him to believe that side of the project had been discarded. Finding the letter in Kluge's papers from the Nazis stating they were working together had woken Kristopher to the reality of the situation.

He should have listened to his nightmares far sooner. Despite Kluge's reassurances, Kristopher should have realised far more money was made available for their research than most were aware of. It had been too easy to stick his head in the sand and chant the mantra to himself that they were working for the advancement of science and the good of the Fatherland.

Once he'd finally had the time and distance to think everything through, he'd realised how much of a fool he'd been. Michel had shaken his head and voiced his disbelief that Kristopher could have been so unaware. Kristopher had found it difficult to admit, not only to himself but to Michel, that he'd *chosen* to be unaware. He had clung to the idea that surely, if such a weapon were built, no one would ever use it. He'd always believed that deep down people were good, but now he wasn't so sure. Although David's warning had been a turning point in Kristopher's life, Michel was right. David—an old friend, and a Jew—had risked his life to reiterate what Kristopher already knew but tried to ignore.

Not only had David disappeared soon afterwards but now Kristopher and Michel were being hunted, both because Kristopher knew the final formulae needed to make the weapon a reality and for a murder they didn't commit.

He bit his lip. If Holm discovered the truth about Kristopher and Michel's relationship, he wouldn't need any excuse to arrest them. One man was not allowed to love another, let alone enter into a sexual relationship. Their slim chance of a future together would drop to zero, as would their life expectancy, if they were sent to a concentration camp.

"You're thinking too much." Michel laid down the scissors, walked around to the front of the chair, and pulled Kristopher into his arms.

Kristopher leaned into Michel, the towel slipping from his shoulders to fall to the floor. "There's a lot to think about," he whispered. "You'd think with the time we've spent here it would stop going around in circles in my head, but it hasn't. Not at all."

"You wouldn't be you if it did." Michel kissed Kristopher's forehead. "I'd hoped you'd at least moved on from your feelings of guilt, but I'd be wasting my time, wouldn't I?"

"Yes." Kristopher didn't see the point in lying.

Spending time in close proximity like this meant they'd got to know each other very well. They'd talked a lot, not only about their hopes and dreams but about their regrets. They both had them. Michel told Kristopher he figured most men their age did, especially with the war going on around them. Too many people had died already, too many good people had given their lives for a cause they believed in. Surely it all couldn't be for nothing?

"The past is done, mon cher." Michel lifted Kristopher's head and kissed him deeply. "We can't change it, but the future is unwritten. That, we do have a chance to influence for the better."

"Is it for the better?" Kristopher caressed Michel's cheek, the stubble of his lover's beard rough under his fingertips. "What happens when we get to Switzerland? What do you think the Allies will do with this weapon once they have it? They're just as desperate to win the war."

"You may be right," Michel admitted. "I really don't know. But all we can do is take this one step at a time. For now, I'm more worried about getting you somewhere safe. The longer we stay here, the more we risk Reiniger deciding to come back. We made him lose face in front of his superior when we left him tied to that tree. He is a man who holds a grudge, and he won't rest until he has the opportunity to take revenge."

"I don't know how you put up with him for all those months you were undercover."

"We all do what needs to be done." Michel smiled and placed his hand over Kristopher's. "Some might wonder how you've put up with me these past months. I'm not always the best of company, and these walls are beginning to make me more than a little claustrophobic."

Kristopher pulled Michel onto his lap and kissed him, cupping the back of his head to hold him close. "Je t'aime, Michel," he whispered when he finally broke the kiss.

"Ich liebe dich auch, Kit." Michel's skin looked flushed. He was breathing heavily. "Do you know what you do to me when you do that?"

"Tell you 'I love you' or kiss you?" Kristopher teased. Michel speaking the same words in German never failed to make Kristopher's breath hitch.

"Both." Michel reached for the buttons on Kristopher's shirt. He shuffled forward on Kristopher's lap, his cock straining against the material of his trousers. Michel groaned. He finished undoing Kristopher's buttons and slid the shirt from his shoulders, kissing across his shoulder and nipping at the skin. "After we leave here, I won't be able to touch you like this. We'll have to be very careful so no one suspects."

"Perhaps one of these safe houses will have a room with a lock?" Kristopher suggested. He ran his hands up and down Michel's back. Whenever they made love, he couldn't help but think it might be their last time together.

He glanced at the trap door, making sure the lock was secure.

"You're still thinking too much." Michel silenced him with another kiss. He pulled Kristopher's undershirt over his head. Michel licked his lips. "You're beautiful," he murmured. He dipped his head and ran his tongue over one of Kristopher's nipples, which hardened under his touch. Kristopher gasped and threaded his fingers through Michel's hair.

"Oh, oh." Kristopher tried to force himself to think, to tell Michel that no, he really wasn't, but couldn't get the words to form.

Michel began to undo Kristopher's belt and then reached for his fly. "I want a future with you. I want to be with you when we're old and grey." Michel closed his eyes for a moment. When he opened them, Kristopher saw a familiar desperation there. "I'm yours. For as long as we have together, I'm yours," Michel promised.

"Touch me. Please." Kristopher yanked Michel's shirt and undershirt from his trousers and caressed the bare skin beneath. "I want you." Michel slipped his fingers beneath Kristopher's undershorts. Kristopher scrunched the material of Michel's shirt with one hand, his knuckles white. "Oh God. There. Yes. Right there."

"Right there?" Michel's voice sounded breathy, barely above a whisper. Kristopher reached for, and fumbled with, the clasp on Michel's belt. Once undone, he yanked down the fly and the white cotton material beneath it.

"I want you. Now." Kristopher began stroking Michel, slowly at first, then speeding up. Michel mirrored the rhythm and touched Kristopher the same way. They both withdrew their hands at the same time and rocked against each other, thrusting, bare skin sliding against bare skin, their movements growing faster.

Kristopher moaned loudly. Michel leaned in and kissed him, muffling the noise, exploring Kristopher's mouth with his tongue. He thrust frantically against Kristopher, his body going rigid as he lost control. Michel broke the kiss and buried his head against Kristopher's shoulder. Kristopher followed a moment later, clinging to Michel, holding him close.

"We've made a bit of a mess," Kristopher said shakily, glancing down.

"Just a little." Michel smiled softly. "I do love you, Kit, with everything I am."

"I know you do," Kristopher whispered. "I love you too." He traced Michel's lips with his fingers. When he smiled like this, it was as though nothing lay between them and Kristopher could see into Michel's very soul. If someone had told him a few short months ago that he'd ever feel like this about someone, he wouldn't have believed them. While not the first time he'd felt sexually attracted to another man, what he and Michel shared was more than lust. It felt too emotional, too deep to be anything but love. He didn't speak the words lightly. They came from his heart.

"You—" Michel's words were lost when a familiar loud creak reverberated through their attic room. Someone was coming up the stairs.

Michel placed one finger over Kristopher's lips to quiet him before slipping off his lap and grabbing a cloth. He dunked it in the basin of water by the wall, squeezed it out, and threw it in Kristopher's direction.

They could not afford to be caught with any clue as to what they'd been doing. Not even by someone they perceived to be a friend.

Another creak sounded a few moments after the first. Two of the stairs leading to the attic were loose—an early warning of someone approaching. Kristopher cleaned himself quickly and yanked his trousers up, ready to dive for the hidden room. He was still fastening them when he heard the lock being opened on the other side of the door.

"Oh Lord, thou hast searched me," Sister Magdalene called out the beginning of the psalm that was their agreed code phrase. Kristopher heaved a sigh of relief.

"I'm sorry," he mouthed. Every time they made love, they risked being discovered. Despite the sisters' work with the Resistance and their support for their "guests" so far, Kristopher did not want to risk a less than favourable reaction to the intimacy he and Michel shared. Emotions tended to run high over a person's beliefs. Hell, Kristopher had been no better about his views on certain subjects until recently.

Michel merely shrugged and shook his head. He refastened his fly and called out in the direction of the door. "My apologies. I'm unlocking it now, Sister." They often locked it from their side too when they were sleeping. Sister Magdalene had suggested it, as it would give them more time to get to the hidden room. The telltale creak of the stairs was easier to miss when not awake. Although the door being locked from the inside would be a giveaway someone might be there, it was better than the alternative, and easy enough to argue the stiff old lock was beyond a woman's strength. She'd told them that for two men, they took a "surprising amount of naps for ones so young."

Sister Magdalene's gaze lingered on Kristopher for a moment, and then she smiled. "Hair gets everywhere when you cut it, doesn't it? It's very sensible of you to remove your shirt before you started, although I wouldn't stay like that for too long. The convent furnace is old and not as efficient as it once was, and February is a cold month. Enjoy the heat while you have it."

Kristopher blinked several times before replying. "Yes, it does, and we will." He was never quite sure how to take Sister Magdalene's comments. How aware was she of what went on under her roof?

"Thank you, Sister." Michel had managed to get his shirt re-tucked, although a few buttons were still undone. "The walnut dye you supplied has worked well."

"It should last a good while too, although you may have to reapply it, depending on how long your journey takes." She glanced at Kristopher. "Take care to keep your beard trimmed, as that will draw attention to the difference between the dye and your natural colour. The equipment is set up to take your photograph. You should have the papers tomorrow. I must admit, I will miss both of you."

"Is there any word of my sister?" Kristopher asked. Sister Magdalene had known Clara when she'd first started working at the hospital and had promised to make discreet inquiries.

"As far as I know, she is still in custody. I'm sorry. Security is very tight around Gestapo Headquarters in Berlin, but I will let you know if I hear anything further before you leave." Sister Magdalene sighed. "I pray for the end of this war every day. Too many lives have been lost and too many families separated."

"Thank you." Kristopher hoped and prayed each day for Clara's safety. He'd been shocked to discover she'd joined the Resistance movement in Berlin. Reiniger had taunted him with the knowledge they had her in custody when he'd tried to get Kristopher to give himself up. But once they captured him, her usefulness would be at an end. The best way to protect her was to evade Holm and his men and to complete what he'd set out to do and get the formulae he carried in his head to the Allies.

"Thank you for everything you've done," Michel said. "We know how much of a risk you take in harbouring us."

Sister Magdalene shrugged. "We do what we can to help those in need, Herr Schmitz. It's what we've always done, and I don't see why we should change that now." She peered at Kristopher. "Your shoulder has healed well. You're moving it much better than you were when you first came to us."

"It is a lot better," Kristopher admitted, "but I get a few twinges with the cold weather." He'd expected that. Although he didn't possess his sister's medical knowledge, he had listened to her talk about her work since he was a child and had picked up information that way. She'd also given him some basic first aid training in case he ever needed it. On the run across Germany disguised as a medic was not the way she'd most likely intended him to use it.

"Unfortunately, none of us have any control over the weather," Sister Magdalene said. "My poor joints are already looking forward to the spring." She turned to go. "Sister Claire has been making bread, so there will be that to go with the soup for supper tonight."

"I'll look forward to it." Michel smiled. "Her bread is delicious."

Sister Magdalene chuckled. "You are very polite. The poor dear means well, and I must admit I've tasted worse."

"So have I," Michel told her, "but the experience was one I'd prefer not to dwell on." He waited until she'd left the room before continuing. "You should change into your uniform, Kit. The sooner the photograph is taken, the better. I'll feel happier once we have your papers."

"Do you think we'll need to leave earlier than we thought?"

Michel shrugged. "There's no reason to think we will, but I'd prefer to have your papers before our transport arrives, in case there are any problems."

"I could be Brother Dominic if there was no choice," Kristopher pointed out, referring to the identity he'd used to flee Berlin.

"We got away with that once. I don't want to risk it again. Holm is no fool, and there would have been a reason he sent Reiniger to search for us here. The Oberfeldwebel who stopped us at the checkpoint might have said something in his report that made Holm suspicious."

"Your papers have the same name on them you were using with Sister Brigit at the Klosterkirche. Isn't that as dangerous?"

"Sister Brigit knows far more than my false identity, so if she is arrested, that is the least of our problems."

Michel shrugged, but Kristopher knew the motion was

to hide his fear that might happen. Sister Brigit had been a good friend to them, and Michel had already lost his brother and a close friend, among others, to this war.

"As with all false papers, they won't stand up to too much scrutiny, but we work with what we have. Yours won't either. Nevertheless, I figured as I already have a set of papers with an identity Holm won't be looking for, it makes sense to use them. That way too, we only had to worry about getting yours."

If they were caught at the convent, any papers would be useless, so there hadn't been a great rush for them until needed. They'd hidden Kristopher's original papers. He'd have to convince their contact in Switzerland of his identity some other way. The formulae in his head would go a long way towards that; he was a valuable commodity.

Kristopher shook his head. He didn't want to think about that right now. One day at a time. He'd told himself that ever since their arrival here. He'd have to deal with the fallout of what he'd done with the Allied authorities soon enough. For now, he and Michel were alive and together, and that was what mattered.

He walked over to the bed and the uniform lying on it. "Let's get this over with," he told Michel. "Very soon I'll be Paul Reichel, and you'll be Michel Werner, and we can't be anyone but two soldiers travelling together to rejoin their unit. This could be the last time we have the luxury of just being us. Let's make the most of it."

Michel silently slipped his arms around Kristopher and rested his head on Kristopher's shoulder. "I like that idea." He turned Kristopher to face him. "Whoever you'll pretend to be or need to be, you'll always be Kit Lehrer to me."

"I'll hold on to that thought." Kristopher smiled. He

caressed Michel's check. "You need a shave, my love. Let me do it for you?"

"After supper?" Michel smiled, a genuine one this time, and his eyes lit up. He'd shaved Kristopher when his shoulder was too sore to do it himself.

"Yes, unless there is something else you'd prefer to do?" Kristopher couldn't help but grin. He nodded at the chessboard set up near the window.

Instead of answering with words, Michel kissed Kristopher, long and deep. When he broke the kiss, he leaned his forehead against Kristopher's, both of them breathing hard.

"I'll take that as a no to the chess, then, hmm?"

"Your reputation as a brilliant man is not without good reason, I see." Michel returned Kristopher's grin, ran his hands over his buttocks, and then let him go. "Get dressed, mon cher." He looked Kristopher up and down and swallowed. "Let's not waste the little time we have."

CHAPTER TWO

"No!" Matt Bryant screamed the word, yet couldn't move. Flames surrounded him. He tried to dive through the heat, but it was like watching from a distance as events unfolded in slow motion.

Someone grabbed him and held him tightly.

"Let go of me," he yelled. "I've got to save him. You've got to let me save him."

The flames burned higher, filling the room with smoke. Matt coughed, his eyes watering, tears flowing down his cheeks.

"It's all right. It's all right," a familiar voice said softly. "You're fine, and so am I. Ssh, Matt."

"Ken?" Matt opened his eyes and shivered. Suddenly instead of the heat, he felt cold. He glanced around the room, confused and disoriented. *What the hell? Where was the fire?*

The dark beckoned him, taunting. He couldn't see anything. All around him felt cold, so cold. Fighting his rising panic, he backed up, trying to escape, but had nowhere to go.

"It's me, Matt. It's Ken. Calm down. You'll wake the others. You were dreaming."

Dreaming? Matt took several deep breaths. He felt something soft under him—a mattress, not the hard floor of a cell or the burning timber of a floor about to give way.

He was in bed, safe, and more importantly Ken was safe.

The bed creaked as Ken got out of it. Matt heard the sound of a striking match, and within moments a small glow illuminated the room.

"You'll start a fire." Matt's voice shook. He stared at the candle.

"I'm holding it. It's fine." Ken Lowe climbed back onto the bed. "I'm going to put the candle on the table by the bed so I can hold you. I won't let anything bad happen. I promise," he said, his voice rough with emotion. He shook his head sadly. "It's the same nightmare, isn't it?"

Matt nodded. The further the distance between the nightmare and reality became, the more he began to feel like himself. "I'm sorry for waking you." He managed a shaky grin. "Perhaps you should have taken Juliane's offer of the couch."

"It didn't look very comfortable, and it seemed foolish not to use a perfectly good bed." Ken brushed his fingers across Matt's cheek, then leaned in, and kissed him gently. "It could be worse. You could be sharing with Liang."

"I'm sure he's happy where he is." Matt shrugged and returned the kiss. "Besides, it's more fun sharing with you. Why do you think I waited for him to take the single bed before weighing the other options?"

Juliane had given them the choice of a single bed, sharing a double, or the couch. Zhou Liang had quickly said he'd take the single bed, and Matt insisted he didn't mind sharing. He'd bunked down with other men before when quarters were sparse and was prepared to make the sacrifice.

A chair jammed under the doorknob sufficed well as a makeshift lock, and he and Ken had been careful to be quiet so no one would suspect they were using the bed for more than sleeping.

It had taken nearly losing each other for them to finally admit what they felt was far deeper than friendship, and Matt intended to make the most of whatever time they had. He wasn't fool enough to think getting out of Germany would be easy. The days he'd spent in Holm's custody had fuelled his determination to never be captured again.

Matt had always had issues with the dark since losing his family in a fire when he was a child. Mostly he'd learned to deal with it, but the trauma he'd experienced at the hands of Holm and his men had brought it all to the surface again. He needed some kind of light when he slept to keep the nightmares at bay, and not even being in Ken's arms seemed to help.

"Either the power went out or the bulb died," Ken told him. "I wasn't aware of it until your nightmare." He shook his head. "This is going to be a problem once we leave here. We can't risk drawing attention to our location by keeping a light burning." He glanced at the heavy curtains. "At least without those we'd have the light of the moon. I'm hoping it will help."

"We could stay here," Matt suggested, half joking.

Ken frowned. "You know that's not an option. Why suggest it?" He'd never been one for realising when someone wasn't serious, and his sense of humour took a bit of getting used to. Matt had only seen it a few times.

"It was a joke." Matt pulled the bedclothes around them

and rested his head on Ken's chest, listening to his heartbeat. "Some of us make those occasionally." He slid his hand under Ken's shirt and stroked his chest. "You're right, though. This is going to be a problem. I'm supposed to be leading this team, not being the hindrance I know I am."

"You *are* leading this team," Ken reminded him. "I'm sure as hell not leader material, and Liang isn't military."

Liang had reminded them of that on more than one occasion. Originally a scientist sent to confirm that the plans they were given were what they claimed to be, his role had since changed to validating Dr Lehrer's formulae. Although his priority was still doing what he could to help save their mission, he needed to keep his head down. Being part Chinese, Liang would not be able to pretend to be German if confronted for his false papers at close quarters. Matt had questioned his superiors' sanity in sending Liang into Germany but had been told others with his knowledge were either too old or already serving their country elsewhere and could not be spared.

Their so-called simple mission had all gone horribly wrong. They were supposed to meet with an undercover Resistance operative and retrieve plans for some catastrophic weapon the Germans were working on. Once Liang confirmed the authenticity of the plans, their team would get them back home. No one had counted on Michel —code name Gabriel—helping one of the scientists working on the project to defect. Not only that, but he and Dr Lehrer had since disappeared, along with the plans. The team's orders were to retrieve the plans first and worry about Lehrer and Michel second, yet from what Juliane had told them, that wasn't an option. Lehrer had the plans in his head as well as the formulae needed to complete them. The last existing paper copy, which had been incomplete and missing the final formulae, had perished in the same bombing that had allowed Matt's team to escape from the institute's holding cells.

"Walker dying wasn't your fault," Matt said. "He was a good man, and he made the decision to stay behind to try and save the prisoners." They'd lost both their enlisted men. Palmer had been arrested along with Clara Lehrer.

"Elise wasn't your fault either." Ken grimaced as soon as the words were out of his mouth. "I'm sorry. You don't need the reminder she's gone."

Matt shrugged. "It's not as though I'm going to forget her." She'd given shelter to Michel and Kristopher, and that bastard Holm had killed her. He tightened his grip on Ken. "She would have liked you. I wish you could have met." He'd told Ken a lot about Elise when he'd finally found the strength to talk about her. Someone needed to keep her memory alive, and if Matt couldn't do it for whatever reason, he wanted Ken to be able to.

"With everything you've told me, I feel as though in some way, I have." Ken ran his fingers through Matt's hair. Ken's breath on him felt warm and comforting. "We cannot stay here any longer. This feeling of safety is an illusion. If Holm or his men find us here, the fact Juliane is his sister won't protect her. We have a mission to complete, and the longer we wait, the less chance we have of finding Lehrer."

"Michel knows the location of the safe house in Freiburg. He has his orders, the same way we do. If he and Lehrer are alive, that's where they'll be heading." Matt had no intention of staying in Berlin any longer than necessary.

"If? According to Juliane's contacts in the Resistance, they *are* still alive." Ken snorted. "I'll feel much better once I can make radio contact with London. Coded messages in half-smoked cigarettes and advertisements in newspapers are far from ideal, and I'm unsure how accurate or up-to-date the information is by the time we get it."

"Clara Lehrer wouldn't be held at Gestapo HQ if her brother was already in custody. Holm wants Lehrer as badly as he wants you." Matt shivered. "I still can't believe Holm blames your dad for his father's death. It was during the last war! People got killed on both sides. The man's driven and dangerous. He comes near you again and I swear I'll kill him myself."

"Matt..."

Matt shifted to look at Ken and shook his head. "I know you made some crazy promise to Juliane not to harm her brother, but I didn't. I'm not arguing over this. It's not open for debate."

"Are you pulling rank on me, *Captain* Bryant?"

"No. I'm stating a fact." Matt sighed. "The weather's clearing, and I've never been a good patient. I guess I'm itching to get back into action again."

"You're a lousy patient," Ken agreed. "At one point I wondered whether I was going to have to tie you to the bed in order to make you rest."

Matt's eyebrows rose. He grinned and ran his hand up Ken's thigh. "It's always the quiet ones," he murmured.

Michel slowly opened one eye, then the other. He peered out the window of the truck. The landscape was much flatter than it had been the last time he'd looked. "You were supposed to wake me once we got past Magdeburg," he told Kit.

"You were tired. I decided to let you sleep, as you didn't do a lot of that last night."

"You didn't either." Michel had found it difficult to settle. His mind kept running over the thought of everything going horribly wrong once they left Alexanderdorf. It wasn't like him at all. When he'd taken on the undercover mission, he'd had no problems sleeping. But then everything had happened so quickly he didn't have time to think before being shoved into the mission despite his inexperience. He was their only choice—his German was good enough, and he'd always had a knack for blending in.

"I slept enough." Kit shrugged. "We can swap seats later. It's been a while since I've had the chance to drive for an extended period of time, and I'm enjoying it." He grinned. "Besides, I like watching you sleep, even if you do snore."

"I don't snore!" Michel grumbled. He glanced at Kit in time to see him raise an eyebrow. "I don't, do I? Papa used to lift the roof when he snored, or so Maman used to tell him loudly over breakfast practically every morning. I never heard it, though."

Kit chuckled, a wistful look on his face. "I wish I could meet your parents. From everything you've told me, it sounds as though you were close."

"Perhaps one day." Michel doubted he'd be able to tell his parents about his and Kit's real relationship, but at least he'd be able to introduce him as a friend. He sighed. His mother would take one look at them together and instantly know the truth. Michel suspected she had already figured out where his interests lay, despite it being something they hadn't discussed. His parents were staunch Catholics, and Michel was never going to provide them with the grandchildren they wanted. After already losing their eldest son, Corin, they were probably more concerned with him surviving this madness and coming home to them once it was over.

"It doesn't hurt to dream, does it?" Kit said softly. "To live in the moments we can but without ignoring reality." He refocused his attention on the road, frowning as he peered into the distance. "There's some kind of roadblock up ahead. Do you think we should risk it?"

"I think we're going to have to." Michel sat bolt upright in his seat. "If they've set one up here, they're going to be monitoring any side roads too. How far are we from the nearest town?"

"We're about ten minutes from Helmstedt, if I remember the map correctly." Kit slowed down minutely. "If we take that route, we can head towards Königslutter and get to Wolfenbüttel that way. Avoid Braunschweig altogether."

"I'm sure you do remember it correctly." Michel had been impressed by the way Kit could look at something and retain it.

Getting out a map now to double check wouldn't be a wise move. Neither would stopping the truck to swap seats. As the driver, Kit would most likely have the initial interaction with the soldiers patrolling the roadblock, rather than deferring to Michel as his immediate superior to carry the conversation. Michel would have far preferred the latter, despite needing to take turns driving with the length of the journey. His false identity was only one step above Kit's in the chain of command, although it was hopefully enough to ensure whoever spoke to them directed most of the questions towards Michel.

"Let's keep to our original route," Michel said finally. "We're not going into Braunschweig itself, just around it, and our cover story makes more sense if we stick to the main roads." Whatever decision they made, they'd have to deal with being stopped at some point. If not here, it would be later.

"It does." Kit sounded thoughtful. "There's something I want to discuss with you once we get past this checkpoint." Braunschweig and Magdeburg were within the same military district, and there hadn't been a checkpoint near Magdeburg. Hopefully this wasn't Holm tightening his net around them. "I've had an idea."

"Is it an idea I'm going to like?" Michel asked. If Kit had any brilliant ideas about doing something to draw attention to himself and away from Michel, like he'd done the last time they'd been in this kind of situation, it wasn't going to happen.

"Oh yes." Kit grinned. "Well, not as much as the idea I had first thing this morning, but it's still something I believe has some potential."

Michel grew warm. "I liked that idea you had this morning," he said. "A lot." For someone who was relatively new to the idea of having sex with another man, Kit was a quick learner and liked to explore possibilities.

"So did I." Kit sighed and grew sombre. "I'm going to miss being able to touch you like that."

The next few minutes passed in silence. Kit slowed down again when they approached the roadblock and came to a complete stop several feet in front of the Oberfeldwebel.

The man walked over to the driver's window. Kit wound it down. "Heil Hitler. Good afternoon, Herr Oberfeldwebel," he said politely.

"Heil Hitler. Travel and identity papers, Gefreiter." The Oberfeldwebel motioned to his men, who went around to the back of the truck. "We are searching all vehicles in the area. Please step out of the truck."

Michel and Kit did as they were told and stood a short distance away from the truck as the soldiers searched it. The Oberfeldwebel and his men were all armed with Walther P38s. If this went badly, they outnumbered Michel and Kit two to one, and Michel didn't want to run for it and find out how good their aim was. The afternoon grew, with the snow falling faster. If they managed to escape, they'd have to find shelter quickly.

One of the Oberfeldwebel's men gestured to him. After the Oberfeldwebel looked inside the back of the truck, the two men exchanged several words, although they spoke too quietly to be understood. He walked back to Kit and Michel and examined their papers before speaking. "Where are you headed, Obergefreiter Werner?" He directed his attention towards Michel this time.

"We're delivering some of our supplies to the garrison at Braunschweig, Herr Oberfeldwebel," Michel told him, taking care to repeat the information in their travel papers. "After that we will be continuing on to Kassel to unload the rest."

"And receive your orders as to what unit to join?" the Oberfeldwebel prompted. Michel nodded. "You'll not make Kassel by nightfall in this weather, although I've heard it's supposed to clear in the next few days."

The plan was to leave the truck and its supplies outside Wolfenbüttel and walk the rest of the way to the safe house.

"Our orders are to either stay in Braunschweig overnight and head out again in the morning, Herr Ober-feldwebel, or take shelter in a town midway between the two. We'll be told which once the supplies are unloaded for Braunschweig."

The Oberfeldwebel nodded. "Remember you'll be in the shadow of the mountains again before too long, and night falls quickly. It is important that the supplies get through to Kassel. The town has been in a bad way since the bombings last year." He glanced at the papers again and then back to Michel, his eyes narrowing for a moment. "It's not only those of us who fight who lose our lives in this war, Herr Obergefreiter."

"I lost my father in the recent bombings in Berlin," Kit said softly.

What was he doing? Michel didn't dare risk letting his reaction show. The Oberfeldwebel had shifted his attention from Kit. They were almost about to be sent on their way.

"My condolences, Gefreiter Reichel," the Oberfeldwebel responded "My brother was one of those recuperating in Kassel when the bombs fell. He didn't survive."

"My condolences, Herr Oberfeldwebel," Kit replied. "We all do what we can to ensure this war ends quickly."

"That we do." The Oberfeldwebel nodded. He handed back their papers. "I wish you well on your journey." He motioned to his men to remove the barrier so the truck could pass through. He saluted. "Heil Hitler."

Michel returned the salute and gave the man a brief nod. "Thank you. Heil Hitler."

"Heil Hitler," Kit echoed, following Michel's lead. He climbed into the truck and started the engine. Michel joined him quickly but did not say anything until the roadblock was well in the distance behind them.

"What was that about?" he asked. "You took an entirely unnecessary risk."

"He appeared to be having second thoughts. I saw him glance at your identity papers again and then at you. I thought it important to connect with him in some way, to reassure him that we were loyal Germans who felt the losses of this war as much as he did."

"He never mentioned he'd lost anyone until you did," Michel pointed out.

Kit shrugged. "You also mentioned Braunschweig, and yet his focus shifted immediately to Kassel. Sister Claire told me about the bombings there last October and that there were a lot of civilian casualties. I figured it was a safe enough assumption."

"We need to have a long talk about your definition of safe, mon cher." Michel shook his head. "He might have taken another look at my papers, but he hadn't re-examined yours."

"Not yet," Kit said evenly. "I did what I thought was necessary."

"*Necessary* is another word like *safe*. I'm wasting my time, aren't I?"

"Probably." Kit brushed one hand against Michel's knee. "I'll be careful. I promise."

If that was supposed to put Michel's mind at ease, it wasn't working. He'd already seen Kit's definition of *careful* in action too, and it was no better than *necessary* or *safe*. "I know you will. That's what worries me."

CHAPTER THREE

———————

Michel grew quiet as they trudged through the snow-covered fields outside Wolfenbüttel, and Kristopher had given up trying to make conversation. Michel needed time to work through whatever troubled him. Kristopher suspected it had something to do with what had happened back at the roadblock, but he wasn't about to ask. In spite of Michel's apparent calm demeanour, he carried an underlying fear that this mission would go horrifyingly wrong and they'd never see each other again.

Nothing Kristopher said seemed to reassure Michel that a successful outcome didn't have to result in a future apart. They'd spoken more than once of what they each wanted, within the limits of what society would allow. Although Michel smiled and nodded, he had a feeling of resignation about him as if he thought fate had already conspired against them and it wouldn't matter what *they* wanted.

Once they'd left the roadblock behind, the next part of their journey had been without incident. It didn't seem long before they reached their destination. Although no one was in sight when they'd left the truck, Michel had assured

Kristopher that Resistance members would be there to collect it shortly and they shouldn't make direct contact with each other. The less information someone had, the less could be tortured out of them.

He and Michel would spend the night at a safe house and continue on in the morning. An ambulance would be waiting for them on the other side of the town. Kristopher would pose as an Army medic, and their cover would be that they were delivering the ambulance to Stuttgart. Once past Stuttgart, they'd continue through the Black Forest and to Freiburg. If the information received through the Resistance was to be trusted, Matt Bryant and his team would meet them there. Michel had made sure Kristopher knew exactly where to find the various safe houses between Alexanderdorf and Switzerland in case they were separated, and he'd given him descriptions of the Allied team. If he had any doubts, he should play it safe and not reveal his true identity. Kristopher had decided, until Michel vouched for them personally, he'd continue in his guise as Paul Reichel and pass himself off as a member of the German Resistance.

He was, in a way, he supposed, so his assumed identity wasn't exactly a lie. While still a loyal German citizen, he wanted to help end this war any way he could. Ironically, the information he carried had the potential to do just that.

Kristopher stuffed his hands into his pockets and sped up his pace a little to keep up with Michel. The temperature had dropped quickly the closer they got to nightfall. He'd never been fond of the cold and would be glad when they reached shelter. His stomach rumbled, a reminder it had been several hours since he'd eaten. Although the food hadn't been what he was used to, they hadn't gone hungry at the convent. He'd heard stories about shortages of food and other items in many cities. Sister Claire loved to talk, and it hadn't taken much prompting to encourage her to fill the gaps in his knowledge about what life was really like for the people of Germany.

He hadn't realised how privileged his life had been until a few short months ago. He'd had his head in the sand about so many things, despite Clara's attempts to educate him.

Clara.

She had to be all right. Kristopher clenched his fists. If Holm hurt her— If Holm hurt Clara, it would be to get to Kristopher. The same way Holm or Reiniger would hurt Michel if they got the opportunity.

The thought of Michel at the mercy of Reiniger more than scared Kristopher; it terrified him. He'd heard enough from Michel about what the man was capable of, although Michel had warned him not to underestimate Holm either. Often the polite, seemingly more civilised men and women were the most dangerous.

A hand on his arm dragged him back to reality. "See that farmhouse?" Michel indicated a building in the distance. "That's where we're heading. I'm looking forward to being somewhere warm." He brushed snow from his coat and studied Kristopher for a moment. "I'm sorry," he said softly.

"For what?"

"I haven't been the best of company." Michel shrugged. "Instead I've sought the company of my own thoughts, and that's not always a good idea."

"It's fine." Kristopher gave Michel a smile. As much as he wanted to give Michel a reassuring hug, it wouldn't be wise. Although they couldn't see anyone watching them, it didn't mean there wasn't. "We've both got our demons to deal with. If you need time to work through yours, I'll give you whatever you need. Remember I am here if you do want to talk, though, hmm?"

"I know, and I appreciate it." Michel squeezed Kristopher's arm before removing his hand. He shifted his duffel more squarely onto his shoulder. "You look tired. It's been a long day, and you did most of the driving." He glanced at the farmhouse and then at Kristopher. "We were supposed to share it."

"You look tired too." Kristopher neatly sidestepped a conversation he didn't want. "These people are taking a risk, giving us shelter. They don't know who we are, do they?"

"No. All they know is we're on the same side. People do what they can, and often the real heroes are those history will never know about." Michel smiled sadly. "We'll sleep in the barn, and if we're discovered, we'll deny they knew we were there. Do you remember the code phrases?"

"Yes." Both of them sounded familiar, but Kristopher couldn't quite place them. It had niggled at him, occupying his thoughts for at least part of the walk here, and a welcome distraction from the cold. "Don't worry, I'll follow your lead and quickly if they don't reply with the correct counterphrase."

"Good." Michel began walking again, Kristopher beside him, as they made their way in silence towards the farmhouse in the distance.

The snow began to fall more heavily as they walked, covering the footsteps they'd made. Now they were closer, Kristopher could make out the farmhouse in more detail. They'd cut across the fields instead of keeping to the main roads, which made for slower progress, but at least it was less likely they'd run into anyone that way. The farmhouse was a decent size, with turreted windows along its roof. The barn backed onto the farmhouse, its larger door more noticeable in the failing light than the smaller one belonging to the dwelling.

"See those windows?" Michel said. "They open into the hayloft, so it's another way out. It's not ideal, but it's better than being trapped."

"Anything is," Kristopher agreed, although he would have preferred to avoid needing either option.

Michel let out a breath once they reached the farmhouse and knocked twice on the door. He stood back slightly and waited for the farmer to answer.

"Hello, who's there?" A man called out the greeting, and the door opened a crack, enough to peer outside.

Michel quickly spoke the code phrase, "Ich träumte von bunten Blumen, so wie sie wohl blühen im Mai." The door opened a little wider.

The man who stood before them was older, perhaps in his sixties. He smiled. "Ich träumte von grünen Wiesen, Von lustigem Vogelgeschrei."

Of course! The puzzle Kristopher had been trying to work through suddenly fell into place, and he hummed the familiar tune. That would be why he hadn't remembered it sooner. He had an eidetic memory, so it was easier to retain what he'd seen rather than something he'd heard.

Both Michel and the old man turned to stare at him, both wearing confused expressions.

A woman's voice sounded behind the man. "Welcome to our home." She came to stand beside him. She looked about the same age as the man, and like him was dressed in worn but neatly mended clothing. "Georg, it's cold outside, and these young men must be freezing."

He opened the door wider and ushered them inside. "I

was about to invite them in, Karolina. You're always rushing me. My old brain takes longer to think than it used to, you know." He grinned at Michel and Kristopher and winked at them when she wasn't looking.

The inside of the house was warm, the woodstove against the wall providing a very welcome heat. "Thank you for your hospitality," Kristopher said. "My name is Paul. This is Gabriel."

They'd decided to use the code name Michel had used with the Resistance when introducing themselves rather than the one on his identity papers. Paul had been Kristopher's father's name so was familiar and one he'd respond to if called.

"Take their coats and let them warm themselves by the fire. You must excuse my husband; he needs a bit of prompting from time to time." Karoline smiled and eyed both of them up and down. "Would you like some supper? I have some leftover Eintopf." Michel opened his mouth as though to protest, but she gave him a look that suggested he'd do no such thing. "Sit down, and I'll get you a bowl each and some bread. I'll not have visitors in this house go hungry."

"I could have sworn that originally started as a question," Kristopher whispered to Michel once she'd left the room.

Georg chuckled. "She's always been like that. It doesn't pay to argue." His expression sobered. "She misses our boy. He's away at the front fighting the war. We pray every day he comes home to us safe and sound once this is all over."

"We'll all be glad when this war is over." Michel warmed his hands over the stove.

"I remember saying that during the last war." Georg sighed and settled into one of the armchairs by the stove.

The other one had a cloth bag sitting on it. He gestured for Kristopher and Michel to move two of the chairs from the table closer to the stove, which they did. "That was a long hard war too. I didn't expect there to be another so soon, at least not in my lifetime."

"There you are." Karolina interrupted the conversation as though there wasn't one. She handed them each a large bowl of thick stew full of beans and, by the smell of it, spicy sausage of some kind. "Eat up, and I'll fetch some bread."

"Spoons might be helpful too, mein Schatz," Georg said with a straight face. Karolina clipped him lightly on the side of the head.

"You could always help me in the kitchen instead of sitting by the stove," she told him.

"I'll come and help." Kristopher put his bowl of stew down carefully on the table by the window and followed her out into the kitchen.

Karolina handed him two spoons and a round of bread. "I heard you humming a tune. It's not one I've heard before."

"It's 'Frühlingstraum' from Schubert's *Winterreise*," Kristopher explained as they walked back into the other room. He was surprised they hadn't heard of it, considering the source of the code phrase they'd used.

Both Karolina and Georg still looked puzzled. So did Michel. "I've heard of Schubert," Michel elaborated, "but I don't know much about him. My uncle played a tune by Schubert on the flute once for me."

"The code phrases you used were from a collection of poems by Müller," Kristopher explained. "Schubert set the poems to music. I was humming the first part of the code phrase." He retrieved the bowl of stew from the table and sat down on one of the chairs. The stew smelled delicious. His stomach growled again, echoing how hungry he was.

"We weren't told where the words came from or what they were," Georg said, "only that they were the way to know for sure that you were who we were expecting." He scratched his head. "It sounds as though you're an educated man, Paul. There's not much opportunity or need for that round here."

"Oh." Kristopher paused, his spoon halfway to his mouth. "I'm sorry. I never thought. I didn't mean to..." The words trailed off. Telling them he hadn't meant to embarrass them would only serve to do that.

"I'd never heard the poems before either." Michel glanced at the door, as though suddenly nervous.

"That's the thing with wars." Karolina paused before continuing. "They draw all sorts of different people together, don't they? It doesn't matter who you are. Out there on the battlefield, everyone's the same, aren't they?"

"Yes, they are." Kristopher swallowed a mouthful of beans while he collected his thoughts. "I was a musician. A long time ago. Sometimes it feels as though in another life-time. I've been trying to work out why the code phrase sounded so familiar. I'm sorry. I guess I should have kept it to myself."

"Nonsense," Georg said briskly. "Don't apologise for having a good education, and if it gives you some distraction to get through this terrible time, you should use it." Karolina placed a hand on Georg's shoulder. He reached up and placed his hand over hers. A sad look crossed her face, and she suddenly appeared a lot older.

Kristopher bit his lip. He lowered his gaze and concentrated on eating. He hadn't meant to upset either of them.

Michel had warned him to keep any conversation brief and focus on very general topics.

Verdammt. He wasn't very good at this at all. For a short time, he'd forgotten their situation and been caught up in the moment, remembering his passion for his music and wanting to share it.

"Paul…" Michel spoke Kristopher's assumed name, and he looked up. "Karolina's right. This war has drawn people together who normally wouldn't have met. Perhaps we should take it as an opportunity to learn new things, hmm? We all have something to offer."

"Well said, Gabriel." Karolina squeezed her husband's hand. "It's been too long since Georg and I had the company of young people. You said you were a musician, Paul. What instrument did you play?"

"I play the violin, although I haven't picked it up in years." Kristopher watched the couple, noticing the way they took comfort from each other's touch. He wanted so badly to be able to lean over and take Michel's hand in his and be open in front of others as to how they felt about each other. During the months spent in the attic at St. Gertrud's, they'd had to be careful, but they'd been left alone for much of the time. He hadn't realised how difficult having to hide their relationship was going to be.

"We're not *that* young," Michel said when Kristopher lapsed into silence again. He'd told Kristopher he'd turned thirty on his last birthday. Kristopher was almost a year younger. Where would both of them be by his next birthday, only a few months away?

Georg chuckled. "You're about the same age as our boy, so to us, that makes you young." He got out of his chair. "I'm going to make some tea. Do you want some? Here, Karolina, have my chair. You're not getting any younger."

"My husband, he thinks he's funny." Karolina gave him a light peck on the cheek and went to clip his ear again, but he ducked out of the way and headed to the kitchen. "He's only offering me *his* chair to keep me away from my knitting. He knows full well I'll poke him with one of my needles if he gives me too much cheek."

"How long have you been married?" Michel seemed amused by their banter. Did it remind him of his parents?

"Since just before the last war." Karolina picked up the cloth bag Kristopher had noticed earlier and settled into the other armchair. She opened the bag and took out yarn and a large knitted square on needles. "We'd met the year before, and I waited for him to come home to me and our newborn son. I didn't allow myself to think he might not. Tell me, do you have someone waiting for you?"

Kristopher glanced at Michel. Karolina wasn't exactly following what he'd been told about keeping to safe subjects either.

"I have someone, yes," Michel confirmed finally. "I want nothing more than this war to finish so we can have a life together, but sometimes I doubt that will ever happen."

"It will." Kristopher placed his bowl on his knee, feeling the warmth of it through his trousers. "When you love someone, you wait for however long it takes."

"You're making these boys uncomfortable, mein Schatz." Georg came back into the room carrying a tray. He handed his wife a cup of steaming liquid and then gave one each to Kristopher and Michel. "I keep telling her to make polite conversation when we have visitors and not to embarrass them. Here, drink this and we'll get you settled for the night."

Karolina glanced at them a couple of times during the conversation that followed, then shifted it onto more neutral topics. She and her husband continued to tease each other, but it was all good-hearted and, Kristopher suspected, done to put him and Michel more at ease. He found himself joining in more despite being careful about what he said. Michel was polite and, after answering Karolina's question, more subdued.

Their meal finished, they followed Georg into the barn, carrying the blankets Karolina had given them. Kristopher had been reluctant to leave the warmth of the house, although the barn was far from cold. Except for one of the cows looking up when they entered, the rest of the livestock didn't take much notice. Perhaps they were used to visitors.

"The loft will be the most comfortable place to sleep," Georg explained, showing them the ladder. "It's nice and warm up there too, and you won't be bothered by any of the animals." He gave them both a nod. "It's been good to have your company this evening, and good luck with the rest of your journey. I'm sure you'll be gone by morning, and there will be no sign you were ever there."

"What about the blankets?" Michel asked.

"Oh, those old things?" Georg winked. "Karolina's always telling me they're not fit to be in the house, so we store them in the loft."

"Thank you," Kristopher said.

"Do your bit to finish the war, and that will be thanks enough." Georg turned around and walked out of the barn, then shut the door behind him without waiting for an answer.

"Let's get up into the loft, and then we can talk." Michel adjusted his duffle bag and the blankets and began to climb the ladder.

"How did you know I wanted to talk?" Kristopher followed him and glanced around the loft. The area wasn't large, but they had plenty of room to arrange straw into some kind of makeshift mattress. Stacked bales of hay stood at the front of loft, preventing anyone entering the barn from catching sight of anything that shouldn't be there.

"When we were in the truck, you said you had an idea you wanted to discuss," Michel reminded him. He began to arrange loose straw into a rectangle shape. "This isn't going to be as comfortable as you're used to, but it's not bad."

"That sounds like the voice of experience."

"I'm a farmer, like Georg and Karolina." Michel used one of the blankets to cover the straw and tucked it in around the edges. "I've spent a few nights sleeping in a barn for various reasons."

"You've only made one mattress." As much as Kristopher wanted to sleep with Michel, being found together would be dangerous.

"It's winter. It makes more sense to share body heat." Michel held out his hand. "Come here." He patted the blanket. "Sit with me."

When Kristopher had done so, Michel leaned in and kissed him slow and deep. He smiled when he broke the kiss.

"I've wanted to do that all evening."

"So have I." Michel sighed. "I'm sorry. I know you felt bad in there." He brushed his fingers against Kristopher's cheek. "Don't ever apologise for being yourself, mon cher." He kept his voice very low, almost a whisper.

"I embarrassed not only our hosts, but you as well." Kristopher leaned into Michel's touch. "I never meant to do that. When I talked about all of that, it never occurred to me you wouldn't know what I was talking about."

"I don't have your education. The teacher we had at the local school taught us what we needed to know, but I never felt the need to go to university. I've only ever wanted to have a farm of my own. I never had any need to think past that. As long as I have the knowledge needed to make that happen..."

"Is that what you still want?"

"Yes, but it's no longer *all* I want." Michel let his hand fall from Kristopher's face. "You could be anything you want. Why would you want a life on a farm?"

"You really think after all this is over I could still be anything I want?" Kristopher didn't believe it for a moment. "After everything I've done?" He shuffled up so his back was against one of the hay bales. "You know what I really want? I want what Karolina and Georg have. I want to be able to be with and marry the person I love and not to have to hide how I feel." Tears formed in his eyes, and he blinked them away. "I want to be able to offer you comfort when you need it and not just when we're alone." He stood up abruptly, walked over to the edge of the loft, and kicked at the straw at his feet. "Verdammt. How can what we have be wrong? It's not. It feels so right. I feel complete when I'm with you, like I was missing something before but never knew it."

"It's not wrong." Michel wrapped his arms around Kristopher from behind. Kristopher hadn't heard him move. Michel could be very silent on his feet when he wanted to be. "I want that too." He rested his head on Kristopher's shoulder.

"Do you think the world will ever change to the point where it won't be a crime to be with the person you love?"

"Honestly?" Michel shrugged. "I don't know. In a perfect world we wouldn't be in this situation. There wouldn't be a war, and..." He shook his head. "Without this war, we probably would have never met. A French farmer and a German scientist. We come from two very different worlds."

"Then we'll have to make a new one with whatever is available to us, won't we?"

"You're an idealist," Michel pointed out.

"Is that a bad thing?" Kristopher asked. "With everything that's happened, I need to believe we have some kind of future, or what's the point? We might as well surrender and give up now."

"That is not going to happen," Michel said. "That bastard Reiniger is not getting his hands on you, no matter what I have to do to prevent it."

"He's not getting his hands on you either." Kristopher took Michel's hand in his and held it tightly.

"We need to survive this war first, don't we?" As much as Kristopher wanted to stay like this and pretend the outside world didn't exist, it was a luxury neither of them could afford.

"First things first," Michel agreed. "Do you want to tell me about your idea?"

"Can we get under the blankets first? I want to hold you while we can still do that."

"Of course." Michel led Kristopher back to what would be their bed for the night. They took off their coats, draped them over themselves, and then arranged the other blankets on top of that. If they were disturbed, it meant everything would be close enough to grab if they had to run. One of the windows was directly above the loft with a few hay bales stacked underneath it. He doubted it was a coincidence.

Once they were lying down facing each other, Kristopher took a few minutes to go over his idea in his head before speaking. "I've always used music to think through things," he explained. "It focuses me, and things tend to fall into place. Even though I haven't played for years, I've hung on to that."

"I thought I heard you humming something while I dozed in the truck," Michel said. He kissed the top of Kristopher's head. "What was it? It sounded rather intense."

"The overture from Mozart's *Magic Flute*." Kristopher grinned. "I must admit you were somewhat of an inspiration for my plan."

Michel laughed. "You haven't heard me play. I haven't touched my flute in a very long time. I can't promise you it will sound magical in any way."

"You haven't heard me play the violin either," Kristopher said. It had been far too long since he'd picked up the instrument, but he could still imagine the feel of the strings under his fingertips and hear his favourite pieces of music in his head. "I'll probably be equally as bad, and we'll have to rethink that duet we promised each other."

"I doubt it." Michel slid his fingers under Kristopher's shirt and played a gentle rhythm against his skin. He snaked his other arm around Kristopher's waist and held him in a loose embrace. "So what exactly is this plan of yours?"

"Can you read music?" It had suddenly occurred to Kristopher that perhaps Michel couldn't and he played by ear.

"Yes. Uncle Brice taught me, although I mostly play by ear."

"Good." Kristopher let out a contented noise when Michel's hand moved lower. "If you keep doing that, I won't be able to focus on telling you my plan. In fact, I won't be able to focus at all."

"Sorry." Michel sounded amused.

The little light they had was fading, although the moon

shone through the window above them, illuminating him enough so Kristopher could see his expression. Georg hadn't offered them a lantern. It wouldn't do for there to be any sign of light coming from the barn when the only residents were supposed to be animals that didn't need one.

"You can help me lose my focus later." Kristopher noticed Michel didn't totally remove his hand but instead moved it higher again. "You feel good."

"So do you." Michel stroked the fine hair on Kristopher's chest. If he took his shirt off, it would very obvious that his hair was no longer its original colour. "Your plan?"

"Oh, right. Yes." Kristopher forced himself to think. "I was thinking about if we get separated."

Michel's embrace tightened. "Yes?" The playful tone in his voice had completely disappeared. "I've already told you where the safe houses are and how to recognise Bryant and his team. You're not to wait for me or to try to find me. Your priority is to get to safety. You're too important to risk capture."

"You've already told me that." Although true, Kristopher was tired of hearing it. "I want there to be a way for us to leave a note for each other, to at least let each other know which of the safe houses we're heading for. I want to be able to know you're all right."

"Leaving a note is dangerous. What if Reiniger or one of his men read it? They'd know exactly where you were heading too."

"Not if the note is in code."

"They'll break it. They're very good at what they do." Michel took a sharp breath and frowned.

"I'm not talking about using words." Kristopher kept his voice light. "We could devise a code that uses musical notation. It wouldn't be difficult, and it's not particularly original. Bach did it, and so did Schumann. We can keep it simple and prearranged. It's easy enough to draw a stave on a piece of paper and clefs, a time signature, and notes on it."

Michel nodded slowly. "If it's not obvious, they might not recognise it for what it is. You say it's been done before?"

"Yes, but we don't need to make it that complicated," Kristopher said as Michel started to relax against him. "We both play instruments that use the treble clef. That's a way of addressing it to each other to start with. A minor key for trouble, a major one could mean everything is fine. If I'm heading to Freiburg, the first note can be F. If I have to resort to another location, I can write another note. As long as we know which location means which note, both of us will be able to read it."

"So perhaps if I wrote something using a treble and a bass clef, you'd know I was all right but Reiniger and his men are close behind so it's not safe to stay?"

"Exactly," Kristopher confirmed. "As long as we know what the code means, we can make it as simple or as complicated as we wish."

"I think it's a brilliant idea." Michel kissed Kristopher softly. "I hope we never have to use it, but I feel happier knowing it's a way open to us if we do."

"There's something else I was reminded of when I figured out where the code phrases came from." Kristopher broke the kiss and traced the outline of Michel's lips with one finger. "There's one line of Müller's poem that reminds me of you, of us. Two lines actually, they're from the final poem, 'Der Leiermann.' I thought they were particularly fitting, as it's winter and he wrote about the wanderer during winter." He met Michel's gaze and smiled. "Wunderlicher Alter, Soll ich mit dir geh'n? Willst zu meinen Liedern Deine Leier dreh'n?"

Michel kissed the tip of Kristopher's finger and nodded slowly. "I want to be a part of your journey, mon cher, and you already play the music to *my* songs."

CHAPTER FOUR

Matt took a moment to stretch and yawn, despite the cramped space in the truck cab. He ignored the amused looks Ken and Liang gave him from either side.

"I'm surprised you're still tired, considering how well you slept." Liang glanced at Ken, who was frowning, and hastily amended his statement. "After you kept both of us awake till late, that is."

"Sorry," Matt said, "but I didn't notice you making your apologies and wanting to sleep either." They'd started off discussing different scenarios to try and salvage the mission, the conversation leading into their hopes as to what they'd do once all of this was over. It had been a clear night, and the stars provided more light than he'd anticipated. He hoped like hell his first night with no nightmares for a while wouldn't be the last, although Ken's frown a few moments ago suggested that maybe Matt hadn't slept as well as he'd thought.

Liang looked away, a slight blush tingeing his features after Matt grinned and winked. "What we talked about last night was personal," Liang grumbled. "It doesn't give you the right to tease me." He shrugged. "Just because I gave a beautiful woman a way to contact me after the war doesn't mean she's actually going to do it."

"Juliane likes you." Ken kept his eyes on the road, having volunteered to drive for the first part of their journey. Once they reached Göttingen, Matt would take over the driving, and they'd decide whether to risk the bigger city of Kassel or head to Bamberg instead. "She's an intelligent woman who knows her own mind. A woman like that appreciates someone she can converse with as an equal."

"I didn't know you were so well-informed about such things," Matt said.

"I'm not, but I'm also not blind." Ken snorted. "Only a fool wouldn't have seen how she looked at him."

"Hmm." Matt frowned. Had he and Ken been careful enough so their feelings for each other weren't obvious? He risked a glance at Ken, but Ken didn't appear to notice, or if he did, he didn't respond.

Liang shifted in his seat. "One thing I'm looking forward to when I get back to England is sleeping in my own bed," he grumbled. "I swear I'm stiff in places I didn't know existed. Tell me again what part of my sanity agreed to this plan of yours?"

"You would have preferred to keep hiding in Berlin until Holm and his men found us?" Matt pulled up the collar of his greatcoat. He didn't feel comfortable at all wearing a German uniform, but it was the safest way to travel, and hopefully there would be fewer questions asked of three German soldiers. Every able-bodied man of their age would be serving his country, unless he had a very good reason not to be. As long as Liang kept his head down and no one looked at him too closely, they might pull this off. They'd taken a detour and gone through Helmstedt instead of Braunschweig, and the Oberfeldwebel at the roadblock there had paid more attention to their papers. Matt had kept his captain's rank in his new identity, or rather the German equivalent, Hauptmann. As senior officer of their party, he'd done all the talking. While Ken's German was passable, he spoke with an accent, unlike Matt, who sounded like a native Berliner despite the fact he'd grown up in Pennsylvania. He'd lived in Berlin for years with Elise before they'd parted ways and he'd returned home. Liang spoke several languages fluently, but the less direct contact he had with anyone who might identify him as part Chinese, the better.

"I'm worried about them finding us *here*," Liang said. "Holm knows what we all look like, and I know full well it would be a miracle if I was able to pass myself off as German if anyone looked too closely."

They'd left Liang in the truck when they'd sought shelter at the safe house the night before, only having him join them once their hosts retired for the night. It was another reason they'd left early that morning. While their contacts were sympathetic to the Resistance, taking unnecessary chances would be pointless.

"We do what we can with what is available to us," Matt said. "I wish I could fix this, but I can't. We're all taking a risk being out here, but sometimes the best place to hide is in plain sight. I'm hoping like hell Holm is more focused on finding Kristopher Lehrer than us."

"Considering we need to find him too, that's not very reassuring." Liang leaned back in his seat and closed his eyes. "Wake me when we reach Göttingen."

"He's scared," Matt said after checking Liang was asleep. "I would be too, in his position." He brushed one hand very briefly against Ken's knee.

"I don't blame him, and I know how he feels." Ken glanced at Matt and smiled in response to the physical contact. "I've spent most of my life scared that someone would find out the truth about me."

Ken's father, who he had never met, had been American. His mother was of Japanese descent and was presently in an internment camp, despite only being half Japanese. She'd insisted her son take his father's name and deny his Japanese grandfather's heritage rather than risk sharing her fate. Luckily Ken took after his father and maternal grandmother in looks, so, unlike Liang, he had no outward sign to indicate anything other than the German soldier he pretended to be.

"I think we've all done that in some shape or form." Matt's relationship with Elise was an example. It had been easier to fool himself that he was in love with his best friend than to admit that, while he did love her, he preferred to share his bed with another man. "I don't think it's going to be that easy to go home and be honest either."

"The important thing is to be able to be honest with each other." Ken waved one hand towards Liang. "I don't think it's a good idea if he finds out the truth about me."

"You can't judge one person on the actions of others," Matt pointed out. "What happened to your mother is wrong, and you can't presume Liang will agree with it." Once they got back to America, he'd see if something could be done to get her out of the camp and somewhere safe. Ken had mentioned she had friends and family in Japan, some of the former having returned there since the government had begun rounding up Japanese-American citizens.

"People don't tend to think logically when their families have been murdered." Ken didn't sound convinced. Liang had shared a little of his background with them during the couple of months they'd hidden at Juliane's. He'd been brought up by his grandparents after losing his parents to the influenza epidemic, and had spoken at length about his beloved grandmother's reaction after hearing about the Japanese massacring the Chinese in Nanking just over six years ago. "I'm not about to test that theory. We need to work together in order to get through this. Why upset him about something neither of us can change?"

"Do you think he suspects anything about us?"

"If he does, he's not saying anything." Ken shrugged. "For now I think it's better we don't confirm any of his suspicions, if he has any. We're in enough trouble without adding to it. He's an intelligent man, and I want to think he wouldn't have an issue with it, but I could be wrong."

"Of course he could be faking sleep and listening to everything we've just said."

Ken slammed on the brakes. Pain screamed through Matt's arm as he was flung forward and collided with the dashboard.

"I was joking." Matt hadn't meant to get Ken so riled up. Matt rubbed at his sore arm. He'd been told his jokes could be painful at times, but this was taking that a little too literally.

"What? Huh?" Liang jerked awake. Luckily he'd been leaning into the door so hadn't hit anything when they'd stopped.

"No! Don't you see that?" Ken ignored Liang's reaction and answered Matt instead. He stared into the rearview mirror and then twisted in his seat to look behind them. He opened the door of the truck and stepped out onto the road.

As soon as the door opened, Matt heard a familiar sound. "Damn," he muttered. He climbed out of the truck and stared up into the sky.

"What are you doing outside the truck?" Liang blinked rapidly and looked around. "What the...? We're still on the road. I thought we must have gone off it."

"Stay here, and get into the driver's seat," Matt ordered. "Be prepared to move the truck if you have to."

When he reached Ken, Ken was pointing back towards Helmstedt. Smoke rose up in a pillar of darkness tinged with red. Not from one source but several. "Do you see it?" His voice shook. "We were just there. Hell, we were just there."

A low-flying plane passed above them, seemingly out of nowhere. Matt instinctively dived for the ground, taking Ken with him. They twisted their heads up, watching the aircraft swoop lower.

"We can't stay here!" Matt dragged Ken back to the truck. The plane's direction could only mean one thing. "The Allies are bombing Helmstedt! We need to get the hell out of here." He'd heard too many stories of raids not only hitting the target but also surrounding areas. It didn't take much for a bomb to go off course, and he wasn't about to stop to find out firsthand whether that would happen now.

A loud explosion sounded in the distance. They were far too close for his liking. They'd already been at ground zero when a bombing had taken place. It wasn't an experience he wanted to repeat anytime soon.

More smoke rose behind them from the town. Liang already had the truck running. Matt and Ken climbed inside. "Drive," Matt told Liang.

"Was that one of ours?" Liang had his fingers wrapped around the steering wheel. His knuckles were white. He put the truck in gear and his foot on the accelerator as soon as Ken slammed the door shut.

"B-24," Matt explained. He'd recognised the engine and seen enough of the Liberator heavy bomber to identify it. "And yes, it's one of ours."

"Then we're lucky we left early." Ken glanced behind them more than once as they drove. "Should we avoid any of the major cities? In case they're getting warmed up?"

"Göttingen should be safe, though?" Liang kept his eyes on the road. His voice was strained. "Surely they wouldn't bomb there? It would be like bombing Oxford or Cambridge!"

"I hope not." Matt came to a decision. "We'll stick to our original plan and head there. Hopefully our contact at the Marienkirche will have an update, but I think we should avoid major cities where we can, as they could be potential targets."

"Just what we needed to round off this perfect mission," Ken muttered. "Not only are we being pursued by the Gestapo, but now our own side is shooting at us as well."

"Bombing, not shooting," Matt said absently. He'd seen the effect of the bombings on the citizens of Berlin. According to reports he'd read, there were airfields and factories involved with the aviation industry in this part of Germany. Any of those could be considered potential targets to disrupt the country's war effort. Where exactly the hell were they? He couldn't remember specifics, and they had no way of contacting London directly. Not that that would be helpful anyway, considering the situation. Warning his team of potential targets wouldn't happen, even in a coded message, and their safety wasn't exactly high on the list of priorities. Matt had gotten that impression with the last lot of messages they'd received. They were on their own.

"I have no intention of reliving what happened in

Berlin, thank you." Liang shuddered. "I was in London during the air raids. That was enough. Some of those bombs came a little too close for comfort, despite being in the supposed safety of a shelter." He glanced at Matt. "So, should I keep heading for Göttingen, or have you changed your mind? I know you were thinking about something. I could see the steam from here."

"I haven't changed my mind," Matt told him. "Once we reach Göttingen, we'll rethink our route. Pull over and swap seats with Ken. With all this going on, we don't want to draw any attention to ourselves, and I don't want you interacting with the Germans any more than is necessary."

"You won't get any arguments from me about that." Liang stopped the truck and climbed out. Ken shuffled over while Liang walked around and got in the passenger side. "All this history going up in flames," he murmured. "They'd better not bomb the university. Jacob and Wilhelm would turn in their graves."

"Who?" Ken started the truck and pulled back out onto the steepening road. The fields on the left side of the road stretched until the hills in the distance. A woman had dismounted her bicycle and now stood at the side of the road watching the smoke rising in the distance.

"The Brothers Grimm," Liang explained. "They taught at the university." He shrugged. "I enjoyed their stories, so I read everything I could find about them."

"I enjoyed their stories too, but I hadn't realised they'd lived here." Ken waved a hand back the way they'd come. "Personally, I'm more worried about getting out of Germany alive and the safety of the people who are here now. Isn't it better to focus on the present, rather than the past?"

Matt raised an eyebrow at the way Ken had phrased his reply but didn't say anything. Perhaps it was a reflection of him working his way through the mixed feelings he had for his father? "Buildings can always be rebuilt. Keeping people safe is more important."

"But your past shapes who you are," Liang argued. "As does what has happened in the lives of those who have influenced you in some way and the people who influenced them, and so on."

"History doesn't always tell the truth, *Dr Zhou*." Ken argued.

"That doesn't mean we should disregard it altogether either, *Sergeant* Lowe."

"Pipe down! Both of you." Matt really wasn't in the mood for one of their arguments. Although for the most part Ken and Liang got on well, there were certain subjects, this being one of them, that he'd hoped they'd figured out they should avoid. Living in close quarters for the past couple of months had been a strain on all of them. Given Ken's touchiness about what Holm had told him about their fathers and the fact both he and Liang were probably as scared as Matt was, this conversation could only continue to go one way.

"We were only voicing our different opinions, *Captain* Bryant." Liang narrowed his eyes and glared at Matt.

Matt met his gaze evenly. "Do it later and somewhere else," he snapped. "We have a couple of hours' drive ahead of us, and I know what both of you are like once you start on this kind of conversation. So don't start."

"We already have," Ken commented mildly. He glanced at Matt and cleared his throat. "Sorry," he mumbled. "Let's enjoy the countryside while it's still there to enjoy, shall we?"

Matt cringed. A comment like that really wasn't helpful and would only serve to provoke Liang further. "Ken..." he warned.

"Fine." Liang crossed his arms and leaned back in his seat. "I'll go back to sleep and let you continue your conversation. Wake me if we get hit by a bomb."

"I'll be sure to." Ken rolled his eyes. "You don't really think he was listening to our conversation before, do you?" he asked once Liang appeared to have drifted off into a fitful sleep.

"Probably not."

More likely Liang was being sarcastic. After all, it was a logical assumption they would have been talking about something, right?

"Only probably? Great." Ken glanced over at Liang. "One day that man will realise why we have a chain of command and not argue with everything that sounds even slightly like an order."

"We need him," Matt reminded Ken. "He's part of this team for a reason, unless you've got a couple of PhDs you forgot to tell me about?" He managed a half smile. "Look, we're all scared, and this mission is quickly going to hell in a handbasket. We're military, he's not. It's a long way from university professor to this."

"I need *you*," Ken murmured. "We've all come a long way since this started. I know Liang's a good man. I couldn't have rescued you without him. Let's focus on what needs doing and one day at a time, all right? This mission stopped following protocol the minute I ignored London's directive that rescuing you wasn't a priority."

"Thanks. I was successfully ignoring they'd said that until now." Matt tried to make a joke of it, but it didn't change the truth. None of them were indispensable, and they were in the middle of a war zone. "For now it's only the three of us, and until that changes, we have to bury our differences and work together as a team."

"Liang and I have to bury our differences, you mean." Ken gave a mock salute. "Yes, sir, I'll try my best, sir." He grinned, an almost smirk that suggested he wasn't being serious in the slightest.

Matt laughed. He glanced over at Liang again, making sure he was asleep, and then leaned over and whispered in Ken's ear. "There are a lot of reasons I love you, you know."

"Yes, I know." Ken smiled. "There are a lot of reasons I feel that way about you too."

CHAPTER FIVE

"Wake up, Kit! Wake up!"

Kristopher jerked awake with a start. Michel leant over him, his expression grim. "What's wrong? What's happened?"

They'd been in Feuerbach less than twenty-four hours. Surely Reiniger hadn't found them already?

Before Michel could answer, a loud explosion sounded nearby. Kristopher got to his feet immediately, reaching for his gun, his eyes adjusting to the dim light of the flashlight Michel held. The wooden beams groaned. The building shook. Dust fell from the ceiling. He grabbed his satchel, not wanting to leave it behind.

"Bombing raid," Michel said, already on the stairs of the apartment building, heading outside. Kristopher was only a couple of steps behind him. The wailing of sirens echoed around them. "We need to get out of here."

Outside, people were running. A woman screamed. A baby's wail filled the air. The top story of the building next door was gone, rubble lying in the street in big chunks.

Engines roared. Something swooped low above them.

Kristopher ducked. Michel grabbed him and dived, both of them hitting the ground and landing in the snow.

Kristopher coughed. He wiped wet snow from his face and shivered. Luckily he'd slept in his coat and boots. Smoke filled the air. "The river," he gasped. "We need to get to the river." Someone had mentioned a tower shelter by the Feuerbach River the previous evening.

The ground moved, or seemed to, as another explosion lit up the sky, this time in the distance, from the centre of Stuttgart itself. "Can you walk?" Michel helped Kristopher as he struggled to his feet.

"I'm fine," Kristopher reassured him. "You?"

"Yes." Michel retrieved the flashlight from the ground. It lit up for a moment, and then they were plunged into blackness. "Verdammt!" Michel shook it and switched it off, then on, but nothing happened. He shoved it into the pocket of his coat and glanced around. The streetlights were off—they would have been extinguished at the first sign of attack. All they had for light was the waning crescent moon above them and the fires burning as the aircraft dropped their bombs.

"What about the ambulance?" Kristopher suggested. They'd left it parked out of sight but nearby.

"I'm more worried about us surviving this than the ambulance." Michel gazed up at the sky. "I think the river is this way. We can't stay here."

"I don't remember where on the river the shelter is," Kristopher admitted.

A boy pushed past them. He couldn't have been more than seven or eight years old. "The shelter's this way," he yelled. "Follow me."

Kristopher hesitated. What if the boy was wrong? And even if he wasn't, he might lead them into more of this.

"We don't have a choice," Michel pointed out. "Keep close to me. I don't want to lose you in this." He began to run, Kristopher close behind, his eyes adjusting to the dim light.

The boy tripped and went sprawling. Michel stopped just in time before he too lost his footing.

"Oomph," Kristopher grunted when he ran into Michel. "What happened?"

The boy groaned loudly. Michel pulled out his flashlight and tried it again. Light shone from it, barely enough to see by, but it would have to do. Remains of a shattered chimney from a nearby house were spread across the ground ahead of them. The boy lay next to one of the larger pieces, half on top of it. In his haste and with the lack of light he wouldn't have seen it until it was too late.

Kristopher dropped to his knees and examined the boy. His eyes were glazed over, and he flinched when Kristopher touched him. "He must have hit his head when he fell," Kristopher brought his hand away from the boy's temple. It was covered in blood. "He needs help. I can't do much for him here, apart from try to stop the bleeding." He quickly opened his satchel and pulled out a short length of bandage, bundled it into a wad, and held it against the wound. Although applying pressure probably wouldn't be enough to stop the bleeding, it was better than doing nothing. Head wounds tended to bleed, didn't they? It didn't mean it *was* something serious, but it could be.

He let out a quick breath. Verdammt. He wished he'd paid more attention when he'd watched Clara at work. Why had he agreed to disguise himself as a medic? He was next to useless.

"We can't stay here," Michel said. "Can you tie something around the bandage so it keeps the pressure on it when we move him?"

"Keep holding the bandage against the wound while I look." Kristopher searched around in his bag, ripped some more of the bandaging material, and tied it quickly. His hands shook, but at least there didn't seem to be any blood seeping through the original cloth he'd put over the wound. "I think that should hold it for now."

Michel handed Kristopher the flashlight and then lifted the boy into his arms. "What's your name?" he asked softly when the boy opened his eyes and looked up at him.

"Fritz," the boy replied, his voice wavering. He put his arms around Michel's neck and clung to him. Thankfully, he seemed more alert than he had a few moments before.

"Hello, Fritz. I'm Michel, and this is Paul. We're going to keep you safe, I promise."

"You promise?" Fritz had lost his earlier confidence. "I didn't think it was so dark. I know this place. I shouldn't have tripped." He glared at the ground. "Stupid thing. Stupid, stupid. Everything looks different." He sniffled loudly and wiped one dirty hand over his face.

"Do you remember the way to the shelter, Fritz?" Kristopher asked. Michel watched Fritz carefully, holding the boy close to him. His grip had tightened at the first sign of Fritz's distress.

"I don't need to put you down," Michel reassured Fritz. "You can still guide us while I'm holding you."

"I don't want to walk." Fritz bit his lip. He looked around and then pointed to a street to their left. "If we go down there, it's only about ten minutes away."

They'd never reach the shelter in time before it closed.

"There isn't one closer?" Michel asked.

"It's the one I know about," Fritz said, somewhat defensively. "Mutter told me if something happened I should go to it."

"Where's your mother now?" Kristopher asked. The light from the flashlight was dying quickly. They had to hurry.

"I don't know. She went to get my baby sister, but she never came downstairs." Fritz stuck his chin out. "I waited like she told me, even when I heard the loud noises and people crying."

"You live around here?" Kristopher hoped Fritz's family had survived this. They'd have to try and reunite them or at least find someone who could look after him before they left Stuttgart.

Fritz nodded. Whatever his wound, it had to be superficial or he wouldn't be talking as much as he was. "I went looking for her, and I couldn't find her."

"You sound much better. Do you think you could walk?" Michel asked.

"I don't want to lose you and Paul too." Fritz let Michel put him down and then placed one small hand in Michel's.

"You won't lose us," Michel promised. "Keep holding my hand, and Paul will look after the flashlight. We can work together."

"Michel's very good at working together," Kristopher told Fritz. He shone the flashlight around. The further out into the street they got, the more rubble there was. It wasn't safe to move too quickly, and at this speed they'd never reach the shelter before daylight. He glanced up at the sky. Most of the flashes of light now seemed focused on the city centre. "I'm wondering if it's safer to stay here but get as far away from the buildings as we can and wait for daylight."

"We don't know how long this raid is going to last, but we need to make a decision." Something creaked and groaned to the side of them. "Move!" Michel yelled. He picked up Fritz and ran back the way they'd come. Kristopher didn't stop to see what was going on behind him. He followed.

Moments later, more rubble hit the street where they'd just been standing. If they'd stayed there, they would have been buried in it.

Kristopher shone the flashlight on it and shivered. "I think finding the shelter is the least of our problems. We need to get out into the open. It's not only more bombings that could kill us, but the buildings that are already damaged."

"I know a place," Fritz said after Michel put him down. "I'll show you." He took hold of Michel's hand again. "You and Paul are soldiers." He pointed to the red cross on Kristopher's arm. "You'll stay and help look after all the hurt people, won't you? Vater is a soldier too. He's fighting at the front. Mutter says he's very brave."

"Yes, we'll stay and help." Michel reassured him before Kristopher could say anything. He squeezed Fritz's hand. "We'll also help you find your mother, or at least someone who can look after you." He looked over at Kristopher and gave him a questioning look.

"Of course we will." Kristopher wondered why Michel felt he'd had to ask.

Michel stood upright and stretched. He couldn't believe he'd been clearing rubble for a couple of hours already. Kit and Michel had split up for most of the day. Kit figured wearing the red cross on his sleeve meant he had a responsibility to at least try to help the injured, and more of them had been brought in as the day progressed. They'd taken Fritz to the hospital as soon as it was light in the hope his mother might look there for him. Nothing was left of Fritz's home, and none of his neighbours had seen her. Fritz's lower lip had trembled, and he'd clung to Michel, refusing to stay with the woman who had offered to look after him.

Kit had volunteered to help where he could at the hospital, and Michel had joined those working out in the streets. Kit's decision also meant he was working behind the scenes rather than out in the open where he might draw unwarranted attention to himself. He'd probably not thought of it like that, and Michel hadn't been about to tell him. If Kit thought someone desperately needed help, he'd do what was needed without giving his own safety a second thought. At least Kit had been able to persuade Fritz to stay near the hospital. Given the instability of the bombed buildings, the streets were far from safe, and no place for a child.

"There's someone under here!" Michel yelled. "Help me get her free." He picked up a couple more of the smaller bits of rubble and threw them to one side. The woman's hand—he'd guessed it to be a woman because of the size of it—twitched again.

"Where?" Kurt reached his side in an instant. The German soldier had been travelling in the opposite direction to Kassel to rejoin his unit, and also taken shelter in Feuerbach. Michel and Kit had met him the evening before. He'd sounded friendly enough and insisted they meet for a beer, although he'd had asked a lot of questions. They'd had to work hard to maintain their covers.

"There!" Michel pointed to the spot and continued to dig her free. If she was still breathing, they didn't have time to waste. He shivered in spite of the sweat he'd worked up during the physical exertion of the past couple of hours. The thought of someone buried under there, trapped and knowing they'd probably die…It wasn't something he ever wanted to think about.

"I'll take one side; you take the other." Kurt began to clear the rubble on the other side. "Poor soul. She must have been standing close to the building when it collapsed." He wiped sweat from his brow, his light brown close-cropped hair also damp with perspiration. "This is an awful business, isn't it?"

"War is an awful business," Michel said between breaths. He didn't want to get into conversation with this man, and it didn't seem right to exchange small talk, given the situation. One more heave and a good-sized rock came away. Michel lost his balance and would have fallen, but Kurt steadied him in time.

"I can see her face!" Kurt exclaimed. He pulled away smaller rocks, each one revealing more of the woman trapped underneath. Michel clambered over the rocks to her side, intent on speaking to her, reassuring her that they were working quickly and she'd be out of there soon.

He brushed dirt from her face. And froze. Unseeing eyes stared up at him, her expression one of horror. He felt frantically for a pulse. There was none.

"Mon Dieu," he whispered, instinctively making the sign of the cross.

"Michel?"

Michel spun at the sound of Kurt's voice behind him. *Oh God. But how could this be?* He'd seen her finger twitch. He was sure of it. His stomach heaved, and he tasted bile. He heard Kurt speak again, but it seemed to come from a distance.

"She's dead," Michel said numbly. Had the movement he'd seen been imagination, hope, or a mix of the two?

"She's been dead for some time. She's cold and already stiff," Kurt reassured him. "It was probably instant, so she wouldn't have suffered," he added when Michel made a choking noise. He was watching Michel intently, a mix of concern and curiosity on his face.

Not just curiosity but something much darker. Anger? Suspicion?

Michel forced himself to think back. Had he done something he shouldn't? He replayed the moment in his mind and froze.

Mon Dieu.

He repeated the words in his mind, unable to believe what he'd done. He hadn't thought, just reacted, his false identity forgotten for one dreadful moment. After all these months of schooling himself to speak only German unless he and Kit were alone, how could he have been so stupid? Not only to slip into his native tongue, but in front of a German soldier.

"We should get help," he said finally. He had to get to the hospital to warn Kit. If Kurt had overheard, how long would it be before he reported it to the authorities? If he suspected Michel wasn't who he claimed to be, Kit was also in danger. He could be arrested for being a collaborator. Kurt knew the two men were travelling together and had remarked on the fact they were friends. Apparently, although they'd managed to maintain their cover identities, they hadn't been as successful in hiding their relationship. Better to pass it off as friendship than what it truly was, Michel had decided, so he hadn't denied it. Neither had Kit.

"It's a little late for that, but we need to arrange for the body to be moved." Kurt peered at the woman, taking a closer look. "I wonder if she's the missing mother of that boy you found last night."

"I hope not." Michel's heart beat fast, and his skin felt clammy, yet he forced himself to sound calm. He had to stay in control and appear as though nothing had happened. With any luck Kurt hadn't heard him and merely noticed Michel's reaction to finding her. "I apologise for my reaction. You'd think I'd be used to death by now."

"This isn't a battlefield, and she isn't a soldier." Kurt's expression softened before becoming angry. "She's a civilian who should have been safe in her own home! We're fighting to keep the Fatherland safe from our enemies, but some days I wonder how futile it all is." He stood upright. "Stay here and continue the job we've started. I will go for help."

He was gone before Michel had a chance to protest.

Merde! If Michel left now, it would only further Kurt's suspicions, if he had any. Perhaps he hadn't heard anything? He hadn't immediately pulled his gun on Michel, so that was a good sign. Still, he and Kit needed to move on.

He glanced at the dead woman again and sent a silent prayer that she wasn't Fritz's mother. Fritz had a baby sister. Michel swallowed. Surely another body wasn't under all of that?

If so, he had to find it. Even if the child was dead, she couldn't be separated from her mother. Michel hadn't found the woman in time. At least he could make sure her child, if she had one, wasn't alone.

"I'm from Berlin. Why?" Kristopher noted the number of rolls of cotton gauze left on the shelf and added it to the list of supplies he was checking while waiting for an answer.

"You didn't mention it last night," Kurt said, "and I was curious." He shrugged. "You know how it is. Things occur to you after a conversation, and then they sit in your brain and niggle at you."

"You didn't ask me last night." Kristopher glanced at the patient in the bed to his left when she groaned in pain. He frowned, walked over to her, and held his hand against her forehead. Her fever was still high. "Where are you from? You didn't mention it either."

"Hamburg," Kurt told him. He'd followed Kristopher over to the bed. "Have you been there?"

Kristopher shook his head. He reached for the cloth hanging over the side of the bowl on the table by the bed, rinsed it out in the cool water, and gently wiped across her brow. "My family didn't travel much. My father was busy with work and never saw the point in it. There are better ways of being introduced to one's country than fighting a war." He allowed some of the wistfulness he truly felt to enter into his voice. "I wish I could have had more opportunity to see it before now, especially now that so much of it has been damaged or destroyed."

"That's a shame. What—"

The woman groaned again. Where was Dr Osterhagen? The medicine she'd been given earlier didn't appear to be easing her pain, and Kristopher wasn't sure what else to do. Speaking to her softly had reassured her before. Maybe it would again? "I'm sorry, Kurt, but I am rather busy. Do you want to talk more later?"

Although he had hardly any experience, he'd found that he'd picked up a lot more than he thought from watching Clara work and the little she'd taught him. Dr Osterhagen seemed happy to have an extra pair of hands and had set Kristopher to work taking inventory, making beds, and anything else that didn't require a lot of medical knowledge. Many field medics hadn't received much in the way of training, and Kristopher was not about to put patients at risk by pretending to know more than he did. Dr Osterhagen was getting on in years and had retired from practicing medicine more than ten years ago. Other men and women had also come forward to do what they could. With the number of victims growing as those who were able-bodied cleared away whatever rubble they could, the current staffing levels at the hospital were not enough.

Help was on its way, but it would take a while to get there. News was coming in about daytime raids over Hannover, Braunschweig, and other cities.

People were scared, and frankly, Kristopher didn't blame them. He was too.

"Later is fine. I must get back to work now." Kurt nodded and walked away. The man's behaviour seemed more than a little odd, and the way he studied Kristopher, unnerving. Kurt and Michel had both volunteered to help clear the rubble from the streets. Kristopher hadn't seen since either of them since earlier that morning until Kurt had shown up at the hospital.

A moment's panic rushed through him, but he shrugged it off. If something had happened to Michel, Kurt would hardly be wasting time asking Kristopher which part of Germany he was from.

A tug on his sleeve made him look down. "Hello, Fritz."

The boy had taken to following either Kristopher or Michel around since they'd found him. They'd had no luck in locating his mother or sister, but Kristopher held out hope they would soon. Although the bombings had stopped, there was chaos everywhere, and many children had been separated from their families.

"Michel hasn't come back yet," Fritz said. Michel had refused to let Fritz go with him to help clear rubble. "Can I stay here and watch you for a while? I promise I won't be in the way."

Kristopher sighed and crouched down so he was on the same level as Fritz before he spoke to the boy. "I'm not sure this is a good place to be. There are a lot of hurt people here, and some of what you'll see won't be very pleasant." He'd been at Clara's clinic one day when a patient was brought in and felt faint when he'd seen all the blood. His stomach had churned despite his best intentions to be brave and not let it affect him. He'd been about the same age as Fritz.

Twenty years later and he'd had the same reaction when he'd seen some of the injuries brought in during the past few hours. He'd asked Clara once how she'd got used to it. She'd replied that she hadn't and hoped she never would. She was able to hide it better than he did because she had more practice.

"I don't want to be by myself." Fritz looked at Kristopher with pleading eyes. "I still haven't found Mutter, and you promised you'd help."

"Yes, we did." Kristopher hoped they could find Fritz's mother. Michel had spoken to Gretchen, the woman who had taken a lot of the lost children under her wing, but Fritz refused to stay with her.

"Gefreiter Reichel?"

Two men approached. A cold chill crawled up Kristopher's spine when he noticed the metal gorgets they wore around their necks and the patch on their uniforms that signified they were part of the Feldgendarmerie. He addressed the more senior of the Feldgendarme in what he hoped was a calm tone. "Yes, I'm Gefreiter Reichel. How can I be of assistance, Herr Oberleutnant?"

"I need to see your identity and travel papers." The man held out his hand.

"I can assure you everything is in order, Herr Oberleutnant." Kristopher retrieved the papers from his pocket and handed them over. This wasn't a simple check of paperwork. They'd sought him out specifically and asked for him by name.

Fritz edged away out of the corner of his eye. He didn't leave the room but instead hung around the doorway. The ward had two exits, one at either end. The Oberleutnant and the Unteroffizier with him were both armed. Kristopher didn't think much of his chances of reaching either door if they decided to arrest him.

The Oberleutnant studied the papers and then Kristopher.

Stay calm. Act like there is nothing wrong.

Kristopher silently repeated the words. He'd been told to try to avoid close scrutiny of his papers. Although they were a good forgery, they were only that. His palms were sweaty. He fought the urge to wipe them on his trousers.

"Everything is in order," the Oberleutnant said finally. He returned the papers. "Carry on with your work, Gefreiter."

"Thank you, Herr Oberleutnant." Kristopher gave a brisk salute. "Heil Hitler."

"Heil Hitler." The Oberleutnant returned the salute, and both men walked away.

Maybe it had been a routine check, after all? Kristopher took a deep breath. He was shaking. With the destruction around them and his efforts to help the injured, for a few hours he'd almost forgotten the reality of his situation. He was still German and a man trying to help his people. Disagreeing with what the Nazis were doing did not make him any less determined to fight for his country. He wanted this war to end. His people had already suffered enough.

"Paul?"

Kristopher heaved a sigh of relief at the familiar voice behind him. "Michel."

"What's wrong?" Michel looked pale and had an edge to his voice Kristopher hadn't heard since they'd confronted Reiniger and Müller in the park in Berlin. "You look shaken. Did something happen?" He glanced around nervously. Fritz hovered by the doorway; he'd kept his distance since the Feldgendarme had entered the room. Michel saw him and gave him a smile. He had entered the room by the other door and in doing so most likely missed passing the Feldgendarme on their way out.

"I was asked for my papers. The Oberleutnant seemed satisfied with them. It was probably routine."

"I hope so." Michel lowered his voice. "Be careful." A flash of fear and anger crossed his face. "I slipped up earlier, and I don't want you to pay the price for it."

"Slipped up how?" Kristopher followed Michel's lead and kept his voice low. He grabbed the clipboard he'd been writing on before and pretended to show Michel what was written on it. At least that way they had an excuse to be speaking quietly to each other if someone asked.

"I think Kurt heard me speak French." Michel mouthed the last word rather than speaking it aloud.

Kristopher frowned. "What happened? You're usually more careful than that." Michel only spoke French when they were alone.

"I found a woman's body under the rubble. I thought she was alive but..." Michel trailed off. He bit his lip.

"She wasn't?" Kristopher glanced at Fritz, not wanting to put the thought into words.

"No. It wasn't his mother. Someone identified the body. I didn't..." Michel took a deep breath. "I didn't have to tell Fritz what had happened."

Kristopher wished he could pull Michel into an embrace and hold him tightly. "No wonder you—" He stopped himself in time from saying the words. "And you're worried about me being shaken?"

Michel shrugged. "Did anything else happen, anything that might suggest a reason why the Feldgendarme wanted to see your papers?"

"I don't think so." Kristopher thought for a moment. "Kurt came to see me shortly beforehand." He'd nearly forgotten their conversation in the light of everything else. "He asked me what part of Germany I came from."

"What did you tell him?"

"The truth, of course." Kristopher laid his hand on Michel's arm briefly when his eyes widened. "Relax. I told him I'm from Berlin." He was hardly likely to tell Kurt the whole truth. "Do you think he did overhear you?"

"I don't know." Michel glanced around again. Dr Osterhagen was walking towards them. "I'm not taking any chances. It's too much of a coincidence that he spoke to you and then you were asked for your papers. We need to leave."

Kristopher nodded his agreement. "After my shift here is finished. If I leave now, it will raise suspicion, and if we're going to leave, we want a head start before anyone realises we are gone. *If* Kurt has spoken to the Feldgendarmerie, they will be looking for you. Kurt knows we are friends and have been travelling together. It makes sense that the Feldgendarme would want to check my papers." He looked up, gave Dr Osterhagen a smile as he came closer, and continued quickly before the doctor was near enough to overhear. "Go ensure we have a vehicle that is in one piece and works. I'll meet you there as soon as I can."

"Paul..." Michel looked as though he was going to protest, but Kristopher shook his head. If the Feldgendarmerie were looking for Michel, he needed to get away from here as soon as possible.

"Ah, Herr Dr Osterhagen," Kristopher said, changing the subject before Michel could protest further. "I wanted to ask you about a patient and whether you could do anything to help with the pain." He indicated the woman who had been groaning in her sleep. Although she'd had her bandages changed fairly recently, blood was already beginning to seep through them. Given her fever and remembering what Clara had told him, were the woman's wounds infected?

"Let's take a look, and you can tell me what you've observed, hmm?" Dr Osterhagen walked over to the cot, his brows furrowing in thought. He was a pleasant man but hadn't asked too many questions, for which Kristopher was thankful. Dr Osterhagen also appeared to truly care about his patients, often showing frustration over how little he could actually do for them given the lack of facilities and medicine.

Michel stepped back out of the way as soon as Kristopher and Dr Osterhagen began speaking. After a few moments, he slipped out of the room.

Kristopher had only an hour left of his shift. He could do this. Images went through his mind of Michel in handcuffs and flanked by the Oberleutnant and his men.

He shivered.

"Paul?" Dr Osterhagen was looking at him, a concerned expression on his face. "Do you need to take a break? You're distracted." He sighed. "It's difficult being around all this, I know. Pain and suffering is never easy to watch, no matter what the cause."

"I'm sorry, Herr Doktor." Kristopher forced himself to focus. He would miss Dr Osterhagen, although they hadn't known each other long. "It's not easy," he admitted. "I lost my father during the bombings in Berlin, and I wasn't there for him." Although he and his father hadn't agreed on much near the end, Kristopher still loved and respected him. Paul Lehrer had always done what he'd thought was right. Seeing the results of a bombing raid up close like this brought home what it must have been like in Berlin. He hoped his father hadn't suffered, that his end had come quickly and without too much pain.

"It isn't easy when you can't be there for loved ones." A sad expression crossed Dr Osterhagen's face. "My wife died when I was away fighting the last war. I remind myself that I was there in spirit and would have been by her side if I could."

"I didn't mean to bring up painful memories."

"Sometimes it's easier to avoid them, but that doesn't mean we should." Dr Osterhagen gestured towards his patient. "Now, why don't you tell me what's been happening here?"

"I've made some notes." Kristopher folded back the first sheet on the clipboard so Dr Osterhagen could read what was written on the one underneath. "I thought that way you'd have the information in case I didn't have the chance to speak with you about it."

He took the clipboard from Kristopher and read the notes. "You've been writing everything down, good. You're very observant. The medics I've worked with before often didn't report everything in such detail."

"My sister is a doctor." Kristopher suspected his own

background and training was also coming through, but he wasn't about to reveal that to Dr Osterhagen. "I've watched her work on occasion."

"What's her name? Perhaps I know of her?" Dr Osterhagen's interest was definitely piqued. Kristopher kicked himself for having mentioned it, as he could hardly share the information.

"I doubt—"

A loud noise at the other end of the room made him jump, jarring him from his train of thought. Helga, one of the nurses, glanced around apologetically and bent to pick up the tray she'd dropped. She seemed somewhat nervous.

Kristopher looked past her to see what had upset her. A man in a SS uniform stood inside the entrance to the ward. He was talking to the Feldgendarme who had asked to see Kristopher's papers.

The SS Obersturmführer glanced up at Kristopher. Their eyes met. *It couldn't be.* Kristopher would have known that face anywhere, especially the coldness in his expression and the intensity of his gaze. This wasn't a man who merely carried out orders. He enjoyed hurting others. So did the Oberscharführer with him, Müller.

"Verdammt!" Kristopher exclaimed before he could stop himself. He lowered his head, but it was already too late. He'd seen the recognition in the man's eyes.

"Lehrer!" Reiniger shouted. "Stay where you are! You're under arrest."

He had to get out of there. Kristopher glanced around wildly, looking for an escape route. Müller drew his weapon. So did the Feldgendarme next to him.

Kristopher backed up instinctively, Müller closing the distance between them and blocking the way forward. He and the men with him were between Kristopher and the door they'd come through, preventing him from using it as an escape route.

The door at the other end of the ward was his only chance. He heard Dr Osterhagen say something but didn't register the words.

He turned tail and ran for the remaining exit, hoping, praying, he'd reach it in time. He heard footsteps behind him, the sound of boots getting louder as they began to catch up.

He had to reach Michel or at least find some way to warn him.

"After him!" yelled Reiniger. "He must not escape."

CHAPTER SIX

"Who's there?" Michel spun around, his gun already in his hand.

A timid voice came from the shadows of the building behind him. "It's just me. Don't shoot!" Fritz stepped into view, his hands raised above his head. He looked scared.

Michel lowered his gun. "I'm not going to shoot you." He reholstered his weapon. "I thought I told you to stay with Paul. Does he know you're here?"

He doubted Kit did. When Michel had left Kit, he had been in conversation with Dr Osterhagen. Knowing Kit, he'd want to ensure he'd briefed Dr Osterhagen about everything he'd been tasked to do. That Kit didn't like leaving jobs half-done was one of the first things Michel had learned about him when he'd been given the assignment to keep him under observation at the institute.

Michel allowed himself a smile at the memory of Kit speaking softly to one of the women who had been brought in. She'd been scared, but Kit had soothed her and listened to her talk about her experience. He was good with people, and they seemed to trust him. Michel could relate to that.

"No." Fritz took a step closer. "I didn't want you to leave."

"You didn't have a problem staying with Paul when I was helping to clear rubble this morning."

"I didn't think you were leaving then." Fritz shoved his hands into the pockets of his worn coat and shivered.

"So why do you think I'm leaving now?" Michel sighed. He didn't need to explain himself to a child, but even a child talking about something out of place in the presence of the wrong people could be dangerous. "Go back to Paul, Fritz. He's probably worried about you."

He didn't want to have this conversation with Fritz yet. He'd promised to help the boy find his family, but it was too risky to stay in the area any longer. While he wasn't sure sending Fritz back to Kit was a good idea either, at least it was safer than leaving him alone, given the reports of daylight bombing raids taking place elsewhere. As the sun had come up, people had emerged from hiding, concerned for their friends and loved ones and wanting to help. Many of those people had survived the attacks by hiding in tunnels dug into the sides of the hills surrounding the area. The news spreading from Stuttgart about the air raid and the amount of damage there didn't sound good.

Michel glanced at his watch. Kit's shift would be finished soon.

The more distance Michel put between himself and the hospital, the more the uneasy feeling grew that he should not have left Kit. What if Kurt *had* overheard Michel and spoken to someone about it? He'd thought at the time that their journey from Wolfenbüttel had gone a little too smoothly, especially as their presence hadn't been questioned too thoroughly in either Kassel or Frankfurt.

He needed to check on the state of their vehicle so they

could leave as soon as possible. If the bombs had damaged it too badly or destroyed it, they'd have to find some other means of transportation. They had to get to Freudenstadt, which was a good distance into the Black Forest.

But he had to get Fritz somewhere safe first.

"I didn't want to stay at the hospital." Fritz stared up into the sky, watching the snow fall. He held out his hand and caught a snowflake, then closed his palm around it. "Do you think Vater is safe? Why are those planes dropping bombs on us? We haven't done anything to hurt them."

"War doesn't always make sense," Michel said after a few moments. How could he explain that he and Kit had to leave without lying to him? Fritz asked a lot of questions. He reminded Michel of Kit in that, and in other ways. He ruffled Fritz's hair, which was blond like Kit's natural colour. Fritz's eyes were also the same pale blue.

"Do you have children? They must be worried about you like I worry about Vater." Fritz took Michel's hand and held it tightly.

"No, I don't have children." He never would. He'd thought a couple of times about how he'd like a family, but it wasn't about to happen. His parents and Kit were his family. "One of my cousins has two children about your age." They'd followed him around like Fritz did too. At first he'd been annoyed by it, then they'd slowly worked their way into his heart, and he enjoyed their company, for the most part. He hoped they were safe. It had been nearly a year since he'd been home.

"Michel?"

"Yes?"

"You look sad." Fritz was staring at him intently.

"I'm thinking about home." Michel wondered how long he'd been distracted by his thoughts. It had only felt like a few moments. He came to a decision, although it probably wasn't a particularly sensible one. "I need to do something. If you won't go back to the hospital, you'll have to come with me." At least this way he'd be able to assess their current situation properly. If he sent Fritz away, there was a good chance he'd continue to follow, but at a distance. His original idea of sending Fritz back to Kit probably wasn't a good one either. Fritz seemed determined not to return to the hospital, and Kit needed time to get away, which would be problematic with a child in tow.

"I could help," Fritz said brightly. "Do you think we'll find my mother? I don't want her to worry about me. My sister is only a baby. I help look after her."

"We'll find her soon, and then she won't have to worry anymore." Michel wished he believed what he was saying. If Fritz did find his family, he'd be one of the lucky ones. Several children had been found wandering and lost, separated from their parents. Some of them would never be reunited. Michel squeezed Fritz's hand.

He couldn't continue to lie to Fritz. He turned the boy so they were facing and knelt down at his level. "Paul and I have to leave very soon, Fritz. I'm sorry, but we haven't time to help you find your mother and sister."

"But you promised!"

"I know, and I'm sorry." Michel took a deep breath. "We can't stay here. It's not safe. We..." How could he word this without upsetting Fritz even more? Dear God, he was tired of having to pretend all the time. He closed his eyes, remembering his brother, Corin's, death—seeing him captured, knowing what would happen and not being able to stop it, his body jerking before falling to the ground.

"It's not safe because of the bombs. I know that." Fritz

frowned. "There was a soldier at the hospital asking questions about Paul. That's why I left. I didn't like him."

"What did this soldier look like?" Michel let go of Fritz's hand.

"Is Paul in trouble?"

"I hope not." Michel felt cold. *Please no.* He couldn't lose Kit now. Not after everything they'd gone through. Why had he left him? Why hadn't he stayed at the hospital? They could have gone to the ambulance together.

"He was an SS officer. I've seen them before, so I know what they look like." Fritz spoke slowly, as though collecting his thoughts. "He was tall, but not as tall as you. I couldn't see his hair under his cap, but I remember his eyes. They were dark, and he stared at me like I'd done something wrong. He scared me."

"Reiniger." Michel spoke the name aloud. If Reiniger was here and asking after Kit, it could already be too late.

Fritz nodded. "That was the name the Feldgendarme called him. I couldn't remember it until you said it. Do you know him?" He pulled away from Michel, suddenly nervous. "He's not your friend, is he?"

"No, he's not my friend." Michel stood quickly and reached for his Walther P38, making sure it was still there. "Listen, Fritz. This is important. Reiniger is not a good person. If he finds Paul, he will hurt him, and I can't let that happen." Kit wouldn't cooperate unless he was forced to, and Michel had seen enough to know what that force would entail. "I don't want him to hurt you either." He couldn't keep Fritz with him now this had happened. "Go back to Gretchen at the hospital and stay with her. If anyone asks, you haven't seen me."

"Can't I help?" Fritz bit his lip. "I don't want him to

hurt Paul. You and Paul are my friends." He wiped at his eyes. "Is that why you have to leave? So he won't find Paul?"

"Yes." Michel gestured back the way they'd come. "Go now, Fritz, I don't have time for questions."

"Paul's not a bad man, is he? That's not why the SS are after him?"

"No, he's not." Michel managed a half smile. "Paul is my closest friend, and I need to make sure he's safe. That's what friends do for each other."

"Yes, they do." Fritz seemed satisfied with the answer. "That's what I can do, isn't it, by going back? If I pretend I didn't see you, it will help you stay safe?"

"Yes, it will."

A thought struck him. Kurt had seen Fritz interacting with them. He could have told Reiniger. "Fritz, this is very important. Remember the place we hid from the bombs last night? I want you to go there and hide until these men leave. You can't have anything to do with them. Understand?"

"But you said you wanted me to go to the hospital."

"I think it's more important for you to stay out of sight. These men are dangerous."

Fritz nodded slowly. "Stay safe. Say good-bye to Paul for me." He hugged Michel quickly. Michel returned the unexpected gesture with an intensity that surprised him.

He ruffled Fritz's hair before letting go of the boy. He didn't want to walk away, but there was no choice. Merde. He'd carried out this mission successfully, avoiding any kind of emotional attachment, until Kit entered his life.

Perhaps their relationship changed him more than he'd thought? It had been a long time since he'd allowed anyone other than Kit to affect him like this. He couldn't do it again. He couldn't afford to.

This mission was the priority. He had to keep Kit safe

and deliver him and the knowledge he possessed to the Allies.

"Now go. Run, and don't look back." Tears formed and Michel blinked them away. He'd fully intended to stay long enough to find Fritz's family and make sure he was safe. "I'm sorry," he murmured, hoping like hell the time he and Kit had spent with Fritz wouldn't put the boy in additional danger.

He couldn't think about that now. If Kit had been caught... Michel had wasted enough time, but he couldn't leave Fritz without saying something, without making sure he'd at least be safe for now. He could hear Kit's voice in his head agreeing with him. Fritz was an innocent. They'd made their choices in this—he hadn't. Michel had to make sure he was safe.

Always the idealist, mon cher.

If Kit had escaped, he'd be heading for the ambulance. If he hadn't...

Be safe. Please, be safe.

Check the ambulance first, then the hospital. There was no point in running into Reiniger and getting captured. Whatever way this had gone, Michel could help Kit better by staying free.

Kristopher ducked behind the Kübelwagen and hoped like hell the vehicle's owner didn't return anytime soon. It was an officer's car. *God, what if it was Reiniger's?* But Kristopher couldn't keep running. His heart beat fast, and his breathing came in gasps. He drew his gun with shaking hands. While he could aim it well enough to hit a target, the thought of killing someone, whether on purpose or by accident, made him sick to his stomach.

Footsteps sounded close by, boots against concrete as soldiers ran past. He held his breath, hardly daring to breathe in case someone heard him.

"He can't have got far," Reiniger said, his voice louder as he came nearer.

Two sets of boots—Reiniger's and someone else's—stopped as the men continued their conversation.

Move away, Kristopher urged silently. He had nowhere else to hide, and if he ran now, they'd see him for certain. He wasn't sure he *could* keep running. His legs trembled, protesting the way he'd pushed himself since fleeing the hospital. He slid down silently so he was sitting on the ground.

"I have men searching the area, Herr SS Obersturm-führer," Müller said. Kristopher would have recognised his voice anywhere.

He tightened his grip on his gun. Beads of perspiration trickled down his face into his eyes despite the cold, but he didn't dare move to wipe them away. The metal of the vehicle behind him felt hard against his back. The snow beneath him was already beginning to seep through his trousers.

"Keep me informed of your progress, Unterschar-führer." Reiniger had a thoughtful edge to his voice. "I need to question Dr Osterhagen further. I am certain with some persuasion he could be most useful. If anything, he needs to learn that there are consequences for enabling the escape of an enemy of the Fatherland."

Surely Osterhagen had done nothing wrong? He had no clue as to Kristopher's real identity. But that small detail wouldn't stop Reiniger from hurting him.

"It is doubtful his actions were the accident he claimed," Müller agreed.

"Exactly. Oh, and Müller?"

"Yes, Herr SS Obersturmführer?"

"It is highly probable Obergefreiter Werner is Schmitz, given his description. It does not surprise me that he and Lehrer are still travelling together. Lehrer would not be capable of getting this far on his own. Both have been seen in the company of a boy. Find him and discover what he knows. If they have formed an attachment to him, he may be useful."

Kristopher pulled himself up into a crouch. He couldn't stay hidden and allow Fritz to be hurt or worse. He was only a child, an innocent.

He put his gun down and slowly rose to his feet.

Someone yanked him down and placed a hand over his mouth. Before he could struggle, he was pulled around so he could see his attacker.

Michel.

Michel was supposed to be blocks away, readying the ambulance so they could leave, not here where he might be found. If Kristopher gave himself up now, he'd surrender Michel too.

Kristopher jerked one hand in the direction of Reiniger and Müller. Their conversation had finished, and they were beginning to move away. Michel nodded but kept his hand over Kristopher's mouth.

When they were finally alone, he removed it.

"There was no need for that!" Kristopher hissed. "Not after I knew it was you."

"You were thinking about giving yourself up to save Fritz." Michel sighed. "I know you, Kit. Don't try to tell me you weren't."

"Yes, I was." Kristopher glared at him. "I'm not about to let Reiniger hurt a child if I can do something to prevent it. I know *you* too, Michel. You wouldn't either."

He bit his lip. Surely Michel would have also known that Kristopher wouldn't have given him up to Reiniger? He would have found another way to surrender without endangering Michel. He only needed to persuade Michel to turn his back for a few minutes to give him time to find Müller and surrender to him before he found Fritz.

"You're still thinking about it." Michel kept his arm snaked around Kristopher, holding him in a tight embrace. "There's no need. He's safe. I told him to hide until Reiniger is gone."

He let go of Kristopher, who retrieved his gun from where he'd dropped it and reholstered it.

"Good." Kristopher shifted into a crouch and peered around the Kübelwagen. Reiniger's men seemed to be concentrating their search elsewhere, at least for the moment. He studied Michel before speaking. Michel's face was almost expressionless, which made it difficult to read his emotions. Kristopher had seen that look before. Michel was scared and trying not to show it.

"I've already checked the ambulance," Michel said in a calm voice. "It's not an option. Half a building fell on it, and it's damaged beyond repair."

"I wouldn't have given you up." Kristopher tried to sound calm like Michel but failed. His voice wavered. "I couldn't let him hurt Fritz. I would have found another way once I knew you were here with me."

"I know." Michel leaned in closer so his mouth was against Kristopher's ear. He spoke softly to avoid the risk of being overheard. "It's one of the reasons I love you. However, it also scares and frustrates me. You're too much of an idealist, mon cher. I fear one day it will literally be the death of you."

"I'm sor—" Kristopher started to say.

Michel shook his head. "Don't. We both know you'd do it again in a heartbeat." He shrugged and turned away to survey their surroundings, although not fast enough to hide the sadness in his eyes.

"So what now?" Kristopher shivered. Snow was beginning to fall again. They had a few short hours before nightfall, and they couldn't spend the night out in the open. The only hiding place that might work was probably where Michel had sent Fritz, and they couldn't risk being caught with the boy. "We can't walk to Freudenstadt. It would take too long, and it's going to get a lot colder in a few hours." He closed his eyes and pictured in his mind the maps he'd studied. "If we find a vehicle, we could probably reach Wildberg by nightfall. It would at least get us away from the area."

Michel looked thoughtful. "We won't get far without a vehicle." He glanced around and then stood. "Cover me."

"What? Why?" Kristopher drew his gun but kept his current position. If no one could see him, it would at least give him the element of surprise. "What are you planning?" He knew that look.

"You're right. We need a vehicle." Michel waved a hand at the Kübelwagen. "There's one right here." He opened the door and peered inside. "No keys," he muttered, climbing into the driver's seat.

"We can't just take it!" Kristopher protested. The military vehicle would be missed fairly quickly.

"We don't have time to look for another one." Michel reached down and yanked at a piece of the dashboard near the ignition. It came away cleanly in his hand to reveal exposed wires. "Most civilians don't have much in the way of fuel. This makes sense for a lot of reasons." He grinned. "Call it poetic justice if it makes you feel better."

"You've done this before."

"A few times," Michel admitted. "One of the first lessons Corin taught me was how to bypass the ignition to start a car."

"Was that part of your Resistance training?" It didn't surprise Kristopher that it was Corin who had taught Michel this particular skill. Michel's older brother hadn't been happy at first that Michel wanted to be a part of the Resistance, but once they were working together, Corin had made it his mission to take Michel under his wing and teach him well. Michel had fled to the nearby hills with many of the young men in his village to avoid being pressed into compulsory labour service in Germany. He'd joined the Maquis and the fight to free the French people from their German occupiers and those who worked with them.

"Oh, he taught me this many years before the war. Papa was constantly misplacing the keys to the car, so it was a useful thing to know." Michel looked up at Kristopher as the engine roared to life. "Get in. We're leaving."

Kristopher ran around to the passenger side and jumped in. "You're enjoying this," he murmured.

"I can teach you if you'd like." Michel shoved the Kübelwagen into gear and put his foot down on the accelerator.

"Stop!" yelled a familiar voice from somewhere behind them. "Get them!"

Kristopher ducked instinctively as bullets whizzed past them.

"Idiot!" Reiniger shouted. "Aim for the tyres. That's *my* Kübelwagen." He sounded angry. Kristopher turned around and risked a look behind them. Soldiers ran after them.

Others fired their weapons. Michel swerved to avoid being hit.

"Even better," muttered Michel. He twisted the steering wheel, sending the vehicle hard around the next corner. Behind them men rushed for vehicles to give pursuit.

"Yes." Kristopher grabbed the side of his seat and hung on tightly. How could something so terrifying be so exciting at the same time?

"Yes, what?" Michel asked, not taking his eyes off the road.

"Yes, you definitely need to teach me how to do this. Not now of course, because that would be foolish, but later. If there is a later."

Michel chuckled and rolled his eyes. He took another sharp turn, this time to their right. "Steal a car or how to drive like this?"

"Both."

CHAPTER SEVEN

"Tell me again why we're driving into a potential lion's den when we've actually reached what I like to loosely refer to as safety?" Liang muttered, crossing his arms over his chest.

"You didn't have to come with me," Matt reminded him. He'd given both Liang and Ken the option to stay at the safe house, yet they'd refused. By his reckoning, the aircraft had come down somewhere between Baiersbronn and Freudenstadt. Finding it, and its crew, in the forest terrain wouldn't be easy, but he was determined to at least give it a good shot.

"You honestly think either one of us would leave you to go on this wild goose chase on your own?" Liang snorted. Their conversation that morning was one of the few times Matt had heard him and Ken agree about something. "Give us some credit."

"It's not a wild goose chase. More like looking for a needle in a haystack." Ken pulled onto the side of the road and shaded his eyes against the rising sun. The truck engine idled while he surveyed their surroundings on all sides.

"We all heard the aircraft come down last night," Matt said. "We can't leave our own people out here."

They'd barely made it to Freudenstadt before dark, and it had taken a while to find the safe house. They'd found a key hidden outside the deserted house where they'd been told it would be, so they'd let themselves in and decided to worry about finding their local contact in the morning.

Sleep hadn't come easily. Matt had lain awake for hours listening to the steady rhythm of Ken's breathing. As much as he'd wanted to put his arms around him and be held, it wasn't an option with Liang sharing the room with them. Instead he'd focused on the candle Ken had left burning and tried not to think about the memories it brought with it. He was tired. The past few days had been exhausting without enough sleep, yet as soon as he nodded off, the nightmares woken him.

He had more nights with them than without.

At the first sound of the familiar Rolls-Royce Merlin engines, he'd hurried to the window, careful not to disturb either Ken or Liang. The aircraft was in trouble. The engine stalled and then picked up again before the sky lit up in a beacon that would most likely be seen for miles around. It was soon joined by more aircraft—Messerschmitts, if the engine noise was anything to go by—most likely taking another shot at their prey.

The burning plane fell from the sky, plummeting, engines screaming as the pilot fought a losing battle to keep it airborne, before it dropped from sight.

"Are you sure it was one of ours?" Liang asked again. He'd woken the night before shortly after Matt. So had Ken.

"Yes," Matt told him. "I *can* tell the difference in sound between one of ours and one of theirs."

"Matt was a mechanic before the war," Ken added. "He knows his engines."

"I must have missed that conversation. Sorry I doubted

you." Despite Liang's casual tone, his apology did seem genuine. Not that it mattered if it wasn't. Matt knew what he'd heard and wasn't about to argue the point. "Have you any idea *how* we're going to find it? It's a lot of ground to cover, especially as we don't have any idea where to start looking. If we saw it go down, my guess is so did the Germans."

"I'm hoping they're distracted enough by all the bombing in the area to not worry about looking for one aircraft," Matt said. The Allies were attacking day *and* night. They'd done a considerable amount of damage so far with no sign of it easing up anytime soon. Although, if the weather closed in again, they'd have to shift their focus elsewhere.

"I can see smoke." Ken climbed out of the truck to get a better look. He pointed to a thicket of trees over the next rise. Black smoke rose into the air. "That's definitely more than someone burning wood to keep warm."

"It's worth checking out," Matt agreed. "If that's what's left of the aircraft, let's hope the crew managed to bail out." He waved Ken back into the truck. "Let's get this off the road first. I don't want to leave it too close to where we're heading, so it's better we go the rest of the way on foot."

"We won't be the only ones who have seen the smoke. It's foolish to think the Germans won't investigate. I'd say all these bombings would be more likely to make them want to find the aircraft. They can't afford to dismiss it." Ken drove the truck over the rise so they could survey the valley below and then turned off the road into a small clearing. While the vehicle wasn't exactly well hidden, at least it wouldn't be visible from the road. He climbed out of the cab and pulled out his binoculars. "I'm surprised the area isn't crawling with soldiers already. They'll want to get their hands on the crew."

He handed the binoculars to Matt after he came to stand next to him.

"In case they have information about the bombings?" Liang buttoned up his greatcoat and joined them. "That would be a sensible move on their part, especially with the scope of this operation." He glanced up at the sky, as though expecting to see something. "If we are chasing a downed aircraft, the pilot's rather off course, isn't he? Wouldn't he have been heading for somewhere that *was* bombed last night?"

"It's an aircraft, or what's left of it. I can see what looks like part of a wing, but it's difficult to see much more. The trees are blocking the view. We'll have to get closer." Matt gave Liang the binoculars so he could see for himself. "He probably tried to keep it airborne as long as possible, and it depends on the target as to how off course he was. Stuttgart is my guess. It's taken one hell of a beating over the last few days."

"You can stay in the truck if you want, Liang," Ken suggested.

"It's fine. If we split up, we can cover more ground and be back at the safe house for lunch. I figure we can head towards the smoke fifty paces apart and keep an eye out for any survivors. Once we reach the wreckage, we can head back a further fifty paces apart." Liang shrugged. "At least that way we've given it our best shot." Putting it that way made it sound so simple, like they were taking a walk in the park.

Except the park was in the middle of the Black Forest, a mix of farmland and forest stretching on either side of where they were.

"Exactly what I was about to suggest, although if the crew have any sense, they'll keep their heads down," Matt said. For all his talk, Liang did appear to consider himself a part of the team, more so since he and Ken had worked together in Berlin. "Don't take any chances. I'm more concerned with finding anyone who is injured and needs our help. If that happens, they're probably going to be desperate and act accordingly. Speak in English to reassure them, but if they don't want to cooperate, walk away. We can assess the situation once we're back here and then go from there. I also don't want either of you in a situation where you'll be asked for your papers or to explain what you're doing here, so if you do come across any Germans, remember your cover. Don't interact with them unless you have no choice. That goes for you in particular, Liang." He glanced at his watch. "Meet back at the truck in three hours if we miss each other at the wreckage."

"I have no intention of being anything but careful." Liang took another look through the binoculars before giving them back to Ken. "If I see anyone in uniform, I plan on hiding until they're gone and then running very quickly in the opposite direction. What if there's no one else here when I get back to the truck? Do I wait?"

"I'm not leaving anyone behind." Ken gave Matt a pointed look. "We've already had to mount one rescue operation. That was enough."

"I'm not about to get myself captured again." Matt shuddered at the memory.

"It wasn't exactly deliberate last time either." Ken shrugged, but Matt caught a look of real fear in his eyes before he turned away. "Are you sure this is a good idea? We have a mission to complete."

"I'm not leaving one of our own out there for the

Germans to find." Matt met Ken's stubborn look with one of his own. "You disobeyed London to rescue me. This is—"

"No different?" Ken snorted. "Right. You're determined to do this, and you're sure as hell not doing it on your own, so I figure let's get it over and done with."

"You haven't answered my question." Liang looked between Ken and Matt. He seemed more amused by their argument than anything. "Do I wait or not?"

"No."

"Yes," Ken spoke at the same time as Matt. He glared at Matt. "We don't leave one of our own behind. Ever."

"Right." Liang rolled his eyes. "Now we've cleared that up, I guess I'll take the situation as it comes and make a decision then."

"You wait for another half an hour if it's safe to do so, and then you get back to the safe house and wait," Matt clarified. "We all know the way back on foot, and we can make it by nightfall. There's no point risking the truck or getting caught by the enemy." He narrowed his eyes. "Are we clear?"

"Yes."

"Yes, *sir*." Ken turned away and began walking, the stiffness of his posture showing his anger loud and clear.

"That went well," Liang remarked dryly. He watched Ken for a few moments. "He was worried about you after Holm arrested you and blamed himself for it."

"It wasn't his fault," Matt protested.

"I know that, but try not to do it again, hmm?"

Liang closed his eyes and rubbed at his temples. He'd never seen the appeal of flying and had bad memories of his one and only time in an aircraft. He wasn't scared of heights, but more of falling, and not convinced about the safety of the aircraft, despite numerous reassurances.

Seeing this one in pieces didn't help.

Although the wing he'd seen through the binoculars was a part of the aircraft they'd sought, it lay some distance away from the rest of it. The bloodstained cockpit stood empty. The top transparent part—he didn't remember the correct name for it—had shattered into pieces.

Liang shuddered. He hoped like hell that had happened after they'd crashed and not in mid-air.

Fresh snow covered any tracks the missing crew might have made. Liang rubbed his gloved hands together and debated his next move. He hadn't come across anyone or anything that might give a clue to their whereabouts on his way here, but he'd take another look on his way back. Although he wouldn't wish this on anyone, he rather hoped he wouldn't be the one to find the bodies of the crew. He was going to have enough nightmares without that.

A sharp crack made him duck behind a nearby tree. He cocked his head in the direction of it. "Wonderful," he muttered when he heard voices. It appeared the local branch of the German military had turned up in force to investigate. He glanced at his watch. They'd obviously not started at dawn like he and his team, but then perhaps they'd had further to travel. He'd split up from Matt and Ken about an hour ago, and so far he hadn't seen any soldiers.

However, that didn't mean Matt or Ken hadn't already been there. The different routes they'd taken might be faster or slower, depending on the terrain and whether they'd come across any distractions on the way. They could already be heading back to the truck.

The voices grew louder, and so did the sound of barking dogs. He couldn't stay there. The aircraft would act like a beacon, drawing the men and their dogs closer. They'd check out the wreckage and look for the crew, as Liang and the others were doing.

What was it Matt had said? Keep his head down and not let the Germans see him up close. Liang preferred his idea of running in the opposite direction very quickly. Unfortunately, hiding until they'd gone wasn't likely to work in this situation. If these men had any sense, they'd leave someone guarding the aircraft and then thoroughly search the area around it.

If he was going to make a run for it, it needed to be now before they got any closer. Bloody hell. He should have stayed in the truck and let Matt and Ken argue about Matt's decision to play hero. Yes, because that would have been a whole lot safer. If the Germans had found it, he'd be a sitting duck, waiting for them to come and get him. Better to stay on the move, wasn't it?

Damn this. Liang thought about his nice warm office at the university and sighed. He'd pointed out that he wasn't trained for this when his services had been volunteered for him. He'd head back for the truck and hope it hadn't been compromised. He didn't fancy a long walk back to the safe house.

"The dog's got a scent," a man yelled in German. "Quick, this way!"

Time to go. Liang glanced behind him and heaved a sigh of relief when he didn't see anything. But going that way would only serve to take him further into the forest, and he needed to get back the way he'd come. The last thing he needed was to get lost and his skeleton be found months later because he'd starved to death after wandering aimlessly for days.

Enough of that kind of thinking. He needed to act, rather than waste time thinking about it. Yes, because he was a great man of action, wasn't he? Liang snorted. His nice safe tree was only going to stay that way for a short while longer.

He took a deep breath and stepped out from behind it, nearly losing his footing on a gnarled branch in front of him.

"I heard something! Over there!" The voice was different from last time but didn't sound like someone Liang particularly wanted to meet.

Shit.

It wasn't him they'd heard. It didn't have to be him.

If he ran now, wouldn't that prove he was someone they should be after? Liang took a deep breath. He could do this. Of course he could do this. He was armed, although he didn't think much of his chances of actually hitting anyone with the damn thing. What had the man told him during training? "Only use it if necessary, bluff that you can use it if you have to, and for God's sake, don't blow your own foot off with the blasted thing."

Why hadn't he noticed the soldiers before? They wouldn't have been sneaking around in silence. Liang glanced back at the wreckage. He'd definitely let himself retreat into his thoughts for a little too long. Matt had warned him of that before they'd started this bloody mission, when they'd first got to know each other. Liang had listened but apparently not as intently as he should have.

If he didn't get out of here, there wouldn't be much point in chastising himself. Staying alive and in one piece looked very appealing about now. He'd worry about the details of how he'd screwed up later.

Stay calm. I can do this.

Careful to keep his head down to avoid eye contact, Liang began to walk. He belonged here. He had a better chance of not being noticed if he hid in plain sight.

Two soldiers approached from the opposite direction. Liang made a point of glancing around as though looking for something. He crouched down and studied the ground.

"Have you found something, Gefreiter?"

It took Liang a few moments to realise the man was addressing him. He looked up briefly, long enough to note the officer's rank, and adjusted his helmet to shade his eyes. "I thought I saw a footprint, Herr Obergefreiter, but I was mistaken."

"Keep looking, Gefreiter," the Obergefreiter said. "Heil Hitler!"

"Heil Hitler!" Liang saluted, then breathed a sigh of relief when the men moved away. A thought struck him, and he changed direction slightly so he was heading off on an angle rather than obviously in the opposite direction to the wrecked aircraft. He hadn't heard anyone yell they'd found it yet, and he'd been close to it when questioned.

"I've found the wreckage!"

Right on cue. Liang couldn't help but grin. He heard more voices, this time off to his right. He veered left to avoid them. Up ahead two officers were having a discussion. Liang hesitated. Should he risk walking past them or go around? His footsteps faltered before he realised what he'd done.

"Is there a problem, Gefreiter?" one of the men asked, looking up. "Have you found something?"

Oh God, no.

Liang knew that voice. The last time he'd heard it was when Clara Lehrer and Trevor Palmer had been arrested.

The bastard had shot Palmer in the leg to try to get him to give up the rest of the team.

"No, Herr SS Obersturmführer." Liang kept his head down. "I thought I saw something, but I was mistaken." He saluted and turned to go.

Don't run. Don't run. Walk slowly.

"Gefreiter?"

"Yes, Herr SS Obersturmführer?" Liang froze. He hadn't done anything wrong. Had he?

"Look at a superior officer when he addresses you." Reiniger turned to the officer with him. "There are far too many civilians drafted into the military these days, and it shows. They need to be taught about the chain of command."

Liang took a deep breath. Both men were armed. If he ran now, he was probably as good as dead. He raised his head. "Yes, Herr SS Obersturmführer."

"What is your name, Gefreiter?" Reiniger smiled before continuing to speak, his tone casual. "Sometimes what we seek comes to us, Herr Hauptmann," he told his companion.

"Gefreiter Lorenz Sachs," Liang said, "Herr SS Obersturmführer."

He didn't like the sound of Reiniger's last comment. It had that "oh hell the jig is up" feeling about it.

Don't panic. Don't run.

He wasn't the target, he wasn't Lehrer, nor Matt or Ken. He hadn't interacted for a period of time with either this man or his superior, Holm. He was no one. Reiniger didn't have a reason to put a bullet in him because he could.

And at this distance, the man wouldn't miss. The fact he hadn't drawn his gun wouldn't matter. It would be in his hand all too soon. Liang had seen how fast a trained soldier could draw, aim, and fire.

Reiniger took a step closer.

Perhaps he hadn't figured it out?

"I meant your real name." Reiniger examined Liang closely. "Herr SS Standartenführer Holm said a man on Lowe's team appeared to be part Chinese. I thought he must be mistaken."

Liang stared at him defiantly. He said nothing.

"You're under arrest," Reiniger told Liang. He gestured to a nearby soldier, who pulled Liang's arms roughly behind him and handcuffed him. "I'm sure Herr SS Standartenführer Holm will want to make your acquaintance again." Reiniger *tsk-tsked*. "From what I heard, you didn't bother to introduce yourself properly. This meeting will be quite different, I assure you."

CHAPTER EIGHT

Michel parked the Kübelwagen off the road, under a canopy of trees where it wouldn't immediately be noticed. Hopefully the falling snow would hide the tyre tracks well enough from any casual observer. He turned to Kit. "Are you sure you want to do this?" The question was foolish, but one he needed to ask.

As expected, Kit gave him an incredulous look. "After everything that has happened, do you honestly expect me to sit here and do nothing while someone might need our help?"

"No, not really, but I thought I'd ask anyway, in case you'd changed your mind in the last two minutes."

They'd seen the aircraft early that morning and watched it fall out of the sky. Michel had been keeping guard while Kit slept but hadn't had to wake him. The sound of the engines above them had done that.

After they'd lost Reiniger and his men, they'd continued on to Eutingen. Michel had parked the Kübelwagen off the road, and they'd slept in the vehicle rather than risk being caught in a house-to-house search. Kit had insisted he take first watch, and Michel had taken over from him several hours later.

"It doesn't matter whose aircraft it is. The crew are still men who might need help." Kit gave Michel one of those stubborn looks he was beginning to know all too well.

"If it is an Allied aircraft, the area is probably already swarming with soldiers looking for the crew." Michel shrugged. He wasn't sure whom the aircraft belonged to, as he didn't have the experience to distinguish one from the other. It sounded similar to what he'd heard in Feuerbach before the bombs had struck, but he wouldn't want to stake either of their lives on it, which was exactly what they could be doing.

"Then we need to find them first." Kit climbed out of the Kübelwagen and looked around. "The area is a mix of open farmland and forest. Where would you aim for if you were a pilot with an aircraft you knew couldn't stay airborne for much longer?"

"It would depend how much control I had over it and whether the rest of the crew had already bailed out. An open space might make for a safer landing, but it's also more exposed, and he'd have to find somewhere fairly flat among all these hills." Michel pointed to an area south of their location. "Does that look like smoke to you?"

Kit peered in the direction Michel was pointing. "Yes," he said, "I think it is." A thin spiral of black smoke rose into the sky in the near distance. "How long do you think that will take to reach?"

"It's hard to say; it depends on the terrain. If it is the aircraft, it seems to have come down in the middle of the forest. I hope the pilot found a decent-sized clearing, or there's not going to be much of him and his crew or the plane left to worry about." Michel shuddered at the thought.

Kit watched the smoke with interest. He glanced at his watch. "Of course, if the crew did survive and aren't too badly injured, they could already be heading towards us."

"Ever the optimist." Michel didn't want to stay in the forest any longer than was necessary when they were so close to reaching the safe house in Freudenstadt.

"If I let myself lose hope, I'm back in that dark place reliving my nightmares," said Kit quietly. "I won't let that happen again."

"I don't want you to." Michel brushed his hand against Kit's arm lightly, the motion brief enough that it wouldn't be noticed if there was anyone watching. "I need you to keep that hope alive for both of us." Kit had told him of his nightmares about the project he was working on. Although they'd been a part of what finally prompted him to act, hearing about them had been disturbing enough.

"It's better than allowing myself to consider the alternative." Kit smiled at Michel's touch. "It's also easier to cling to it for both of us than just myself."

"I know." Michel waved his other hand in the direction of the smoke. "We should start walking. I don't want to be caught in the forest with soldiers looking for anything out of place. The crew of this aircraft are not the only ones at risk of getting caught." He studied Kit for a moment. "If we don't find anyone within a reasonable amount of time, we need to leave. We'll look for the crew, but I don't want Reiniger getting his hands on you because of it."

"How much of a chance do you think there is that Reiniger is in the area?" Kit began walking as he spoke. Michel fell into step beside him.

"A very good chance, I would think. We won't be the

only ones who saw the aircraft or the smoke. He's as likely to investigate in case we're doing exactly what we are doing."

"Reiniger didn't strike me as someone who would think things through to that degree. He's a bully who uses the excuse of following orders to inflict pain on others. He enjoys it."

"Yes, he is," Michel agreed. "However, his orders come from Holm, who is a man who considers every scenario." Despite them being on opposite sides, Michel had come to respect Holm to some degree in the months he'd served under him. "Holm also believes in what he is doing, and that makes him very dangerous." He hesitated before continuing.

"Whatever it is, just say it, even if it's something you think I won't like."

"You don't miss much, do you?"

"I know you. Now is not the time to be keeping thoughts to yourself. I'd much prefer to be going into a situation aware of the facts."

"You'd go into it, despite those facts." Michel kept his voice light. He cleared his throat and continued before he changed his mind. Not that he'd have the option not to now Kit suspected he had something else to tell. "Holm was in charge of security at the institute for most of the time you worked there, yes? You'd been there for several years?"

"Since I graduated from the university and Dr Kluge asked me to join the project, yes." Kit glanced at Michel. "Get to the point."

"Holm is an observant man. One of the first things I noticed in the six months I was there was your compassion and willingness to help those in need. Holm will be well aware of that too, and I doubt he thinks you would have changed that much despite what you've been through. In fact, those events have made you more inclined to help someone regardless of any risk involved."

"So you think Holm would send Reiniger here because he knew if we saw it we'd have to investigate and help?"

"Not we, Kit." Once there was any sign of soldiers in the area, Michel fully intended to grab Kit and run. Convincing him of the need for it wouldn't be as easy. "*You*. And yes, I do."

Matt hated having to pull rank. More than that, he hated having to pull rank on Ken. Ken wasn't any happier about being on the receiving end of it either.

Although he knew the reason Ken would never agree to leave any of their team behind, Matt had to do his job and ensure the safety of that team. However, he couldn't leave whoever was in the downed plane to the mercy of the enemy either—the thought of anyone going through what he had... Matt shivered. If his team did a quick search and got out fast the risk would be minimal. Waiting for stragglers would only increase their chances of being caught. Why couldn't Ken see that?

Hell, it wasn't as though he *was* condoning leaving anyone behind, but they had to be practical. At least if they were able to get back to the safe house on their own, they could regroup and work out their options. Then they'd go after whoever hadn't made it back. All of them getting captured out here meant no one would be left to mount a rescue. The several days Matt had spent as a guest of SS Standartenführer Holm had been several days too long.

There was no way in hell he'd allow that man to get his hands on Ken.

Or Liang, for that matter.

The three of them were a team, and as such, responsible for one another. Why had they argued? Neither he nor Ken intended to leave any of their team behind, but they had different strategies for getting the job done. For all that he loved Ken, the man could be infuriatingly single-minded at times. Once he'd decided *how* something should be done, he followed it through to the bitter end.

Matt was more about improvisation, and while he preferred to have a plan in place, he'd also make up another if his original idea decided to jump ship.

As much as he enjoyed company, it was good to get out in the fresh air on his own for a time. The months spent at Juliane's had been several weeks too long. Despite the cold weather, this walk was helping to clear his head.

He glanced at his watch. If he'd correctly calculated how fast he'd been walking and the rough distance to where he'd spotted the aircraft wing through his binoculars, he should be on top of the crash site very soon. Matt had talked to a couple of men who had been in an aircraft in flight when it had caught fire. Although they'd been lucky and survived, it wasn't just their bodies that needed to heal, but their minds. They definitely weren't the same men Matt knew before. One of them was jumpy as hell and continuously looking over his shoulder, and the other had an edge to his voice that suggested he'd lost the optimistic outlook on life he'd once possessed. Matt could relate to how they felt after his own experiences. While he liked to think he was the same man he'd been before he'd been captured by Holm, something had changed. Ken hadn't said anything, but Matt knew he'd noticed it too.

Had it only been three months since he'd spent that time in the cells at the institute? His nightmares sure as hell were convinced it was yesterday.

"Damn it," he muttered a few minutes later. He let out a low whistle. Sections of aircraft were scattered around the clearing. Matt could see the front end of the fuselage, but the back end of it was nowhere in sight.

It would have only taken a small fire to give the illusion of the entire aircraft being alight, as the dark sky made it difficult to see much of anything. He'd hoped it wasn't as bad as it looked, or there would be no point in hunting for survivors. Matt wasn't about to go search for the rest of the aircraft. He doubted there would be much left worth looking for.

Despite the damage, he could see the marking on the wing—the distinctive brown and blue circle that meant the Mosquito was RAF. So the crew were either British or from some country working with them. He'd spoken with people of assorted nationalities in the short time he'd spent there before his team had flown out.

He cautiously climbed up over the one intact wing. Although he could see the shattered top of the empty cockpit from the ground, he wanted to check to see if there were any clues as to what had happened to its crew. Both seats were empty, but it looked as though the navigator had managed to get out while they were in flight. At least Matt hoped he had. A quick search revealed that one of the para-chutes was missing, so he'd work on that assumption until he found out otherwise.

Matt ran one gloved hand over the seat on the left. Blood. Probably the pilot's. Matt would have been surprised if he'd come down unhurt with the aircraft in this state.

How far he'd gotten and how badly hurt was he? Matt

took a close look at the other seat, to dismiss the blood being the navigator's, but the red smear was definitely only on the pilot's side. A couple of drops of blood had dribbled onto the floor, with more across the wing. Matt undid the screws fastening the first aid kit to the armour plate above the pilot's seat, grabbed it, and swung it over his shoulder. What the hell had the pilot been thinking, leaving that behind? Unless he'd panicked and focused on getting himself out? He'd heard stories about how young some of these pilots were. First time in combat and coming up against a situation like this didn't tend to lend itself to logic, despite the training. Add in a serious injury, and that would definitely explain it.

A careful study of the snow-covered ground revealed more drops of blood underneath to the front of the wing and another very faint red smear across the top of it. An untrained eye might have missed them. Hell, Matt had nearly missed them. Matt dumped snow over both of them to mask them. He didn't want anyone else working out which direction the pilot might have gone.

He looked around for more clues and saw one set of footprints, but they went in the opposite direction to the trail of blood. Perhaps Liang or Ken had already been here and moved on? Matt bent down on one knee to examine the footprints more closely. There was only one set, and they were heading back the way Matt had come. Hopefully they belonged to Liang and he was making his way to the truck to report what he'd found.

Ken? No, they were too small to be Ken's. His shoe size was at least one bigger than Liang's, and besides, the stubborn bastard wouldn't return to the truck if he'd found this. He'd do what Matt was about to do and follow the trail to find the pilot.

The relative quiet of the forest suddenly erupted into noise. "The dog's got a scent," a man yelled. A dog growled. It sounded close. Too close.

He couldn't stay here. The small window of opportunity they'd had to find the aircraft before the place was overrun by soldiers was up. Matt listened closely for a moment, trying to figure out what direction they were coming from. *Damn it!* It sounded like they'd taken the same route he and his team had. He'd have to double back to avoid them. He glanced around, trying to figure out the best way to go. It appeared as though the pilot, whoever he was, had the right idea. He'd follow the trail the man had left for as long as he could and hope he found him before the Germans did.

"Did you hear that?" Kit held up one hand, gesturing Michel to be silent. They'd been walking for a while, but they were some distance from their destination. So far, they hadn't come across anyone else, but Michel wasn't sure how long that luck would hold.

"You're imagining things," Michel said after he listened carefully for whatever Kit had thought he'd heard. "There's nothing..." He froze, his words trailing off.

A low moan came from a thicket to their left.

"That's what I heard before." Kit ran towards the sound, Michel right behind him. What had happened to being cautious? They didn't know what this was. It might well be some kind of trap.

Michel caught up to Kit and laid a warning hand on his arm, stopping him in his tracks. "We need to be careful and check what is ahead first."

"That noise is being made by someone in pain. I heard enough of it at the hospital to recognise it." Kit pushed aside Michel's arm and shot him a glare. "Don't worry, I'm not about to do something stupid."

"I didn't say that."

"You didn't need to." Kit kept his voice barely above a whisper and dropped down to a crouch behind a nearby tree.

A metre in front of them a figure leaned heavily on an old branch, using it as a cane. He took a couple of steps forward, dragging one leg behind him, before sliding down to sit on the ground. The man moaned again—the same noise Michel had heard before—and tried to crawl to the nearest tree.

"He's hurt!" Kit hissed. Before Michel could stop him, Kit stepped out from their hiding place, his arms held above his head in a universal sign of surrender.

The man turned around. He was young, younger than either Kit or Michel by at least five years, maybe more, which meant he'd be in his early to mid twenties. Strands of light brown hair stuck out from beneath his helmet. His goggles were shoved back off his face, and he wore a flight uniform and flak jacket. Fear reflected in his bright blue eyes, and he held a knife in one trembling hand. His nose had dried blood smeared underneath it. He said something in English but spoke the words too quickly for Michel to understand.

Given his condition and his clothing, it seemed fairly safe to assume this was one of the men he and Kit had come to find. Some aircraft only had room for a pilot, others a bigger crew. Depending on the aircraft, this man might be the pilot and its only crew.

Kit replied in the same language. The man looked

puzzled but didn't lower his weapon. "Do you speak German?" Kit asked in English.

Although Michel's English had improved, it still wasn't that good. However, he understood what Kit had said as he'd practised that phrase when Kit had begun teaching him.

The pilot shook his head, eyeing Kit warily. He took a swig from the water canteen slung over his shoulder.

"I'm going to continue speaking English to him," Kit said. It took Michel a few moments to realise Kit was addressing him and had given away that he and the Englishman were not alone. "I think it will reassure him, and we can find out more that way."

Michel sighed and stepped out from behind the tree. He hoped Kit knew what he was doing, although the man did not seem to be in a fit state to pose too much of a threat. "Can you at least ask him to place his knife on the ground before you get close enough for him to use it on you?" The man might not be pointing a gun at Kit, but that didn't mean he didn't have one, and Michel wouldn't risk mentioning it in case. Although he'd *said* he didn't understand German he could be lying.

"I was just about to." Kit spoke a few more words in English. Michel recognised some of them and the assumed names he and Kit were using.

The pilot nodded. He looked Kit and Michel up and down and spoke again, his voice trembling.

Kit turned to Michel. "I've told him we only want to help, but he doesn't trust us. He says my accent sounds British, but he wants to know why I'm working with a German officer."

"Does he speak French?" Michel asked, continuing to speak German.

"A little," the pilot replied in French. "I understand more than I speak." He nodded at Michel, his frown reflecting his uneasiness. "I understand a little German but not much." He pulled a face. "My French is better," he continued in French, "but still not well."

Michel came closer and stood beside Kit. They had to get the pilot to trust them or he wasn't going to let them move him, and they didn't have the luxury of time. If he panicked and made too much noise, it could raise the alarm, and they'd be surrounded by soldiers too quickly to be able to make their escape.

"I am undercover and part of the Resistance." Michel spoke softly in French. He wasn't telling the man anything their pursuers hadn't probably already figured out. "Paul and I are working together. He speaks English and German well, but his French is about as good as my English." He waved his hand to signify it wasn't that good.

The man's eyes widened, and then he smiled. Given the situation, he probably didn't have much choice but to believe them. Michel hadn't lied to him, merely omitted a part of the truth. "Leonard Dawson. Leo." He tried to stand and hissed in pain. "My knee. It hurts. I can't straighten it."

Kit helped Leo to sit back down again. "I only understood some of what you said to him," he told Michel. "Language is going to be a problem, isn't it?"

"Speak to him in English and me in German," Michel suggested. "You have a common language with each of us, so you can translate."

"I can do that." Kit spoke a few words to Leo in English. Leo nodded and closed his eyes. "I'm going to take a look at his knee, although there's not much I can do for him. I had to leave my medical satchel when I fled the hospital." He glanced at Michel. "We can't leave him here for the soldiers to find. Do you think we could get him back to the Kübel-wagen between us?"

"We could, but our progress would be very slow."

If Reiniger discovered Leo had seen and spoken with them, it wouldn't bode well for his chances of survival, especially as he was already injured.

Kit gently pulled up Leo's trouser leg. Leo gritted his teeth, beads of perspiration running down his face. "Oh my, his knee is very swollen," murmured Kit. "There's also a nasty graze below it, which needs covering at the very least."

Peering quickly at Leo's leg, Michel took a deep breath. The graze didn't look too bad, but the knee was another matter. "You're right. His knee is very swollen. He's not going to be walking unaided until it goes down."

"I'm not sure what's wrong with his knee and whether it will go down on its own or if he needs further treatment." Kit took a closer look at the graze. "I can't see anything in it, but that doesn't mean there isn't. I'll cover the graze for now. It's all I can do. We'll need to find a doctor when we reach Freudenstadt. Do you think the Resistance there will be able to help?"

"I don't know. At least we have a contact there. You remember her name in case we're separated, and how to contact her?"

Kit nodded. "We're not getting separated, but yes, I remember." Leo grabbed Kit's arm and said something in English. Kit replied in kind. "Help him remove the padded vest he's wearing on the outside of his clothes. I'm going to tie it around his knee. It should act as cover for the graze and give his knee some support." He shrugged. "I don't think ripping clothing to use as a bandage is a good idea, and there isn't anything else. It's cold out here, and we need to keep warm."

"Do you know what you're doing?" Michel asked. Kit sounded confident, but Michel hadn't missed the glimpse of fear in his eyes when he turned away from Leo.

"No, not really," Kit admitted but did not alter his tone. "As I told Dr Osterhagen, my knowledge is very limited, but Leo doesn't need to know that, at least not yet." Hopefully Leo didn't know enough German to work out what he was saying. "He's scared. If we're caught before we reach the safe house, it won't matter either way, will it?"

"It's not like you to be so pessimistic," Michel said.

"I'm being practical. There's a difference." The three sections of the vest were held together by some sort of mechanism that seemed connected to the red strap at the back. Kit yanked on it. The jacket parted at the shoulders, and the strap around Leo's waist disconnected. Michel picked up one section of the jacket and examined it. The padding wasn't soft, as he'd first thought, but instead appeared to be made up of small two-inch plates of some sort of metal. Wrapped around Leo's leg, it would cover the graze below his knee and act as a makeshift splint.

"Flak vest." Leo pointed to the piece Michel was holding. His eyes were bright, yet his voice shook. When he spoke, his accent was different from Kit's, the words not as clipped.

"Talk to him while you do this, Paul. Distract him." Michel managed a smile. "Like I did for you when Clara treated your shoulder after you were shot. Ask him where he's from, although I doubt he'll confirm he's the pilot of that aircraft we saw. I wouldn't in his situation."

"Good idea." Kit wrapped one of the pieces of the vest around Leo's leg, with the inside of it against his skin. He gestured for Michel to hold it in place. Leo went white and took a sharp breath. "I'll be as quick as I can." Kit wound the straps from the vest around the fabric, pulling the buckles taut to secure them in place. He spoke in conversational tones to Leo as he did so. Leo clenched his fists but nodded.

"New Zealand. Wellington. You?" Leo gestured to both Kit and Michel.

Kit glanced at Michel. Before either of them could answer, a loud noise sounded close by. He froze and put his fingers to his lips.

Straining, he listened intently yet after a few moments couldn't hear anything. Perhaps he'd imagined it? As he began to relax, he heard it again: a sharp crack followed by a low murmur. Someone or something was nearby.

Supporting Leo between them would slow them down. They couldn't afford to walk straight into whatever was out there. Although both he and Kit carried guns, they wouldn't be able to get to draw them in time, and it would be foolish to take on a platoon of armed soldiers. "Stay here," he whispered to Kit. "I'm going to investigate."

Kit opened his mouth to protest, but Michel shook his head before he could speak. Kit could converse with Leo and they understood each other.

If they were about to be discovered, Michel might be able to lead the soldiers in the opposite direction and double back later.

"Stay safe," Michel said. "If I don't return within an hour, head for the Kübelwagen and get to the safe house. I'll meet you there."

If he had to, Kit could help Leo walk. Their progress would be very slow, but they'd reach the Kübelwagen in time to get to Freudenstadt before nightfall. Better that than waiting for someone to find them.

"Stay safe." Kit's voice shook, and he met Michel's gaze

for one brief instant as he turned his face away from Leo. "I love you," he mouthed silently.

Michel smiled but couldn't reply, as Leo would see it. Instead he took one last look at Kit and slipped into the forest.

CHAPTER NINE

"Shit!" Matt swore before he registered what he'd done. He ran to the tree a few yards ahead of him, hoping like hell the man propped up against it was still alive.

Too late.

The man sat slumped forward, his head against his chest. Matt felt for a pulse, but found none. He lifted the head; the man's sightless eyes stared straight ahead.

His parachute lay half buried a few feet away, the regulation-issued spade next to it. It looked as though he'd tried to get rid of it as he'd been taught but hadn't the strength to complete the job. If his injuries were anything to go by, he'd had a rough landing and had died shortly afterwards.

Poor bastard. Matt shook his head. No one should have to die alone like that. Matt felt around the dead man's neck and pulled out the leather bootlace his dog tags were attached to. He cut off the lower tag, leaving the other one intact.

Fraser, AK, he read silently. *RAF.* He shoved the tag into his pocket. He'd find a way to get them to Fraser's family so they at least knew what had happened to him.

This had to be the navigator of the aircraft. Otherwise what were the chances of someone with RAF dog tags out here? His guess that the navigator had bailed out must have been right. The pilot would have stayed at the controls. Hopefully he'd survived longer than this man.

"Did you hear that?"

Damn it.

Matt glanced around quickly but couldn't work out what direction the voice had come from. The words had been spoken in German... He sighed. Well, of course they would be. He was in Germany, after all. For a moment, lost in his thoughts, he'd almost expected to feel the touch of Ken's hand on his shoulder, offering support as he always did and whispering comforting words. Those would have been in English. Ken tended to lose his German when either he or Matt got emotional. He said he had difficulty enough finding the right words in his native tongue, so he wasn't going to try in another language.

Matt ducked behind some nearby bushes just in time. A couple of soldiers walked past his hiding place. Matt held his breath. One of them spoke again; it was the same voice he'd heard before.

"I could have sworn I heard something. You're..." The man trailed off. "You. There! Raise your hands!"

They sprinted over to Fraser's body. This was Matt's chance, before the soldiers realised they were talking to a dead man. He edged back further into the forest, taking care to act as though he was meant to be there. He kept his head down as he passed another soldier. The man gave him a brief salute. Matt returned it but didn't stop, knowing he wouldn't be questioned by someone of lower rank.

After ten minutes he stopped to catch his breath. His intention to walk slowly hadn't lasted long, and he'd picked up his pace as soon as he'd gotten past the soldier he'd saluted. It had begun snowing again, and he shivered despite feeling warm from the exercise. At this rate he was never going to make it back to the truck in time. If Liang had any sense, he would be getting ready to drive back to the safe house while the Germans were preoccupied searching the forest. Finding one RAF crewman would only serve to make them all the more determined to find the other.

The search seemed focused back the way he'd come. He'd heard several voices and sounds of movement, but they'd grown quieter the further north he'd gone. He took a moment to get his bearings. If he stayed on his planned course, there should be another road about half an hour ahead. His stomach rumbled, a reminder that it had been several hours since breakfast. A check of his watch confirmed it was now early afternoon. Getting back to the safe house from here on foot was still an option, although it would take a while. Once he found the road, he'd follow that but keep to the outskirts of the forest.

He caught movement from the corner of his eye, something up ahead in the distance. Matt stopped and focused, then saw it again, a red patch of colour that didn't quite fit the mix of brown and white of the forest. He moved quickly but silently, closing the distance between himself and whatever or whoever he'd seen. Although tempted to give it a wide berth, it might be the missing pilot.

The man sat on the ground, his back against a tree. A quick scan sized up the situation. The pilot appeared to be injured; his leg was wrapped in the remains of his flak jacket. He wore his goggles and flight helmet, and when he moved, he hissed in pain.

The red strap of the flak jacket lay on the ground, the emergency pull release no longer attached to it. Even so, the strap should have been buried or at least tucked out of sight where it couldn't be seen.

A German soldier, gun in hand, stood over the pilot. The soldier glanced around nervously. He seemed about the same age as Matt, but if his demeanour was anything to go by, he hadn't seen much in the way of action. The pilot looked much younger than both of them, not much more than a kid. He looked up, and his gaze met Matt's. His eyes widened.

The soldier spun around quickly, aiming his gun at Matt. His knuckles were white where he gripped it with both hands. He was shaking. "Drop your gun and raise your hands," he said slowly and clearly.

Matt took a couple of steps closer. He already had his own gun out and aimed at the German. "Lower your weapon, Gefreiter. You're pointing it at a superior officer. We're on the same side."

Michel moved silently through the forest, heading for the sound he'd heard. He stopped at intervals to get his bearings and to try to get a better idea of the position of his prey, yet it seemed to be getting further away rather than closer.

He hadn't wanted to leave Kit, despite it being a better option than waiting for someone to find them. Hopefully whatever he'd heard turned out to be nothing, and they could be on their way. If Reiniger and his men had tracked them this far, it wouldn't be long before they found the Kübelwagen. Reiniger's efficiency had been one of the reasons he'd risen through the ranks so quickly, despite his shortcomings.

What the...?

Michel froze. He could have sworn he'd heard voices close by. In the distance, a dog barked. Up ahead was a patch of dense undergrowth. He sprinted towards it and ducked behind it, considering his next move.

After a few moments, two soldiers walked past. "Nasty way to die," one of them said.

The other shuddered and nodded. "I wouldn't wish it on anyone," he agreed. "I'm happy I'm not the one keeping watch over the body. Dead bodies make me uneasy. I don't think I'm ever going to get used to that."

"I don't want to get used to that." His companion's words trailed off into silence.

Suddenly both men sprung to attention. "Heil Hitler!"

Michel parted the bushes cautiously and peered through. One glance at who had provoked the response from the soldiers and he closed his peek hole quickly and stayed as still as he could.

"Heil Hitler!" Reiniger returned the greeting. "Stay attentive!" he snapped at them. "Now is not the time for idle conversation. Anyone caught doing so will be disciplined accordingly. Do I make myself clear?"

"Yes, Herr Obersturmführer," both men chorused.

If Reiniger had heard any of their discussion, they were lucky to get off with a warning. Someone in their unit at the institute had been caught shirking his duties. Michel shuddered, not wanting to dwell on the details. The man's punishment had been harsh, without mercy, and far in excess of what was required for his so-called crime.

"Our enemy is close by. We've already caught one, and I suspect his companions will not readily abandon him." Reiniger snorted. "That weakness can be used to our advantage, so it is important we are prepared. Do I make myself clear?"

"Yes, Herr Obersturmführer."

Caught one?

Michel took a sharp breath. Surely Reiniger hadn't found Kit? Kit was with Leo. If two men had been discovered, Reiniger would have said so. Wouldn't he? Unless Kit had left Leo and been caught a distance from him.

No. Kit wouldn't... Michel mentally groaned. Of course he would, if he thought it necessary, and especially if he'd decided Michel might be walking into some kind of trap. He'd try to warn him and to hell with the consequences.

Reiniger turned, his eyes narrowing as he glanced in Michel's direction. Michel held his breath, praying, hoping his hiding place hadn't been compromised. "What are you standing here for?" Reiniger snapped at the two soldiers. "They're somewhere close, and I want them found." He gestured in the direction from which Michel had come. "Get on with it."

"Yes, Herr Obersturmführer."

The soldiers saluted and moved off. Reiniger stood for a moment, as though thinking, his face creasing into a frown, and then he headed in the opposite direction. He muttered something under his breath, but Michel couldn't make out the words.

He heard breathing behind him. Close behind him.

Merde! He reached for his weapon, but before he could draw it, he felt the barrel of a gun pressed against his back.

Michel slowly raised his arms. He'd let himself become distracted, first by Reiniger and then by thoughts of Kit. He usually wouldn't have let someone get this close.

The person holding the gun on him slid one hand around Michel and retrieved his Walther P38 from its holster.

"Turn around slowly and keep your hands where I can see them," a man said.

Michel did as he was told, keeping his body tense, ready to move if the chance presented itself. A gunshot fired now would only bring Reiniger and more soldiers. While Michel might overpower one man, attempting the action while outnumbered and unarmed would be foolish.

"You!" To Michel's surprise, he recognised the man holding the gun on him. He lowered his arms. "Ken Lowe," he hissed. "What the hell are you doing here?"

Ken shrugged but didn't lower his gun. "I should ask you the same thing, Gabriel." He looked Michel up and down. "Or should I call you Michel? You seem to be a man possessing several names."

"Michel is fine." His papers gave his identity as Michel Werner, so he preferred Ken used it in case someone over-heard a later conversation. "Gabriel is my code name. Put the gun away. I mean you no harm. We're on the same side."

"Is Lehrer with you?" Ken, like Michel, was dressed in a German uniform. "And I'll ask you again, what are you doing here?"

"Yes, he is," Michel answered. Although Ken didn't seem particularly trusting, it wasn't wise to stay in one place for too long. He needed to be persuaded to lower his weapon. "We were on our way to Freudenstadt and saw an aircraft come down in the Black Forest earlier this morning. Kit—Kristopher insisted we attempt to find the pilot."

Ken raised one eyebrow. "What happened to getting him to a safe place?"

"He can be rather persuasive when he wants to be." Michel kept his voice neutral. "Stubborn too. Besides, he had a point. What are *you* doing here?"

"Clara Lehrer said you could be trusted." Ken handed Michel back his weapon and reholstered his own. "I hope she's right."

"Thank you." Michel returned his weapon to its holster. "Are you alone?"

"No. We should collect Lehrer and meet up with the rest of my team." Ken glanced around. "You said he was with you?"

"Nearby." Michel hoped that was still true. "The forest is swarming with soldiers. We had a run-in with Reiniger yesterday. I doubt he's only here to find the crew of that aircraft."

"Wonderful." Ken's expression didn't change. He was a difficult man to read. "I found the wreckage, but there's no sign of the crew. It's a Mosquito, so there should be a pilot and a navigator, although it looks as though one of them bailed before it crashed."

"Kristopher's with the pilot," Michel told him. "We haven't seen any sign of the navigator." He hesitated. If they were going to work together, Ken needed to have all the facts. "Did you hear anything of Reiniger's conversation?"

Ken shook his head. "No. I missed him." He narrowed his eyes. "Why?"

"He said they'd 'caught one,'" Michel told him, no longer able to ignore his growing sense of dread. "The way he phrased it, I doubt he meant the missing navigator. I'm hoping he's not talking about Kristopher. I shouldn't have left him." He turned and began to walk back to where he'd left Kit and Leo. Reiniger had told his men to search in that direction. He only hoped he wasn't too late.

"Caught one?" Ken's face turned grey. He caught Michel's arm, his next words barely a whisper. "There's another option you haven't thought of. Matt... Matt and Liang are out here too. He might have got his hands on one of them."

~

Kristopher grasped his gun firmly in both hands, determined to at least sound calm. His hands shook. The man holding the gun on *him* had noticed.

He didn't have the option of lowering the weapon, or let Reiniger or any of his men get their hands on Leo. The SS officer would make sure he was part of the interrogation that would follow. Reiniger knew Michel and Kristopher were in the area, and he'd follow any clue, however small, until he got the answers he wanted.

"Put the gun down, Gefreiter," the man barked. He wore a Hauptman's uniform so outranked Kristopher by quite a bit. "That's an order."

"I'm sorry, but I can't do that... sir." What the hell could Kristopher do? Although they outnumbered the Hauptman two against one, he couldn't count on Leo for any assistance.

"I surrender." Leo spoke suddenly from behind him. "Ich ergebe mich," he repeated, this time in German. He raised his hands. He didn't carry a weapon, having discarded his shortly after his aircraft had crashed. He'd told Kristopher it would slow him down, and there was no chance of him shooting his way out if he were surrounded anyway as he couldn't shoot a target if his life depended on it.

The Hauptman glanced from Leo to Kristopher. "He wants to surrender," he told Kristopher. "Lower your gun and I won't pursue this. You won't be in any trouble."

Leo tried to stand. "Do what the nice man says," he said in English. "You can be on your way then. I don't want to cause any trouble." A hiss of pain escaped his lips.

"Of course I won't." Kristopher glanced behind him long enough to see Leo leaning heavily against the tree. Looking back at the Hauptman, he noticed the man had a first aid kit slung over his shoulder. "This man needs medical attention. I'll lower my weapon if you let me use whatever is in your first aid kit to treat him." With any luck it might contain some kind of pain relief, and Kristopher could only keep this standoff going for so long. As soon as his bluff was called, their standoff would be over. He couldn't shoot anyone, and the sound of gunfire would bring soldiers running in their direction.

"Actually..." Leo was peering at the kit with interest. "That first aid kit is mine. I left it behind. What's he doing with it?" He nodded at Kristopher. "Why don't you keep your gun on him and get him to hand the kit to me."

Kristopher raised an eyebrow.

Leo shrugged. "I recognised enough words to guess what you said."

"Hand the kit—" Kristopher started to say. The suggestion couldn't hurt, and it would at least advance the situation somewhat.

To his surprise, the Hauptman lowered his gun. "Why don't we all speak English?" he suggested with an American accent.

"You sound American," Kristopher blurted out in English. He kept his gun pointed at the Hauptman. This could be a trap, but even so, he didn't see the point hiding the fact he could speak English, considering the Hauptman had guessed that much at least.

"And you sound British." The Hauptman pointed at Leo. "I'm not sure about your accent, but you're definitely RAF, and you're right. This kit is yours." He threw it to Leo, who caught and opened it. "Lower the damn gun, will you? I'm guessing you're not about to shoot me with it, not with the way your hands are shaking, and I don't particularly want it going off accidentally. This forest is crawling with soldiers."

"Soldiers dressed in the same uniform you're wearing," Kristopher pointed out.

"You're not exactly trying to be conspicuous either. Look, it's starting to feel suspiciously like we're both trying to get this man to safety, whatever side we're on. Wouldn't it make more sense to work together? It's going to be a lot easier getting him out of here if we do." The Hauptman held out his hand. "Let's start again, this time without pointing a gun at each other. Matthäus Steube. My friends call me Matt."

Kristopher reholstered his gun and then shook Matt's hand. He had a firm grip, and something about the man's manner made it very easy to trust him. Matt. The Allied team Michel worked with in Berlin had been led by Captain Matt Bryant. The first name and the rank were the same. He matched the description Michel had given too. Light brown hair, bright blue eyes, a muscular build, and the same height. Too many details matched for it to be a coincidence, even disregarding the name he'd given.

Often all it took to take another man's identity or to be presumed to be someone else was to be in the right place at the right time.

If the man in front of him *was* Bryant, what was he doing in the middle of the Black Forest? Unless he was heading for the same safe house Kristopher and Michel had been trying to reach.

"Paul Reichel." If Matt wasn't about to reveal his true identity, Kristopher wouldn't either, and besides, he had no proof to back up his theory. He'd trust him as far as he needed to get Leo to safety and find Michel but no more.

"Leonard Dawson," Leo added. "Leo." He frowned. "How did you find us?"

"I found your aircraft. You left a trail of blood." Matt glanced at Leo. Leo had taken a while to staunch his bleeding nose, and the mess it had left had been the last thing on his mind. "I followed it as far as I could, and the rest was luck, really. And, if you really don't want to be found, it's usually best to blend in with your surroundings." He pointed to the red tag of the flak jacket. "Red tends to stand out in the middle of a forest, especially this time of year. Get rid of it."

"Oh. Right." Kristopher had removed it from the jacket but with everything going on hadn't got any further. "Thank you." He picked it up and shoved it in his pocket so it was out of sight.

"Are you two alone out here?" Matt grinned as soon as he'd asked the question. "Apart from the men dressed as soldiers who are really soldiers, that is."

"Yes." Kristopher answered before Leo could. He wasn't about to alert anyone to the fact Michel was out there somewhere and possibly nearby. "We were debating our next move when you arrived."

Leo shot Kristopher a look but didn't argue. "You haven't seen anyone else wearing a flight suit, have you?" he asked Matt. "My navigator bailed before we crashed. I figured he probably came down near here."

"Fraser," Matt said quietly, his tone suddenly much more serious.

"Yes," Leo confirmed. "Alec Fraser, he's a good bloke." He gave Matt a long hard look. "You've seen him, haven't you?"

Matt nodded. "Yes. I'm sorry. He didn't make it."

"Oh." Leo closed his fingers around the strap of the first aid kit. "His wife was expecting a baby. They were arguing about names... Oh hell." He made a choked noise. Kristopher wished he could offer some kind of support but wasn't sure how. Given Leo's reaction, he and his navigator had been friends.

"Tell us about him later," Matt suggested to Leo. "We've stopped here long enough. You'll do better keeping his memory alive by staying in one piece yourself. You knew him. Be the one to give his dog tag to her." He cocked his head to one side. "Those soldiers I dodged earlier are heading this way. Give me a hand, Paul. We can support Leo between us, and we'll be able to move faster."

"But..." Kristopher started to say. He didn't want to leave until there was no choice. Although it was close to the time Michel had told Kristopher to head back to the Kübelwagen, he had a chance of making it back.

When had Matt taken command of their group?

"Unless you've got a better idea? I, for one, am not going to stay here and wait for them to find us." Matt was already helping Leo to his feet. "Do you want morphine before we do this?"

Leo shook his head. "I'd prefer to wait until I really need it. For the moment, I'm fine." Matt raised one eyebrow. "All right, I'll admit it's not an exact definition of the word, but..." Leo shrugged, then lapsed into silence.

"No, I don't have a better idea." Kristopher slid his arm

around the other side of Leo's waist. "Do you have some kind of vehicle? I have one about twenty minutes from here. I can take you to it. It's going to take a long time to walk to Freudenstadt like this."

At least that way they'd be heading in the same direction as Michel. If the Kübelwagen was gone, they could continue on to Freudenstadt on foot and hopefully meet up there.

"Now there's a coincidence." Matt raised an eyebrow. "I'm heading to Freudenstadt too."

"It's the closest town," Kristopher pointed out evenly. "It makes sense to head there." He adjusted his grip around Leo's waist. The younger man was heavier than he looked. "I can do my part to carry him," he told Matt.

"I never thought you couldn't. You'll need to lead the way, as you know where you've parked whatever it is."

"A Kübelwagen," Kristopher confirmed. "German Army issue."

"It's yours?" Matt asked.

"Hardly." Kristopher paused for a moment. "I stole it." Strictly speaking, Michel had stolen it and Kristopher had gone along for the ride, but he wasn't about to tell Matt that.

Matt laughed. "I like it. You're a lot more than you appear to be, Paul Reichel."

"You have no idea," Kristopher muttered. Considering what he'd been doing a few months ago, this situation seemed like a dream. Even more crazy, he'd thought it was one he didn't want to wake from.

Once they got into a rhythm half supporting, half carrying Leo between them, Matt sped up their pace a little. Leo's head had lolled forward about fifteen minutes into their journey, but Kristopher wasn't about to stop and check on him. He could hear Leo's steady breathing, and he didn't sound distressed, apart from the occasional mumbled word under his breath.

They were almost to the Kübelwagen when Matt suddenly stopped and gestured for Kristopher to help him drag Leo under the cover of a nearby patch of undergrowth. A few minutes later Kristopher heard voices. He glanced at Matt, who put his fingers to his lips and cocked his head to signify he was listening. Luckily he'd heard the soldiers before Kristopher had.

Matt kept perfectly still, and Kristopher followed his example. Leo started to stir. Kristopher put one hand over his mouth to silence him, and Leo was instantly awake, his eyes widening in fear. "Quiet," Kristopher mouthed and removed his hand. Leo nodded.

Kristopher peered carefully through a gap in the bushes, making sure not to move any of the branches. Two soldiers stood up ahead. One of them was an officer. He looked familiar, but Kristopher couldn't place him.

"Stand guard, Gefreiter, until more men arrive," the officer said. "Herr Obersturmführer Reiniger will be most pleased we've found his Kübelwagen."

"Yes, Herr Hauptman." The soldier saluted and continued to stand at attention.

Of course! That's where Kristopher had seen the officer before. He'd been at the hospital talking to Dr Osterhagen about one of his patients. If he was here, then more than likely Reiniger wouldn't be far behind.

Kristopher clenched one fist, almost without thinking. He ducked down when the officer turned in his direction, breathing a sigh of relief when the man walked past their hiding place without stopping. Soon this clearing would be swarming with soldiers, as finding Reiniger's vehicle would be a sure sign his prey were nearby or had been very recently.

"Leave. Now," Kristopher hissed once the officer was out of earshot. The soldier had moved closer to the Kübelwagen as soon as his superior had left.

Matt jerked his hand towards a path that would take them away from the Kübelwagen. He picked up Leo, put him over his shoulders, and began to run, Kristopher breathing hard to keep up.

Several minutes later, Matt stopped and carefully helped Leo to sit on the ground, leaning him against a tree. Leo glanced from one man to the other. Both of them were in a half-standing position, hands on knees, catching their breath.

"What was that all about?" Leo asked. "Who's this Reiniger fellow? I saw both of you react to the name. Is he a friend of yours?"

Both?

Kristopher turned to Matt. "You know him?" He glanced around nervously. Had he done the wrong thing in trusting Matt? If Matt was working for Reiniger and this was all an elaborate trap...

Oh God. What had he done?

"Calm down. We're on the same side. I take it from your reaction you like that bastard about as much as I do." Matt watched Kristopher very carefully and rested his hand on his gun. "Unless you didn't steal that Kübelwagen, after all. It is his, isn't it?"

"Reiniger's no friend of mine. And yes, it is his. We..." Kristopher stopped, realising his mistake.

"We?" Matt asked softly. "You told me you were out here alone. What else aren't you telling me?"

"Is Matthäus Steube your real name?"

Matt shook his head. "No. Is Paul Reichel yours?"

"No." Kristopher took a deep breath. "But it's the name on my identity papers, so that's why I gave it to you and why I'm going to continue to use it. I'm guessing the name you gave me is what is on yours too."

"Fair enough." Matt seemed to relax a little.

Leo interrupted the conversation. "Are you Resistance?" he asked Matt. "You sound American."

"His German is also very good," Kristopher pointed out. More than very good, he sounded like a native Berliner.

"I'm working with the Resistance," Matt admitted. "And yes, I'm American, but I spent some time in Berlin. I guess this is the time to put our cards on the table. From what I can see, we have a common enemy, and as the saying goes, any enemy of my enemy is my friend. At least for now. You?"

Kristopher saw no harm in telling a version of the truth. For now, or at least until he found Michel again, working with Matt could be the difference between surviving or dying. And he had to admit, he grudgingly found himself liking the man. Matt had an easy friendliness about him, and Kristopher's gut feeling was that Matt could be trusted, although that didn't mean he had to do so completely.

"You're right. I'm not working alone," Kristopher said, "but my... partner is still out here, and I'm not giving you any information that might put him at risk. We were supposed to meet at the Kübelwagen, but he won't come near it once he sees the soldiers. We can head to Freudenstadt and hopefully meet up with him there."

"And?" Matt prompted. "You've told me about this mysterious partner of yours but nothing about you. You're British, right, and this is your first time out in the field?"

Had his inexperience been that obvious? Kristopher sighed, deciding the answer to that was yes.

"This is my first time out in the field," he replied, "yes. But..." He hesitated. Not confirming a not-quite truth was one thing, but lying directly to someone he expected to trust him was another. "I'm not British, although my mother was. I'm German and doing what needs to be done to save my country and end this war."

CHAPTER TEN

"What part of Germany are you from?" Ken asked suddenly. He kept his voice low so they wouldn't be overheard.

Michel glanced at him and continued walking. Before long they'd be close to where he'd left Kit and Leo. "What makes you think I'm German?" he asked. So far they'd been lucky and not met up with anyone who might recognise them. Michel had no wish to come face-to-face with Reiniger or any of his men. Kit had seen Müller at the hospital, so it was more than likely others in Reiniger's unit who had worked at the institute might also be in the area.

"You're not?" Ken sounded surprised. "You speak like one."

"So does Matt," Michel pointed out. It seemed an odd time to be having this conversation, and Ken didn't strike him as one who wasted much time on small talk. "Why are you asking me this now?"

"I was curious, and I like to know who I'm working with." Ken shrugged. "I know next to nothing about you."

"You don't need to." Michel smiled a little, imagining

Kit's reaction to the conversation and his amusement over Michel's evasiveness. "I'm French," he said finally. He had to admit he was more than a little curious about Ken too. If he ventured some information, it meant he could ask for some in return. "My aunt is German. She taught me and my brother her language so she had someone who would be able to converse with her fluently. Although she had been in France many years, she missed it." She'd most likely corner Kit once they met and spend hours talking about home. At least he hoped so. Kit would enjoy it as much as she would.

"Her husband never learned?"

"He did, but he finds it very difficult. Her French is very good, so they speak that most of the time." Michel's Uncle Brice had learned a few words of endearment in German, which was one of the reasons Michel told Kit he loved him in German. He knew how much hearing the sentiment in his native tongue meant. Just as he treasured the memory of Kit telling him the same thing in French.

"I'm American," Ken said.

Michel chuckled. "I guessed. Your accent gives you away." While Ken could get away with simple conversation if they met any soldiers before it became too obvious, Michel had already decided to step in and do most of the talking. Luckily, according to the uniforms they wore, he outranked Ken, so it wouldn't be questioned. "You speak the language well enough, though."

"I know my limitations, and I'm following most of what you're saying but not all of it. As long as you don't speak too quickly I'll be fine." Ken grew quiet for a few minutes before continuing. "This was supposed to be a simple mission. We were to go in, get the plans, and get out. I didn't expect to be in Germany for this amount of time. Matt would have handled most of the conversation with the locals. He sounds like one. I know I don't."

"None of this has gone to plan," Michel admitted.

"I don't suppose you speak English?" Ken sounded hopeful.

"Sorry. A little, but not well. Your German is much better than my English, but..." Michel frowned and put his fingers to his lips, signifying they needed to be silent. He could have sworn he'd seen something up ahead—the glint of metal—but it was gone when he looked again.

"Keep walking." Ken spoke softly. "We're meant to be here." He slowed down his pace, and Michel fell into step beside him.

A few minutes later, they passed two soldiers, who saluted but kept walking.

"They knew exactly where they were going," Michel said once they were clear. "I would have expected them to be at least looking around if they were involved in a manhunt."

"Perhaps Reiniger has given up and is moving out?" Ken suggested. "If he's found who or what he's looking for..." He shuddered. "I'm going to ignore that. After all, he hasn't found us, right?"

"It depends *who* he's looking for. He knows Kristopher and I are travelling together. If..."

If Reiniger had found Kit with Leo, it wouldn't take long to figure out who Leo was. His dress and lack of language skills would make it very obvious. Reiniger knew Michel; they'd worked together for months. He'd also guess that having Kit in custody meant Michel was probably not far away.

"Do you think this could be a trap and there will be soldiers waiting for us?" Ken asked.

"Maybe. I'm not turning back, though. I've got to make sure Kristopher is all right. If they've found him..." Michel knew how stubborn Kit could be, especially when he was doing what he thought was *necessary* to protect someone he cared about.

"It rather negates the whole mission if they have him, doesn't it?"

"I don't care about the damn mission," Michel muttered. "I've seen what those men are capable of." He shuddered.

"Kristopher is a friend, isn't he?" Ken asked softly. "Is that why you changed the original mission specs? To help him defect?"

"We've spent the last few months together." Michel kept his tone even. "Yes, he's my friend." And so much more, but he wasn't about to tell Ken that.

"I can understand that." Ken smiled a little. "So, how much farther before we reach where you left him?"

"We're almost there." Michel sped up and moved ahead of Ken, not wanting to waste any more time. No soldiers were around, at least none he could see. He broke into a run, suddenly needing to be sure Kit was safe, only pausing to check the mark he'd left on the trunk of a tree before going further. Corin had taught him how to make a small, almost invisible mark that wouldn't be noticed by a pursuer. It would be so easy to get lost in this forest, and one tree had the nasty habit of looking like another.

He heard Ken behind him but didn't look back, sure Ken would keep up with him.

Where the hell are they?

Michel skidded to a sudden stop and crouched down near the tree where he'd left Kit and Leo. "Kit?" he hissed as loud as he dared. "Kit!"

"They're gone?" Ken stood next to him, breathing heavily. "Are you sure you've got the right place?"

"Of course I'm sure," Michel said somewhat testily. He pushed back a pile of snow with his gloved hand. "See that blood? That's where Leo was sitting. He'd had a bleeding nose." He stood and looked around. Apart from the slight discolouration against the white of the snow, no sign existed that anyone had ever been there. Did Kit know enough to cover his tracks like this? He didn't know how to survive out here.

"How close is your vehicle from here?"

"Not far." Michel shaded his eyes against the light through the canopy of trees and peered into the distance. If Kit had only waited the hour he was meant to, they would have got a good start. "I don't like this," he admitted.

"I'm not that happy about it either." Ken crouched down and examined the area around the tree. "That's interesting," he said.

"What?" Michel looked at the spot Ken was pointing to.

"The ground there, to the side of where you were looking before. The snow's been disturbed. See? There's the edge of a boot mark, as though something heavy rested there for a few moments."

Michel frowned. "You're right." How had he missed that before? "Leo's injured and can't put his weight on one leg. If Kristopher's supporting him, that would explain it. But if he's doing that, how would he have time to get rid of their tracks?"

"He wouldn't, and it would be too awkward." Ken shrugged. "It's been snowing on and off for the last few hours. The most recent snowfall would have covered their tracks." He dumped more snow over it. "There. It's not about to be noticed by anyone else now, is it?"

"What if Reiniger's men are using dogs?" Michel pointed out.

"If the dogs get their scent, it won't matter how well they cover their tracks," Ken confirmed grimly, "and unless it snows again soon, it won't cover ours, which will lead them here."

"I was trying not to think about that. I haven't seen any dogs as yet, although I thought I heard one before I met up with you."

"I've seen them. That part of the search seemed based farther south. I haven't seen any since I found the wreckage of the aircraft. The area was crawling with soldiers. I didn't get too close. I'm hoping Matt and Liang steered clear of it too."

Karl Holm put down the telephone and smiled. This was good news, excellent news in fact. "Arrange for my car to be brought to the front of the building," he told Juliane Dunst. "I wish to be on my way within the hour."

"You seem pleased, Karl." When they were alone they addressed each other informally. It seemed foolish not to, considering they were half brother and sister. She collected her papers and stood. "I'll get on to it right away."

"Thank you, Juliane." Karl closed the open folder on his desk. "We will continue my dictation when I return."

"Might I ask how long you will be away?" Juliane asked.

"It will depend on how long this takes." Karl allowed himself a smile. "Given this latest development, I am hopeful that I will soon have Herr Doktor Lehrer in custody."

"Oh?" Juliane raised an eyebrow. "I had not realised

there were any leads as to his whereabouts since Herr Reiniger lost him and Schmitz in Feuerbach."

"One of Lowe's team has been captured. I am meeting Reiniger in Stuttgart." Karl glanced at her. Shame it wasn't Lowe, as Karl wished to continue their conversation which had been interrupted when the institute had been bombed. The American seemed truly ignorant of the truth behind what his father had done during the last war and even had the audacity to make excuses for it. "Shouldn't you be arranging my car?"

"Right away." Juliane gave him a nod and walked briskly from the room.

Karl looked up in annoyance at the sharp knock at the door. "Is there a problem with the car?" he snapped. Juliane was usually very efficient, which was one of the reasons she'd kept her role as his secretary when they'd moved premises after the bombing.

"I'm not here about the car, Herr Standartenführer Holm." Margarete Huber strode into his office although he hadn't told her to come in. She sat in the seat Juliane had vacated.

"What do you want, Fräulein Huber?" The last thing Holm needed was for Margarete to decide now was the time to start playing one of her "games."

Margarete examined one of her perfectly painted fingernails. Although she no longer wore a sling, he'd noticed movement in her left arm was somewhat stiffer than it used to be. "Why, I'm merely reminding you of our agreement, Herr Holm." She smiled at him.

"I haven't forgotten it, Fräulein." Karl was hardly likely to with the amount of times she'd reminded him of it. "I'll ask you again. What do you want?"

She *tsk-tsked*. "I thought it would be obvious, Herr

Holm. Surely you remember telling Fräulein Dunst that you would soon have Kristopher Lehrer in custody?"

Karl mentally groaned. He wondered, not for the first time, what exactly had passed between Margarete and Kristopher Lehrer, given her determination to be present at his interrogation.

"That does not mean he *is* in custody," he told her.

The thought of sharing a car with Margarete to Stuttgart did not sit well with him. She would drive him mad with her incessant chatter. He found it almost impossible to relax with her around, as he suspected she'd put a figurative knife in his back, given the chance. While he wished he knew what her agenda was, he had to admit he hadn't taken the time to find out.

Not yet, anyway.

"Not yet, anyway." Margarete repeated the phrase, as though reading his mind. It was unnerving, like the woman herself. "I'll meet you at your car, Herr Holm. I am looking forward to the journey. I'm sure we have much to discuss."

"It's not here." Michel glared at the spot where he said the Kübelwagen would be as though he could will the vehicle into existence.

"I can see that. Is it possible Kristopher and this Leo decided to drive to the safe house and meet you there?"

"It's possible, but only if they had no choice. We arranged to meet here." Michel crouched down and examined the ground. "There's a lot of boot marks around where I parked it, more than just Kit and Leo here, if they *were* here." He shook snow off his coat, stood up, and looked around again.

"Do you think Reiniger has them?" Although Ken wouldn't wish that on anyone, he hoped Matt hadn't been the one caught. Despite Matt's insistence he was fine, Ken knew him too well to believe it. He'd held Matt through too many nightmares and heard his mumblings. Matt relived his friend Elise's death every night, as well as his own captivity, the events merging with the fire he'd survived as child. The fire that had claimed the lives of his family and left him an orphan.

"I hope not." Michel's expression looked grim. He turned away, but not before Ken caught a glimpse of real fear in his eyes. Whatever his relationship with Kristopher, the two were close. Ken had caught him referring to Kristopher as "Kit" several times; Clara Lehrer had used her brother's full name when she'd spoken of him.

"We'll find them." Ken couldn't sit back and do nothing, especially after what had happened in Berlin. "I have a truck a short distance from here. If we make good time, we could reach it within half an hour. My guess is that Reiniger is probably heading to Stuttgart."

"Probably," Michel agreed. "He'd have to report back to Holm."

"Of course Holm will want to question whoever it is in person." Ken remembered his own experience with Holm and their conversation. He felt torn between wanting to know the truth behind the story Holm had told about Ken's father murdering Holm's during the last war and wishing he didn't. *If* what Holm had said was the truth. Hell if he knew anymore. "Wait here. I want to confirm something." Ken sprinted to the road, following the tyre tracks. The Kübelwagen had definitely turned north towards Stuttgart, rather than south, so if they followed him, they should be able to find out more from the Resistance. Ken had memorised the list of contacts Juliane had given them.

He turned and sprinted back the way he'd come. At first he couldn't see Michel anywhere as he was examining the ground behind some nearby bushes.

"Have you found something?" Ken asked.

Michel held out a red strip of webbing. "This is from Leo's flak jacket," he explained. "They've definitely been here." He pointed to the ground behind the bushes. "See that mark there? Something or someone was dragged out of here."

"Just because it's from a flak jacket doesn't mean it's Leo's." Ken turned it over and looked at it carefully. "I saw enough of the aircraft to identify it. He wouldn't have been the only one onboard, which means there's at least one other crewman unaccounted for."

"From the way Reiniger spoke, I doubt that's who he was talking about. Besides, the crew aren't his target, Kristopher is. Reiniger can be rather... single-minded."

"That's not always a bad thing." Ken had been told he was that way himself.

"Isn't it?" Michel said. "He won't stop until he catches his prey." He took back the strip of webbing and shoved it into his pocket. "I've worked with him. I've seen exactly how he is, and it's not pleasant for anyone concerned."

"Worked with him?" Ken raised an eyebrow. Juliane had told them Michel had worked at the institute, but not that it had been with Reiniger.

"As part of the security detail, so he was my direct superior, and also Holm's right-hand man. He made sure we never forgot it. He's one of those men who are desperate to make a good impression, despite having aspirations much higher than he could achieve. He always found someone to take his bad mood out on." Michel shrugged. "I ended up on the receiving end of his anger several times."

"You could have reported him."

"Not an option while undercover and trying to keep a low profile. Besides, no one would take my word against that of my superior officer, and the institute wasn't run that way." Michel shrugged. "He won't forget what I did to him when Kristopher and I escaped from custody either."

"I hope you got a few good punches in," Ken said.

"Oh, I did." Michel grinned suddenly. "I left him restrained to a tree with his own handcuffs. He wouldn't have been happy." His expression grew sombre. Whatever memory had come next wasn't a pleasant one if Michel's change of demeanour was anything to go by.

Ken knew next to nothing about what had happened to Michel, and by extension Kristopher, since that evening nearly three months ago at Elise's Kaffeehaus. If Juliane knew anything of their whereabouts through her connections with the Resistance, she hadn't passed along the information.

"Perhaps Kristopher left the strap here for you to find?" Ken suggested. "If he got here before us and saw Reiniger, he'd have enough sense to hide." At least Ken hoped he would. "Does he know where the safe house is in Freudenstadt?"

"Yes." Michel shrugged. "That's working on the assumption Reiniger doesn't have him."

"There's only one way to find out." Ken didn't want to think about Reiniger having Matt either, but dwelling on it wasn't going to do Matt any good if that was what had happened. He hoped either Matt or Liang, or preferably both of them, were waiting with the truck.

Damn it, Matt. Be safe.

Ken didn't want their last conversation to have been an argument.

"Come on, we're wasting time," Ken said. "The sooner we catch up with Reiniger, the sooner we can assess the situation and plan a rescue."

"He'll be heavily guarded, and it won't be easy."

"Of course it won't." Ken started walking, knowing Michel would fall into step with him, and quickly. He hid a half smile when Michel did just that. "It never is."

Liang hit the concrete floor with a thud. The door of the cell slammed shut behind him, leaving him alone in the dim light.

He crawled over to the nearest wall, his body aching in places he hadn't thought possible to feel pain.

"Bastard," he muttered. He brought his knees up to his chest and wrapped his arms around them. The wall was freezing cold against the back of his pounding head. He gingerly felt around with his tongue. The cut on his lip seemed to have stopped bleeding although it still hurt.

His throat felt dry. Reiniger had offered him water, but Liang had refused it, determined not to show any sign of weakness. In hindsight, that hadn't been a wise move on his part.

He shifted position and immediately regretted it. God, he hurt. Was there anywhere on his body that hadn't been hit? Not only hit but beaten over and over in an attempt to get him to talk.

Liang had politely asked if he could have some tea and suggested they talk about this like civilised gentlemen. Reiniger hadn't appreciated the idea. Liang had already known the man was a bully. Matt must have downplayed what had happened to him, although he'd said Holm was responsible for most of it.

Most, not all of it. The pupil had been taking lessons from the teacher. Holm was on his way from Berlin, and the hospitality Liang had been shown so far was the warm up for the main event. He'd heard Reiniger talking to one of his men while he'd feigned unconsciousness, not only to buy himself a few moments recovery time but to learn what he could.

He would have been better off not knowing.

Liang shivered. He tightened his grip around his knees and closed his eyes.

He wouldn't think about what Matt *had* told him. This had been bad enough. The thought of a whip...

Bloody hell. He needed to think of something else. Anything else.

Juliane.

If he focused, he could see her in his mind as she'd looked the last time they'd talked. He'd run his fingers through her blonde hair, tucking a stray lock back behind her ear. She had the most beautiful deep blue eyes. He'd lost himself in them several times and felt himself blush when she'd repeated herself because he hadn't heard what she said.

Her name formed on his lips. He stopped himself uttering it just in time.

He wouldn't betray her. Being Holm's sister wouldn't save her if Holm discovered she was a part of the Resistance. She was a brave woman, one of the many Germans doing what they could to bring this awful war to an end.

She'd told him that although she was a loyal German who loved her country, she couldn't agree with what Hitler and the Nazi party were doing. Standing up and proclaiming her beliefs would only serve to get her thrown into prison. If she remained free, she could do more good and play her part to help those in need.

A faint laugh escaped Liang's lips. He'd been foolish enough to think she might come to Britain after the war. He'd even told her where she'd be able to find him.

Why would a sophisticated, beautiful woman want him? He still couldn't believe it, yet she'd told him she did, and that she loved him.

They'd kissed that last evening. He'd finally found the courage to act on his feelings. If it was the only kiss they ever shared, it was worth it. She tasted so good, and he wanted more, but he held back, determined to be a gentleman. His grandmother had told him that a good woman should be treated with respect and be courted properly.

They couldn't have a future together. How could they? Their countries were at war. He'd seen the sadness in her eyes when she told him they could find a way. He wanted to believe she spoke the truth, but now the little time they'd had together seemed like a fading dream.

People met loved ones during wars. They also lost them. *Oh, Juliane. I'm sorry.*

He wouldn't only protect Juliane with his last breath. Matt and Ken were his friends, despite his continued failed attempts to keep them at arm's length. At least it wasn't Matt in this cell. He'd been through enough already.

They hadn't found Lehrer or the plans for this device. Liang's position on their team was next to useless unless they did. He wasn't that great at keeping a low profile either. Getting caught had proven that very quickly.

He had no hope of passing himself off as German, so he was more a hindrance than anything.

All he knew was the location of the safe houses they were heading to and some of the names and locations of local Resistance fighters.

Even that made him a risk. He had very little training, only what was deemed necessary to throw this team of theirs together before sending them into the field.

To hell with it. He was strong. He could do this. He had to.

He wouldn't give up his teammates. He wouldn't give up Juliane.

He'd rather lose himself first. Hopefully it wouldn't come down to that.

CHAPTER ELEVEN

"You seem certain this is the right place." Kristopher had found it difficult to keep track of where they were heading. While Leo had done his best to stay awake, Kristopher and Matt had practically carried him between them for most of the journey. Between that and dodging soldiers, the couple of hours it took them to reach the outskirts of Freudenstadt had felt much longer.

"It is. Can you hold Leo up alone for a couple of minutes? I need to grab the key."

They stood in front of a house that looked like all the others in the street. The number of the door matched what Michel had told Kristopher, but if he'd had to find the place by description alone, he would have been hard-pressed to do so. Matt hadn't glanced at street names. He'd seemed to know where to go once they were out of the forest.

Finding their way out of the forest had been the least of it. Kristopher had suggested following the tiny knife marks Michel had left to retrace their steps to where he and Kristopher had parted ways, but Matt decided it would be easier to follow the road from a safe distance, skirting the edge of the forest. His truck was parked off the road, so if they followed it, they wouldn't get lost. He'd muttered something about being lost in a forest once and that being more than enough. Not having the energy to argue, and as Matt seemed to know what he was doing, Kristopher let him take charge. It was easier to do so, at least for now. But if he suggested something Kristopher disagreed with, he'd state his opinions very clearly.

Matt's reaction to finding his truck gone had been unexpected. Instead of being angry or fearful, he seemed almost relieved. He'd explained to Kristopher it meant there was a good chance one of his men had taken it and would be at the safe house when they got there.

The fear, although he'd hidden it quickly, had come when they reached the house and it was locked, with no sign it was occupied.

"Maybe they're hiding? After all, it's not meant to look as though there's someone there, is it?" Kristopher glanced around nervously. They'd been out in the open where they could be seen for far too long. He'd felt very exposed as they'd made their way through the farmland areas of the Black Forest. They'd only reached their destination through luck and that would only last so long.

"True, but considering the houses on the other side are occupied, it's going to draw attention if this one appears vacant." Matt pulled out a loose brick to the right of the front door and retrieved a key. "It also doesn't explain why the key is still here. Locking the house from the inside buys time while whoever is after you has to break in."

"I'm looking forward to finding a bed and sleeping for a week," Leo said. "I can lean against the wall if it's easier," he told Kristopher. "I know I've been a burden. Sorry."

"It's fine," Kristopher reassured him. "We'll get you

inside, then take another look at your leg." It wouldn't heal unless Leo rested, and that had hardly been an option so far.

"I'm thinking the morphine wouldn't be a bad idea either." Leo grunted when Kristopher helped him into the house.

The living room had two couches. He eased Leo down onto one of them and surveyed their surroundings. The room and the rest of the house were a decent size, judging from what he'd seen so far, but much smaller than Kristopher's family home in Berlin. In the far corner of the room stood a large bookcase with stacks of paper on it as well as an assortment of books and newspapers. The upright piano on the opposite room caught his attention. Both the lid and top were closed, and the latter, like the bookcase, had a stack of papers on it. Probably sheet music, Kristopher decided, which would work well in regard to the coded note he would need to leave for Michel.

A door led to a kitchen on their right. Presumably the bedrooms and bathroom were on the next floor.

"The bedrooms are upstairs." Matt confirmed Kristopher's thoughts. "I suggest at least one of us stays down here. There's a back door if we need to get out in a hurry. One of the upstairs windows opens onto the roof, but that's not going to work. Get him as comfortable as you can. I'm going to check upstairs." He laughed at Kristopher's raised eyebrow. "My team and I slept here the night Leo's aircraft came down. It's how I knew where to find it. We were supposed to meet back here afterward."

After Matt sprinted up the stairs, Kristopher heard doors opening and closing. Matt would be making sure they were alone, despite the house appearing empty. If Matt's friends were there, they would have recognised his voice and made their presence known by now.

"Bring down some blankets," Kristopher called up the stairs. "And the first aid kit." Matt wore it slung across his shoulder.

Leo was already beginning to close his eyes. If he could sleep without the morphine it would be better, as they only had one dose.

The kitchen was small, but Kristopher found a couple of pots and a cupboard full of tins of food. A kettle sat on top of the stove. He lit the stove, filled the kettle with water, and put it on to boil. He picked up one of the tins, which contained some kind of stew, and frowned. How was one supposed to heat the contents?

"What did that can ever do to you?" Matt asked from behind Kristopher, making him jump. "You look as though you're about to interrogate the thing."

"I... um..." How could he put his thoughts into words without sounding like a total idiot? He'd never cooked a meal in his life and had no clue how to start. His father's servants had always dealt with everything like that. The only thing he knew how to do was boil water for tea and coffee. At the convent the nuns had brought supper to his and Michel's hiding place, and this was the first time since leaving there he'd had to deal with the issue.

"Give it here. I'm too hungry to watch you staring at it when I could be eating it." Matt took the tin from Kristopher, found an opener, and emptied the contents into the pot.

"Oh." Kristopher watched Matt intently so he'd know what to do next time. He hadn't been sure whether he was supposed to empty the tin and heat the contents or place the tin in boiling water and do it that way.

"Oh?" Matt grinned. "Do you want to explain what you mean by that, or do I have to guess?" He put the pot on the top of the stove. "See if you can find some plates while I'm doing this."

"I don't know how to cook," Kristopher admitted, relieved he could turn his back to Matt while he hunted through the cupboards for the plates. At least that way he didn't have to see Matt's reaction.

"This isn't cooking. It's just heating food that's already been cooked."

"I haven't done that either." Kristopher found a stack of plates and started looking for cutlery. "I've never needed to, so I didn't learn."

"So who did the cooking in your house, then?" Matt seemed more curious than anything. "Your mom?"

"My mother died when I was born." Kristopher pulled out an assortment of cutlery and counted out three sets, although he doubted Leo would wake for a while yet. "My father... my father had servants. They did the cooking, and I wasn't allowed in the kitchen. It wasn't... done."

"I'm sorry about your mom." Matt stirred the contents of the pot. "I lost my family when I was young, and was brought up in an orphanage. They were very good to me, but it's not the same, even though we all looked after each other."

"My father died during the Berlin bombings. I don't think anything really prepares you for that, no matter what age you are." Kristopher shrugged. For the most part he'd worked through his loss, yet some days it hit him hard and in ways he didn't expect. "We didn't agree on much, but..."

A low moan came from the living room. Leo must be waking.

"It still hurts." Matt nodded. "Look, we don't need to talk about this. I was only teasing about the cooking."

"It's fine." Kristopher managed a smile. "Thank you."

Talking to Matt had been a little too easy. He would have to be careful not to let any information slip he shouldn't. "I'll go check on Leo."

"Good idea." Matt put a lid on the pot and picked up a tea caddy. He shook it, then opened the lid and sniffed it. "I'll make some tea. At least I think this is proper tea. It's hard to tell these days with everything being rationed."

"Tea sounds wonderful." Kristopher walked out into the living room. "Leo? What are you doing?"

Leo stood balanced against the edge of the couch, upright, although barely, sweat running down his face. "Thinking this wasn't such a great idea?" he mumbled, collapsing back onto the couch. "I thought I'd feel better after some sleep, but I don't. In fact I feel worse."

"You haven't been asleep that long. Give yourself a chance and try again."

"I was having this really strange dream." Leo pulled a face. "I was on my uncle's farm over in the Wairarapa, and we were chasing sheep."

"What's so strange about chasing sheep?" Kristopher helped Leo to lie down again. He pulled over a small side table and propped Leo's injured leg on it. "Keep talking. I'm going to look at your knee, and it might hurt."

"It already hurts." Leo closed his eyes. "There's nothing strange about chasing sheep. It was the sheep. They had..." He cracked open one eye. "Promise you won't laugh?"

"I promise." Kristopher carefully opened the makeshift splint. Leo's knee was swollen, but Kristopher had expected that. The graze below concerned him.

"Bloody hell," Leo hissed. He gripped the couch, his knuckles white.

"Tell me about the sheep, Leo." Kristopher knew enough about what he was looking at to realise it didn't look right. Michel had given him the name of a local nurse who could help. They'd have to find her in the morning.

He briefly placed his hand against the graze. The skin and the area around it was red, hot to the touch, and seeping blood.

"The bloody things had fangs. I haven't been back to his farm since the quake in '42. Not sure why I'd dream about it now." Leo shivered. "Is it only me or is it cold in here? I can't seem to get warm. My head hurts too."

"You could have a fever." Matt spoke from behind the back of the couch. "That would explain the dream too. It is cold but warmer than it was outside. You've been through a lot, so there could be some shock and concussion in there too." He handed Kristopher one of the bandages from the first aid kit. "Sorry, thought I'd left this out here before."

"Thanks." Kristopher redressed Leo's wound, then refastened the splint. It was probably a good idea to keep his knee immobile, at least till they figured out what to do.

"I've made tea." Matt felt Leo's forehead and covered him with the blankets lying on the end of the couch. He must have brought them down when Kristopher was in the kitchen. "You don't feel too hot, so if you do have a fever, it's probably not much of one. You want some tea, Leo? I hunted for coffee but couldn't find any. I'm guessing that's harder to get hold of."

"We're lucky to have tea," Kristopher told him. "Why don't I come out to the kitchen and help you?"

"I don't need..." Matt glanced at Kristopher and then Leo. "Oh, what a good idea." He grabbed Kristopher by the arm and manoeuvred him into the kitchen.

"I was trying to be subtle." Kristopher lowered his voice. "I don't want to worry Leo, at least not yet."

"I thought the running through a forest avoiding the

enemy at every turn would have given him some hint that things aren't great," Matt said dryly. Kristopher shot him a look that suggested very strongly he wasn't amused by the comment. "It was a joke, Paul. I know you're worried about him. I can see it on your face. He will too, if you're not careful."

"The graze on his knee is hot to touch. From the little I do know, I think that might mean it's infected. We don't have any sulpha drugs to combat it, and…"

"How much *do* you know about medicine?" Matt asked. "You looked as though you knew what you were doing, so I figured I'd let you get on with it."

"Not a lot," Kristopher admitted. "I was posing as a field medic and helped out a little in a hospital while we were in Feuerbach. I have a… friend… who is a doctor. Most of what I know I picked up by watching her. She'd often explain what she was doing and why." He'd told the truth, just not the whole truth.

Matt poured the tea and gave one cup to Kristopher. "Take that out to Leo. It's not going to take him long to work out we're taking more time than it should to make the tea."

"I have the name of a nurse who will help. She works with the Resistance in Freudenstadt."

"Give me her name, and I'll find her in the morning."

The temperature had fallen further with the dwindling outside light.

"Her name is Isa Beckert, and she lives on one of the streets off the square." Kristopher told Matt the address, and he repeated it. Better they both had the information. "I can go," he offered.

Matt shook his head. "I want you to stay with Leo. You might not know what you're doing, but you act like you do. There's no need to worry him until we have to."

"Hopefully it won't get to that point." Kristopher hoped they were doing the right thing waiting until morning, but trying to find someone at this hour of the night would be foolish. He took the tea out to Leo, Matt following behind with the other two cups. They sat at opposite ends of the other couch.

"I guess I'm sleeping down here." Leo sipped his tea. "The couch is comfortable enough, and I'm not stupid enough to think I can manage those stairs." He smiled at Matt. "You make a decent cuppa. My mum always said most of life's problems could be solved with a cup of tea." His hand shook a little as he brought the cup to his lips again.

"I'll sleep on this couch." Kristopher gave Matt a look he hoped would be taken to mean it wasn't open for debate.

"Good idea. I'll bring down some more blankets and pillows. There are beds upstairs. I'll take one of those."

"Perhaps your team will be here by morning?" Kristopher tried to sound hopeful. Where was Michel? He was supposed to be here by now too. He could look after himself, but what if he'd run into Reiniger and his men? He wouldn't have stood a chance. Would it be too risky to ask Isa if she'd heard anything? It was safe to ask someone in the Resistance, wasn't it?

Whatever had happened, Michel had to be alive. Reiniger needed leverage to persuade Kristopher to surrender. Kristopher had offered to give himself up to save Michel in Berlin. Reiniger would remember that.

Wouldn't he?

So if Reiniger had Michel and wanted to trade, why hadn't Kristopher heard anything?

"I hope so." Matt leaned over and placed a hand briefly on Kristopher's shoulder. "I'm sure your friend will be here by then too." He drained the rest of his tea and yawned. "Time for bed. It's been a long day, and tomorrow will be early too. Once this war is over, I swear I'm going to sleep for a week."

"I know the feeling." Although Kristopher had got plenty of rest while they were at the convent, the last couple of days had been very tiring. He caught Leo's empty cup when it fell from his fingers as his eyes started to close. Luckily it was empty.

Leo jerked awake again. "Sorry, I need to sleep I guess."

"Do you need the morphine?" Kristopher asked. "There's also some food heating on the stove."

"I'll see how it goes without it," Leo said. "The morphine, I mean." He managed a crooked smile. "If I wake screaming in the middle of the night, it probably means I made the wrong decision."

A peculiar expression crossed Matt's face. The mix of fear and guilt was gone so quickly that Kristopher wondered if he'd imagined it. Neither of them had been forthcoming about their true identities, and it made sense that Matt would have his own secrets. Michel had heard through the Resistance that Matt had been captured by Holm and held for several days. Kristopher wasn't about to ask him about it, even if Matt did eventually confirm his identity.

"I can come get the blankets," Kristopher offered. "Get yourself settled. There's something I want to do before I sleep." Hopefully Leo would eat later when he was ready.

"All right." Matt ran one hand through his hair. "Good night. I'm going to take a plate of that stew upstairs with me. If you need me, yell."

"Don't worry, I will," Kristopher reassured him. He pulled the blankets up around Leo, who nodded his thanks. "If you need anything during the night, I'll be close by."

"Thanks, Paul." Leo yawned. He lowered his voice, gesturing for Kristopher to come closer. "You trust Matt, don't you? I notice you haven't mentioned Michel very often or used his name. You weren't going to tell Matt about him if he hadn't caught your slip."

"I trust him. As much as I can, anyway. Michel told me, and more than once, that the less people know, the less can be tortured out of them if they're caught."

"You're worried about Michel?" Leo frowned. "But I know about him and can describe him. So do you. I'd like to think I could tell the Hun..." His voice trailed off, and he looked suddenly aghast. "I'm sorry! I forgot for a moment you're German. I didn't mean it like it sounded."

"I don't like this war any more than you do, and I want it over." Kristopher had flinched when Leo had used the word. He hated it and the connotations that came with it. "I *am* German, and as I told Matt, I'm doing what is needed to save my country. I'm a loyal German first and foremost, but that doesn't mean I agree with what Herr Hitler and his Nazi party are doing." He shivered, remembering the letter he'd found in Kluge's paperwork, knowing full well what the Nazis would do with his work if they got hold of it. "Go to sleep. Please. I'm tired. We all are."

"I *am* sorry." Leo sounded very subdued.

"I know," Kristopher said softly. He gathered up the cups, took them out to the kitchen, and put them in the sink. He could hear Matt moving around upstairs.

Where are you, Michel? I miss you. I'm worried about you.

I love you.

If Leo had issues coming to terms with Kristopher being German and not acting like he expected, how the hell would he cope with Kristopher being a homosexual?

God, he couldn't go back to his previous life, could he? Not that Kristopher wanted to, but he'd truly put everything he'd once thought important behind him. His priorities had changed so much, he hardly recognised the man he had become.

Hopefully, that was a good thing. A small smile played across his lips as he served himself some of the stew. Michel had told him he though rather than Kristopher changing that much, he'd become more aware of who he really once, and what he deemed important. He'd always been a good man, or why would his conscience have irked him persistently after David had spoken with him until he'd finally taken action and done the right thing?

Michel always knew what to say, although sometimes the words weren't always what Kristopher wanted to hear.

A glance at the couch confirmed Leo had drifted back to sleep. Kristopher found a pencil and a couple of pieces of paper on the bookshelf on the far wall and sat at the table. If he left a message for Michel on the piano, no one would think twice about seeing a half-written music manuscript there. He'd write both versions of the note now, as they would require some thought, and leave the appropriate one when the time came. Although he wanted to believe he wouldn't need either of them and they'd be reunited before he had to leave, he wanted to be prepared in case.

He'd finished his meal and written the first note—using the code they'd devised—to tell Michel to meet him at the safe house in Freiberg and that their current location had been compromised, when he heard a noise from upstairs.

It sounded like someone crying.

Matt?

Kristopher turned the light on at the bottom of the stairs and sprinted up them. A quick glance through the doors of the first room confirmed the noise wasn't coming from there. The door at the end of the hallway was ajar. He walked over to it quickly but then paused, resting his hand on the door handle.

If Matt was upset, did Kristopher have the right to walk in on a private moment?

"Ken!" Matt called out the name, his voice cracking with emotion. "Don't leave me! Come back! Don't go in there. The fire..."

Fire?

To hell with this. Kristopher couldn't leave Matt alone to deal with whatever troubled him. He couldn't feel any heat through the door, and the handle felt cool to the touch. He sniffed the air but couldn't smell any smoke. Who was Ken? Was this some kind of nightmare?

He pushed open the door. A dim light shone from somewhere on the floor, barely illuminating the room. Kristopher located the light—it was a low-wattage night-light—and placed it back on the bedside cabinet.

Matt sat huddled in the corner of the bed, against the wall, bedclothes pulled tightly around him. He shivered, his eyes open but unseeing. He looked up when Kristopher sat on the bed, but he doubted Matt registered who or what he was seeing.

"Ken?" he whispered hoarsely. "I'm sorry. I tried to sleep, but the nightmares came again. It's worse without you. God, they're worse."

Ken?

Michel had spoken of a Ken Lowe. He was a member of Matt's team. Could that be who Matt was talking about? By the way he spoke, it sounded as though the two men were close friends and Ken had helped him through what must be recurring nightmares.

"I'm not Ken," Kristopher said softly, choosing his words carefully. "I'm Paul. Ken's not here, Matt, but he's safe." At least he *hoped* Ken was safe. "There's no fire, I promise. It's only a dream."

Matt stared blankly for a moment, then jerked back as though suddenly realising where he was. He looked up at Kristopher, their eyes meeting briefly before Matt turned away.

"I'm sorry," he murmured, "I'm so sorry." He looked down at his fingers, white knuckled and clutching the edge of the blanket.

"We all have nightmares," Kristopher said. "There's nothing to be sorry for. Do you want to talk about it?"

After a few minutes silence, Matt finally looked up. He spoke quietly and didn't sound at all like the confident, good-humoured man Kristopher had thought he was beginning to get to know. "How much did you hear?" he asked, an edge of fear in his voice. "It's not true, you know. It's only a nightmare. Ken..." Matt bit his lip. "It's just me. He had nothing to do with this."

Kristopher frowned, not understanding what Matt meant by the words. Ken wasn't here. Why try to protect him?

"*It's worse without you.*" Matt's words echoed through Kristopher's mind.

Realisation hit.

When Michel had nightmares, Kristopher held him, spoke softly to him, and told him he loved him. The same way Michel did it for him when he needed the reassurance that the person he loved was there and safe.

"I won't say anything," Kristopher told Matt. "I didn't hear anything. I promise."

"Thank you." Although he still sounded on edge, Matt

seemed a little more like himself. "I... I have nightmares," he said haltingly. "They're worse in the dark, which is why I left the light on, why I wanted to sleep up here by myself. I thought I wouldn't wake you that way—that you wouldn't need to know."

"I won't tell anyone," Kristopher promised. What had happened to Matt while he was in custody? Surely he wouldn't have been sent on this mission if he already suffered from these nightmares.

Matt nodded but didn't say anything.

"You didn't wake me," Kristopher reassured him. "Is there anything I can do to help? Perhaps I could sit with you until you go back to sleep?"

"You don't have to—"

"I know that. I want to." Kristopher smiled a little, remembering waking several times to find Michel watching him. "As I've already told you, we all have nightmares. I've found knowing I have a friend nearby helps."

"We've only just met," Matt said.

"Friends are made and lost quickly during these terrible times. I've already lost too many friends and family because of this war. Let me at least do this for you, hmm?"

"All right." Matt looked hesitant, yet lay back down on the bed and pulled the blankets up over himself.

"Don't worry. I won't repeat anything I hear, and this stays between us." Kristopher got off the bed. He shifted the chair from the other side of the room closer to the bed and grabbed a couple of blankets off one of the other beds. "Now sleep."

"I don't expect you to stay here all night." Matt's eyes were already beginning to close again. "You need your sleep too."

"I'm not intending to stay here all night." Kristopher

settled into the chair and arranged the blankets around him. Upstairs was colder. Their first night at the Klosterkirche, Michel had spent the night bundled up in blankets in a chair watching Kristopher sleep. He'd sung a lullaby to him in French, a soothing song that Kristopher had since learned.

As Matt's breathing began to even out, Kristopher started to sing softly, his memories echoing the simple tune, remembering that night. Once Kristopher knew the song, they'd sung it together, Michel changing his part slightly so he was singing a harmony.

Kristopher faltered. His voice hitched, tears forming in his eyes. He didn't rub at his face but instead let them fall.

Je t'aime, Michel.

He wanted so badly to be able to hold Michel, to tell him he loved him, to kiss him softly and hear the words Michel loved to say.

Ich liebe dich auch, Kit.

Matt slept peacefully, seemingly free of his nightmares, at least for now. Kristopher hoped Matt would find his Ken again too.

It was always worse without the one you loved.

Be safe, Michel. Take care, my love.

Kristopher stood quietly so he didn't disturb Matt, folded the blankets neatly on the chair, collected the empty plate from their makeshift meal, and slipped out of the room. As much as a part of him yearned for company and for the reassurance it brought, for now he needed to be alone.

CHAPTER TWELVE

Michel paced back and forth across the room. Max, the Resistance operative Michel and Ken had contacted as soon as they'd reached Stuttgart, had told them to keep out of sight. Although sensible advice, it didn't make the waiting any easier.

The longer they waited, the longer Holm and Reiniger could be doing God knew what to Kit, or whoever they had in custody.

"Do you want a cigarette?" asked Ken. "It might calm your nerves." Despite his offer, he lit one then stubbed it out a few moments later.

"No, thank you. I'm fine."

Ken's talk and seemingly calm demeanour didn't quite hide his apprehension. When they'd reach his truck, only to find none of his team there, Ken had faltered for a moment. The words he'd muttered under his breath were in English, and although Michel hadn't heard them before, the meaning and tone easy to guess. His concern for Matt matched Michel's uneasiness about Kit.

Sleeping alone the night before, without Kit close by,

had been harder than Michel had thought it would be. Over the months they'd spent together, he'd grown used to sharing his bed and waking to either Kit propped up on one elbow watching him or listening to Kit's breathing as he slept. Michel often laid his head on Kit's chest so he could hear his heartbeat. He found the sound comforting and a confirmation that, at least for now, they were together.

It had been late but not quite dark when he and Ken reached Stuttgart. Ken already knew where to find Max, as they'd met when he and his team had taken shelter in Stuttgart on their way to Freudenstadt. Max had been surprised to see him again but had wasted no time in finding them somewhere safe to spend the night. The truck was parked off the street in a nearby deserted warehouse used by the local Resistance.

"Why don't you try to get some sleep?" Ken said. "I know you didn't get much last night."

"If you know that, then you obviously didn't get much yourself," Michel pointed out. He poured himself another cup of coffee. "Sorry, I didn't mean to keep you awake."

"I wasn't sleeping anyway." Ken grimaced. "Some of those bombs sounded too damn close. I swear I'd just gotten to sleep when the sirens went off."

"I would have thought they would have stopped bombing by now," Michel commented, somewhat dryly. "It's been going for several days now, day and night."

"I don't like this any more than you do," Ken said. "I didn't join up to kill innocent people either." He examined his cigarette stub, reached for his matches and lit it again, although instead of smoking it, he watched it burn. "I don't think anyone really wins a war. We're fighting for victory, yet there are already too many people who have lost too much to ever go back to the way things were. I'm not only talking about lives being lost, but dignity and the way we perceive ourselves." He shrugged. "I've never..."

"Never what?" Michel asked softly when Ken trailed off. The tone he used suggested his opinions had been formed by something very personal. His words weren't the result of some abstract theory but from a very raw experience. His voice hitched in places, which was unusual, apart from when he spoke of Matt.

"Never mind." Ken shrugged again. "If Max does not return soon, I'm wondering if it's wise to keep waiting. His cover could have been compromised, and I don't want to sit here only to have Reiniger or his men arrive to arrest us."

"Give him a bit longer," Michel suggested. "I'd prefer to know what we're up against before we try to mount some kind of rescue. Knowing where to go would be helpful too. The longer we're out there, the more chance there is of getting picked up." Reiniger had probably circulated their descriptions by now. He knew Michel and Kit were in the area, and if he had one of Ken's teammates in custody, he now knew Ken most likely was too.

"I have no intention of getting arrested by the Gestapo." Ken picked up the cigarette and took a long draw of it. "One meeting with Holm was more than enough." He looked up at Michel. "What were your impressions of the man? Or didn't you see that much of him to form one?"

"I saw enough of him. He... liked to be well-informed about everything going on." Michel took a moment to put his thoughts into words. "He struck me as a man who wanted to be in control, whatever the situation. The few times something unexpected happened, I learned quickly to make myself scarce before the civilised gentleman he projected disappeared. Holm is a dangerous man. Don't be fooled by his demeanour. He's very calculating and won't hesitate to destroy anyone who gets in his way."

"You've seen it?"

"Yes." Michel put his hand out for the cigarette and took several puffs of it, breathing the smoke in deeply. "People make the mistake of thinking Reiniger is the dangerous one. He is, but although he's learned everything he knows from Holm, he lacks the finesse of the master." He held out the cigarette to Ken, but Ken shook his head.

"Finish it." Ken pulled up the other chair in the room and propped his legs up on it. He put his hands behind his head and leaned back, half closing his eyes. "Holm believes in what he's doing, that's for sure. In his mind he's justified all his actions. That came across loud and clear."

"How long did you talk with him?" Michel was curious now. Whatever had passed between Holm and Ken didn't sound like merely an interrogation between an SS officer and his captive.

"Long enough." Ken glanced at Michel. "Apparently our families have a history. I had no idea." His tone grew bitter. "I also apparently look like my father. Not that I'd know. I've never met the guy."

"Sorry."

"Don't be." Ken rolled his eyes. "The more I learn about him, the more I think I was probably better off not knowing him."

"You can't take whatever Holm said to you as the truth. He twists things to suit himself." Michel had noticed that very quickly, and listening to the whispers between some of the scientists working on the project had confirmed it. Many of them spoke as though their guards were not in the room and acted like Michel's role within the institute was that of a servant, which therefore made him invisible. Their attitude had puzzled him at first, but he'd soon learned to use it to his advantage, and it had become a way to pick up information.

"So do most people. It's getting harder to work out who the good guys are." Ken studied the floor. "Nothing's black and white. I keep reminding myself that Hitler and the Nazis are the bad guys and we need to stop them. But I've seen the effect of these bombings on civilians, seen women and children hurt and dying. How can I justify that? Sometimes I feel as though I'm no better than Holm."

"You wouldn't torture someone and enjoy it," Michel said softly. "Holm does." He seemed to get the same perverse enjoyment from ordering someone else to carry it out for him too. "I've seen it in his eyes and in Reiniger's. Reiniger doesn't hide it, nor does he bother to justify it. Holm is more subtle. He tells his prisoners it's their choice they're getting hurt. It's not. He could stop it any time he wants to, yet he chooses not to."

"You've been present when he's tortured someone?"

"Yes." Michel finished the cigarette and took a swig of now-cold coffee. "I'll never forget it. Holm kept going until he got the answers he wanted. It didn't matter that his victim had already told him the truth from the onset. He wanted a certain answer, a specific variation of the truth, and he was going to get it." He slammed the cup onto the table, brown liquid swishing over the rim of it like thin mud.

The thought of Kit at the mercy of Holm... Being hit over and over, the crack of Holm's whip as it connected with bare skin...

The same skin—perfect, smooth, apart from the scar on one shoulder—that Michel had caressed and kissed when he and Kristopher made love.

Michel blinked back tears.

Please, God, no. Don't let him have Kit.

"Michel?"

"What?" Michel looked up to find Ken watching him closely. He'd swung his feet off the chair, his brow crinkled in concern.

"I know you're worried about your friend. We won't leave Stuttgart until we rescue whoever Holm has in custody. Whatever it takes."

Michel nodded. "I know. I wasn't planning to." He managed a grim smile, knowing similar thoughts must be going through Ken's mind. He'd heard Ken mumbling in his sleep the night before and recognised the tone he'd used and some of the words. "Whoever it is and whatever it takes."

Kristopher opened one eye, then closed it again. "Michel?" he murmured, feeling around for the familiar warm body next to his.

His hand collided with something hard and cold instead. He jerked back, sitting up, his eyes fully open, his sleep-fogged brain trying desperately to make sense of his surroundings. "Michel?"

This wasn't the convent, and he wasn't in the comfortable double bed he'd shared with Michel either. Instead he was on a narrow couch with an assortment of blankets over him and a hard pillow under his head. His hand had connected with the wooden edge of the couch.

A brown-haired man slept on the couch across from his, only the top of his head visible over the edge of the blankets he had pulled around him. He shifted uneasily in his sleep, a low groan escaping his lips.

Leo.

Memories flooded back. Kristopher pushed off the blankets, relieved Leo was asleep and hadn't heard him call Michel's name. He let out a breath, and it hung in the air, white smoke that disappeared after a few moments.

It had been late when Kristopher had finally slept. He'd composed a second, much more positive note, for Michel, taking the time to get it exactly right. Hopefully it would be the one he'd have to leave, as it would mean a reality in which Reiniger hadn't found them, so they were safe, at least for now. He'd reread it and sighed. If that was the case, why would they have to leave? They could stay here and wait for Michel. He'd taken it out to the kitchen, fed it into the stove, and watched it burn before starting again. The only difference between the two would be their destination, so Michel would know which safe house to head for. Kristopher wouldn't leave Freudenstadt before Michel unless Reiniger was closing in. Then the note would be a warning and left in the hope it wasn't already too late for either of them.

A key turned in the front door lock. Kristopher got to his feet instantly and reached for the gun he'd tucked under his greatcoat, which hung over the side of the couch, within reach in case he'd had to lunge for both. He'd taken his boots off for the first time in days, wanting to be free of them badly enough to risk it.

Leo hauled himself up into a sitting position, apparently woken by the noise. He glanced at Kristopher. "Should we hide?" he whispered.

"There's no place like home," Matt called as the door began to open.

"We're not in Kansas." Kristopher replied with the counterphrase. He lowered his weapon, glad they'd decided to agree on a code before they'd reached the safe house the night before, although he had no idea why Matt had chosen that particular answering phrase.

A young woman entered the room a few steps ahead of Matt. She had blonde hair and blue eyes and wore a dark-coloured coat. She held a medical bag.

"This is Fräulein Beckert," Matt explained. He carried a paper bag, which he put down on the piano. "She's a nurse and has offered to take a look at Leo's knee."

"Good morning." Kristopher said politely. "I'm Paul Reichel."

"Call me Isa," she suggested, taking off her coat. Matt took it from her and draped it over the back of a chair. "It's probably safer to use first names only, and only hearing your last name once means I'm less likely to remember it." Isa smiled which made her seem much younger. "Matt tells me you know a little medicine and have been treating my patient."

"A very little," Kristopher confirmed. He glanced over at Matt, who grinned and nodded. When had Matt left the house to go find her? Surely it couldn't be that late? How long had he slept?

"I didn't want to wake you." Matt shrugged. Had Kristopher's concern been that obvious? "I figured if I took the front door key, no one else could get in that way, and you'd be able to make a run for it through the back."

"I'm still practicing my hopping," Leo muttered. "It's not going so well."

Isa took off the splint and was now unwinding the bandage. "How did you do it?" she asked in English.

"I jumped down and misjudged the distance." Leo winced when she examined his knee. "I heard something pop and found out very quickly it was me. Or rather my knee. I can't straighten it."

"I suspect you've torn a tendon," Isa said. "You've done the right thing, though. If it doesn't require surgery, keeping it immobile like this is about all we can do for it."

"So no magical cure, then?" Leo asked.

"Sorry, but no." Isa peered at the graze below his swollen knee. "This is more of a concern. It's infected. Do you remember how it happened?"

"No, sorry. I didn't take much notice of it, as my knee was distracting me somewhat." Leo flinched when she touched it. "Ow, that hurts!"

Isa opened her bag. "I'm going to clean it out and then sprinkle sulpha powder on the wound. Hopefully it will help with the infection, but you're going to have to keep it clean and redress it. I'll leave a course of sulphanilamide for you to take." She turned to Kristopher. "Watch what I'm doing so you know what to do. You did a good job with what you had."

"Thank you." Kristopher knew this part was going to hurt. He remembered all too well Clara cleaning out the bullet wound in his shoulder. "Do you want something to bite down on, Leo? It helps."

"I'll be... fine," Leo grunted. He gritted his teeth and turned his head away.

"If you're not, don't try to hide it," Isa suggested. "There is no shame in reacting to pain. I'll be as quick as I can." She retrieved a bottle of surgical spirits from her bag and set to work.

"I went through this a few months ago." Kristopher struck up conversation while he watched Isa work. Michel had talked to him and taken his mind off the pain a little. "I know how much it hurts. I didn't enjoy it." He held out his hand. "If you want something to squeeze, that's fine. I bit down on a piece of leather. It helped a little, but mostly I listened to a friend talk to me. I focused on that rather than the pain. Do you want me to keep talking, or would you prefer I stayed quiet?"

"Talk," Leo whispered. "Please. Tell me about what happened..." He trailed off when Isa poured the sterilising solution over the graze. "Oh... hell." He grabbed Kristopher's hand and squeezed tightly.

Kristopher forced himself not to react to the vice-like grip. "I was shot in the shoulder." It seemed like almost a lifetime ago and more like a dream now, if not for the way his shoulder felt stiff on occasion. The area was still sensitive; he shivered at the memory of how it felt when Michel kissed him there. "Luckily it missed anything important, but it still hurt like hell."

Matt listened intently. Isa seemed more focused on what she was doing. Kristopher hesitated, unsure as to how much he should say.

"I was very lucky," he continued. "The doctor treated it much the same way Isa is treating your graze. It's worth going through this to get rid of any infection." He had been lucky his shoulder had healed cleanly without complications.

The wound cleaned out, Isa sprinkled sulpha powder over it and rebandaged it with cotton gauze. "I'll leave you more medical supplies. Contact me if it gets any worse, and change the dressing twice daily. Don't get it wet. Rest up as much as you can, Leo, and let yourself heal."

"Thank you." Leo looked pale. "Not meaning to be rude, but I think I'll take a nap now. You'll have to excuse me not offering you tea or escorting you to the door." He let go of Kristopher's throbbing hand. Leo had a strong grip.

"It's fine. I'll leave you to rest now." Isa stood and gestured to Matt and Kristopher to follow her into the other room. Once Leo was out of earshot, she spoke further and in German. "Now we hope and pray. With luck he will be all right, but there is always a chance of the antibiotics not working. Keep a close eye on him."

Kristopher nodded. "We will. Do you have any suggestions if it does get worse and we're not in a position to contact you?"

If their location was compromised, they'd have to move on, and it was doubtful they'd be able to stay for as long as it would take Leo to heal.

"Did the doctor who treated you tell you what to look out for?"

"Yes." Kristopher had already known, courtesy of an earlier lecture from his sister, and he'd presumed she'd told Michel. Kristopher had lost consciousness before they'd left Clara's surgery, and Michel hadn't been particularly forthcoming about the conversation that had passed between him and Clara. "It's already red and hot to the touch. If that doesn't go away and it swells or there's a discharge or bad odour, it means he's in trouble."

"Exactly." Isa looked from one man to the other. "Do either of you know how to cauterise a wound?"

"I do." Matt didn't look happy about the idea. Kristopher didn't blame him. "Do you think it will come to that?"

"I honestly don't know." Isa glanced back to the living room where Leo had fallen asleep. "He's young and strong, but it could go either way. When he wakes, help him to change into the clothes I brought you and bury what he's wearing now. At least with his injury, no one will question the fact he's not in uniform."

Kristopher guessed that must be what was in the bag

Matt had carried into the house. "What about identity papers?" he asked. "Matt and I have them, but Leo doesn't. Do you have any contacts in the area who could help?"

It would be dangerous to try and move Leo if he didn't have papers, as that would be the first thing the authorities would ask for.

"There is a group in the area who can help," Isa confirmed. "There's a butcher's shop by the square. Do you know it?"

"I passed it on the way to find you," Matt said. "Is there a code phrase I should use?"

"Buy four sausages and tell the butcher you're waiting for a letter from Simon. There will be a message telling you where and when to meet him in the parcel of meat." She smiled her thanks at Matt when he helped her into her coat. "Be very careful, and don't venture out unless you have to. I heard from one of my contacts this morning that an SS officer who is usually based in Berlin arrived in Stuttgart this morning. Apparently he travelled all night to get there, so it must be for something important."

A shiver crawled up Kristopher's back. "Do you know his name?"

"Yes." Isa glanced at him. "Do you know something about this?"

"I hope not. His name?" Kristopher realised how abrupt he sounded and dipped his head in apology. "Please, Isa. It's important."

"SS Standartenführer Holm. Yes, that was his name. Standartenführer Karl Holm."

CHAPTER THIRTEEN

Liang hadn't realised he was dozing until the door to his cell opened, tired hinges creaking loudly enough to jerk him awake. He peered up at the guard leaning over him and shaded his eyes against the unwelcome light. "What now?" he muttered.

"Get up," the guard ordered.

"I'm getting a tour of the facilities? How nice." Liang struggled to his feet and straightened his clothing as best he could. He'd already decided that, despite the situation, he would behave in a civilised manner for as long as he could. Doing so also gave him something for his sanity to cling to, which had become more of an issue the longer he'd remained in the cell.

It hurt to move so probably a good thing he couldn't see the bruises he could feel. He forced himself not to give in to the ache, to move as though everything was normal.

Nothing about this was "normal." Hell, he'd forgotten the meaning of the word.

But the longer he could fool himself it was, the better.

He'd lost track of how much time had passed since his

arrival in Stuttgart. Since his capture. He hadn't been able to see his watch with his arms behind his back, and it had been taken from him before he'd been thrown into his cell. He supposed he should be thankful they'd removed the handcuffs. Bloody things weren't very comfortable. He doubted they were supposed to be.

Feeling the building shake the night before hadn't helped his composure any either. He'd huddled in the corner and hoped like hell the ceiling wouldn't come down on him. If it had, there would have been no way out.

A blonde woman stood outside the cell. He didn't recognise her. She nodded at him in way of a greeting, and he instinctively returned the gesture. She smiled when he did, but something about her manner made him uneasy.

The guard stood to attention when he saw her.

"Oh, there's no need for that." Despite her words, she seemed pleased he'd treated her with such deference. "I'm here to accompany the prisoner to Herr Holm."

Herr Holm?

Bloody hell. Holm was here already? Liang swallowed. He'd hoped to avoid that meeting indefinitely. Reiniger's actions paled in comparison to the pain Holm was capable of inflicting. Liang had seen the scars on Matt's back, and although he refused to go into detail about exactly what had passed between him and Holm, it didn't take a genius to work it out.

"As you wish, Fräulein Huber." The guard seemed unsure, and Fräulein Huber laughed.

"Naturally you are to perform your duty and take him to Herr Holm yourself. After all, I might need protecting if he decides to be difficult." Fräulein Huber smiled at Liang again and then took a step closer. Her eyes were a darker blue than Juliane's, and the look she gave him was more scrutiny than curiosity. He shivered. "You aren't going to be difficult, are you, Gefreiter Sachs?"

"I'm not going to be difficult." He noted she'd used the name on his forged papers. The longer he could pretend to cooperate, the higher his life expectancy.

"That's almost a shame," she murmured. "Oh, where are my manners? We haven't been properly introduced. I'm Margarete Huber." She held out her hand as though she expected him to shake it.

He hesitated. The guard behind him had a gun. One move out of place and the man wouldn't falter to use it. A bullet didn't have to kill to be effective. A shot could disable him in a lot of nasty places and hurt like hell.

"Shake my hand, Gefreiter," she murmured. "We both know you're going to behave, don't we? After all, you gave your word, and besides, I doubt you want to risk being shot."

"No, I don't," Liang agreed. Attempting to take her as a hostage would be foolish and only succeed in hastening his own demise. He wasn't sure how fast he could move either, given how much it hurt to move. He shook her hand briefly. Her skin felt cool, and he got the impression she carefully considered each word and movement she used. She was a dangerous woman, that was for certain, but exactly how much power did she possess? "Lorenz Sachs. I'm surprised to see such a beautiful woman in these surroundings, Fräulein."

His response seemed to please her. "You'll do nicely. Come along now. We don't want to keep the Standarten-führer waiting."

This whole situation felt surreal, he decided, as they walked down the corridor. Despite his being a prisoner of the Reich, she behaved as though they were taking a social walk through the park. He'd also expected more than one guard. Surely, given his known association with Ken and Matt, the Germans considered him dangerous.

Or perhaps they'd already figured out he wasn't a trained soldier like his teammates? His refusal to be foolish enough to attempt pretence could be used to his advantage.

Despite being lightly guarded, it didn't take long for Liang to realise he had no way to escape. The guard led him through a narrow but well lit corridor, with a locked door at each end. The two well-armed soldiers guarding each door wouldn't hesitate to shoot him. Once through the door at the far end of the first corridor, he found himself outside what appeared to be some kind of office a few minutes later.

Holm sat behind the desk. He was writing something in a notebook and looked up when the guard knocked lightly on the open door. When Holm saw Margarete, his expression darkened. "What are you doing here, Fräulein?" he barked.

The last time Liang and Holm had met, it had been briefly, and Liang hadn't taken much notice of Holm's appearance. He'd been limping, and his demeanour had come across as very calm. Interesting that Margarete's appearance now evoked more of an emotional response than the institute going up in flames behind them had then.

Now that he could see Holm up close and under decent lighting, Liang could see a faint resemblance to Juliane. His hair was blond like hers, but trimmed very short. His eyes were grey while hers were blue. He and Juliane shared a mother; Liang could see her in Holm. Juliane had showed him some family photos and told him that Holm had never forgiven their mother for remarrying after his father had died.

"We have an arrangement, Herr Holm," Margarete reminded him. "Surely you have not forgotten it already?"

"I have not. However, as I recall, your request was very specific, and as Herr Lehrer is not in custody yet, your presence is neither required nor welcome."

"It is only a matter of time." Margarete glanced at Liang and smiled. "I'm sure you'll keep me informed."

"I'm sure I will. Good morning, Fräulein."

"Good morning, Herr Holm." Margarete left the room.

Liang caught sight of two guards outside the door. Had they been there before? He was sure they hadn't. Oddly, Holm's office had been the only one without guards. Liang had the nasty feeling their appearance now was for his benefit, to remind him of his place.

Two more guards entered the room. One of them closed the door before both men took up position in front of it.

"Please sit down, Gefreiter." Holm gestured to a chair opposite the desk. "I must apologise for Fräulein Huber. She is keen to renew her acquaintance with an old friend. Hopefully she will not have to wait much longer."

"Hopefully," Liang agreed, at least vocally. The silence after Holm's comment had strongly suggested it was the only acceptable answer.

The mention of Lehrer had definitely been intentional, and probably not only on Holm's part. Liang had been careful to hide his recognition of the name. Were Margarete and Lehrer really old friends? Or was their friendship because of family expectations? No wonder Lehrer had run. The thought of a lifetime with someone such as Margarete would have been enough to make Liang head for the hills.

"Would you like some tea?" Holm stood and poured from a fine crockery pot before Liang had the chance to answer. "You strike me as an educated man, Herr...?"

"Sachs." Liang took the tea when Holm handed it to

him but didn't drink it. The cup rattled in its saucer, and he willed his hand to stop shaking.

Holm sat down again. He walked with a slight limp, but nowhere as pronounced as when Liang had last seen him. Liang hoped he wouldn't regret his decision not to shoot Holm when he'd had the chance.

But taking someone's life made him no better than those he was fighting. Once he lost his principles and did that, what was the point of any of this?

"Oh, come now." Holm picked up his cup but didn't drink from it. "I know that isn't your real name. How can you expect us to have any kind of conversation if we haven't been introduced properly?"

"I already know who you are, Herr Holm." Liang took a sip of the hot sweet tea and forced himself to drink slowly. His mouth was dry after his time in the cells and the journey to get here. One of Reiniger's men had ordered him to drink the water he'd been given, as they wanted to ensure he'd be fit to answer any questions, but it had barely quenched his thirst.

Holm chuckled. "Do you play chess?" His expression hardened when Liang nodded. "Please keep in mind that you are not the king on this board, or even a knight. You are merely a pawn, and those are easily sacrificed. Now, I'll ask you again. What is your real name?"

If Liang appeared to cooperate, he might survive this. His name was unimportant. From what Juliane had said, Holm already knew the reason for their team's presence in Germany. There was no harm in giving him information he already knew or that would not jeopardise their mission.

"My name is Zhou Liang." Liang looked up and met Holm's gaze directly.

"See, that wasn't so difficult, was it, Herr Zhou?" Holm

leaned back in his chair. Juliane had addressed Liang correctly when they'd been introduced. Given that, it figured her brother would be aware of such things too. "I'm surprised someone of your background is in Germany." He studied Liang for a moment. "I see some European in you. You're not fully Chinese, are you? I suppose that is why you were chosen for this mission. In a dim light, you could be mistaken for something you are not."

"My mother was English," Liang admitted, not seeing the point in denying the obvious. His mother had had blonde hair and blue eyes. He remembered her voice as she'd told him stories, but with each passing year, his memories of her grew dimmer. He'd been a small child when the influenza epidemic claimed his parents.

Holm nodded thoughtfully. "That explains it, then." He took a long drink of tea. "It's difficult denying a part of yourself, isn't it? Family is important, after all."

"Denying a part of myself?" Liang couldn't work out what Holm was talking about. If there was a point to all this, he needed to get on with it.

"Well, it's the only reason you'd be working with Herr Lowe, isn't it?" Holm placed his cup on his saucer and steepled his fingers.

Liang frowned. "I don't understand."

Matt had said Holm had some issues with Ken, but Liang sure as hell wasn't about to confirm he knew about that. He wasn't about to deny knowing Ken either, though, as that would be foolish, considering Holm already knew they were working together.

"Oh dear. My apologies. I thought you knew." Holm poured himself more tea before offering to top up Liang's cup.

Liang shook his head, declining the tea. "Knew what?"

he asked. Holm was behaving like a perfect gentleman. What was he up to? Did he honestly think Liang was so stupid he'd give up information, and trust that easily?

"Your friend, Lowe, is Japanese," Holm explained. "Not fully of course. His mother is Japanese, his father American." He shrugged. "But I doubt it matters, does it? After all, you're British, and that's what is important, yes?"

"You're lying."

Holm had to be mistaken. Ken and Liang were friends, or at least Liang thought so. Ken was American and came from Chicago. His father had served in the last war. Surely he would have told...

No. Why would he?

Liang curled one hand into a fist. He'd lost family in Nanking during the massacre. His beloved grandmother still cried about it. He'd heard far too many stories about the atrocities done to their people by the Japanese during that time. About how they all deserved to rot in hell, except that would be far too good a fate for them.

"You're lying," he repeated. Ken didn't act like the Japanese Liang had heard about. He'd never been foolish enough to judge one man on the actions of others. Juliane was German, but no Nazi. She did what she could to help bring this war to an end, risking her own life to shelter those in need. They'd spent months with her while they waited for Matt to recover from his injuries and until they'd received word that Lehrer and Gabriel had survived the bombing of Berlin.

"I assure you I'm not." Holm appeared concerned, but Liang doubted the sentiment was genuine. "I've seen his birth certificate. The facts do not lie. I'm sorry, Herr Zhou. Sadly, there are many people who are not what they appear to be, especially in this war we're fighting."

"Dr Zhou," Liang corrected absently. He unfurled his fist and took several deep breaths. "What do you want from me, Herr Holm? I'm not about to betray my colleagues, no matter their presumed nationality. You'll have to try harder, if that was what you meant this to do."

"*Dr Zhou.*" Holm smiled. His expression grew colder. "As to what I want from you? Merely information, nothing more." He put his cup and saucer to one side, opened a folder, and pushed a photograph over to Liang. It was of a man about the same age as Liang. He had blond hair and was staring with some annoyance at the camera, as though he'd been interrupted from something important.

"Who's this?" Liang asked. "Is he someone I am supposed to know?" He peered at the photograph more closely. There was something familiar about the man, but he couldn't place it.

"Herr Dr Kristopher Lehrer," Holm said.

That explained it. Liang had met Lehrer's sister, Clara. He could see the family resemblance between them, especially around the eyes, but if he hadn't been told this was Lehrer, Liang doubted he would have made the connection.

"Is he someone important?" Liang asked.

"Don't play me for a fool, Herr Doktor." Holm did not seem impressed with Liang's answer. It appeared the façade of two civilised men sharing tea and conversation was over.

Oh well. It couldn't have lasted much longer anyway, and to be honest, Liang was tired of it. He hated games, although he had to admit Holm played well.

"You are no fool, Herr Holm." Liang considered his next words very carefully. "I was speaking the truth when I said I did not recognise Dr Lehrer. We have never met."

"What is your purpose here?"

"That depends on how you define purpose."

Holm snorted. "The pawn thinks he is valuable to his own side too. It appears as though you are the foolish one, *Herr* Zhou." He rolled his eyes. "I know why your team is here. You were sent to retrieve the plans held at the institute. Otherwise why include you in the mission? But having *Dr* Lehrer as a part of that mission changes things, doesn't it?" He stood and walked around to the front of his desk. "It makes you dispensable."

"Everyone is dispensable, given specific circumstances," Liang said evenly. Holm was obviously trying to undermine his hope that Matt and Ken would attempt a rescue. They didn't have Lehrer, nor did they know of his whereabouts. They needed Liang's expertise to confirm Lehrer's claim that the rumours about this device were true.

"Then you won't have an issue in telling me where the rest of your team are, will you?" Holm leaned in closer so he was looking directly into Liang's eyes.

Liang flinched, in spite of his intention not to. "I don't quite get the leap of logic from my statement to yours, but if I did, the answer would be the same." He swallowed and stared back at Holm. "I will not betray them."

"I beg to differ, Dr Zhou." Holm collected his paperwork from the desk and walked over to the door. One of the guards opened it for him and let another man enter.

"Herr Standartenführer Holm," Reiniger said, saluting his superior officer.

"You know what I require, Obersturmführer." Holm returned the salute then glanced at the floor. "Do please try not to get too much blood on the carpet. I'm sure the Major would prefer his office returned to him in the state in which we acquired it. Blood stains terribly, as you well know."

"I'll do my best, Herr Standartenführer." Reiniger smiled, his eyes glinting. "Heil Hitler."

"Heil Hitler," Holm replied and left the room.

Liang studied the carpet beneath his chair. He really wished Holm hadn't mentioned bloodstains.

"Get up," Reiniger ordered. "Stand behind the chair and place your hands on its arms."

Liang obeyed. No point in doing otherwise. The action resulted in him turning his back on Reiniger. He heard the clink of something metal behind him. One of the guards moved forward and handcuffed Liang's hands in place. Another one grabbed hold of his shirt and tore the back of it off completely.

Oh God. What now? Please no more beatings. Anything but that.

A loud crack echoed through the room.

No. Liang swallowed. Tasted bile. He knew that noise and what it was.

One guard moved to Liang's right, the other to his left. They each held one of his arms, ensuring he could not move at all.

"The handcuffs were enough," Liang muttered, clinging to the words, trying desperately to sound calmer than he was. If they wanted him to talk, he would, but not about what they wanted to hear.

This isn't real. It isn't happening. Stay calm and pretend. Stay calm and—

The first touch of leather across his bare back sent pain spreading through his body. *Fuck. That hurt.*

Liang gritted his teeth. He wouldn't lose control. Not in front of these bastards. He wouldn't give them the satisfaction. He was stronger than that. "Go burn in hell," he gasped. "I'll not tell you what you want."

One of the guards backhanded him with his free hand. Liang swallowed, tasting blood.

Behind him Reiniger laughed. "They all say that, but even the strongest eventually give in. It is your choice as to how long this lasts, Herr Zhou."

"Like hell." Liang spat at the guard nearest to him. Whatever happened he would not give up his friends. He would not give up Juliane.

"Oh yes," Reiniger told him. "It will be. For as long as you refuse to answer my questions."

"You haven't asked any yet." Liang pointed out. Probably not the brightest thing to say, but the words were out of his mouth before he could stop them. Easier to talk, to focus on that, instead of the pain.

The second stroke of the whip hurt as much as the first.

"Where are the rest of your team?" Reiniger cracked the whip against Liang's back before he could answer. Then again.

Liang gritted his teeth. He closed his eyes. His skin already felt as though it was on fire. He tried to focus on something else, anything else.

Juliane.

No! Not that. He couldn't afford to…

Another crack.

Someone screamed.

Please. Stop.

He didn't want this. He'd done nothing wrong. He wasn't a soldier. He'd been the only one available for the job, the only one *dispensable*.

There was no place to hide.

Focus, Liang, focus.

God, it hurt. A sob tore from his lips, but he did not speak.

He heard his mother's voice. She sang to him in his

memories, a lullaby, words that promised a future that would never be.

She was dead, gone, buried so many years ago. He'd woken and crawled into his parents' bed. They were cold, so cold. He missed them so much. His father had always told him to be brave.

I can't. I can't. I can't.

Pain, so much pain.

"Stop! Bloody hell. I can't... I don't... I can't..."

And this time he knew the scream was his own.

CHAPTER FOURTEEN

"You're taking a huge risk trying to rescue your friend." Max stirred sugar into his coffee while he looked thoughtfully at Ken and Michel.

"Being here is a risk." Ken debated another cup of the so-called coffee but decided he'd had enough.

"We will not leave him there," Michel insisted. "It will also be *us* taking that risk. If we are caught, we will deny any involvement by any of your operatives."

"All right." Max pushed his glasses further up his nose. "From the information I have, you may have to carry him out. I am not sure how badly injured he is."

"If he needs medical treatment, is there somewhere we can go?" Ken remembered the state Matt had been in when they'd escaped from the institute, although some of his injuries had been the result of the institute collapsing around them. It didn't negate the extent of the wounds on his back, though. If Holm or Reiniger had been interrogating Liang, it would be sensible to expect more of the same.

He'd felt guilty about his relief when he'd discovered

Liang was in custody, not Matt. Liang was a good man and totally unprepared for this. He didn't deserve any of it.

No one did. And to hell with the so-called training he and Matt had received. Nothing prepared someone for the reality of torture. Matt was a strong man, but he'd broken down when he'd finally told Ken some of the details of what he'd been through.

If Ken had known about that when he'd first met Juliane, he would never have promised her he wouldn't harm her brother.

"There is a doctor who will help," Max said. "I will tell you where to find him." He retrieved paper and a pencil from a drawer and sketched a quick diagram. "This is the floor plan of the building where they are holding your friend. I have someone who can get you inside, but once you're in, you're on your own." He marked two sections with an x and pointed to the first one. "The cells are here, so start there." He then pointed to the second x. "This is the location of Major Bruhn's office. His name is on the door, although Holm has been using it since he arrived. I'd advise staying clear of it if possible." Max glanced up at them and then ran one hand through his dark hair. "The building is only a few blocks from here, so if you are successful, you need to put as much distance as possible between yourselves and this area. The Gestapo will mount a door to door search, and if you return here, they will find you quickly."

"Once we leave here, if you arrange to have our truck moved to a prearranged spot, we can head for wherever this doctor is," Michel suggested. "How far away is it?"

"He is in Feuerbach. Since the bombings began, he has been working at the hospital there. I will give you directions."

"What's his name?" Michel didn't look happy.

"Conrad Osterhagen," Max answered.

"I am known in Feuerbach, and to Dr Osterhagen. It's probably not a good idea to return there."

"Not all doctors can be trusted," Max said, "but Dr Osterhagen has helped the Resistance since the beginning of the war. He is your best chance."

"He helped K... my friend escape. He is most likely being watched," Michel pointed out.

"Then I will be the one to contact him," Ken offered. "Holm thinks you are no longer in Stuttgart, and you were seen leaving Feuerbach. It probably makes it the safest place to be, as he will not think you'd return there."

"Because it would be the stupid thing to do?" Michel rolled his eyes. "If he is being watched, we should stay clear of him."

"If Holm is focused on Liang and whatever information he can learn from him, we can hope he has shifted his attention from Osterhagen."

"We can hope." Michel didn't sound convinced.

"Unless you have another suggestion?" Ken asked. "I've seen what Holm and Reiniger do to their prisoners. Liang will need a doctor, even if he has gotten off lightly."

"I'm not arguing that he won't." Michel held up his hands in mock surrender. "It wasn't my intention to suggest otherwise."

Max had been quiet through their exchange. "Do you know this man?" He put a photograph down on the table between Ken and Michel.

Michel started, and his eyes widened. His response spoke louder than words. He definitely knew whoever this was. Ken looked at the photograph closely. The blond man was of slender build and looked to be in his early thirties—about the same age as Ken and the rest of his team.

"Is this Kristopher Lehrer?" Ken asked. Given Michel's response his guess was an educated one.

"Yes. Where did you get this?" Michel asked Max.

"Through my contacts," Max told him. "Holm is circulating Lehrer's picture. He's wanted for murder and treason."

"He's no murderer." Michel didn't deny the accusation of treason, but considering why Ken and his team were also looking for Lehrer, from Holm's perspective that one was accurate. "He's a good man who is following his conscience, despite the risk to himself in doing so."

"I figured as much from what my contact said. The official story does not mesh with what I've heard of the man through my other sources." Max gave Michel a nod. "Your description is also being circulated as someone working with him."

"It doesn't surprise me. No photograph, though?"

"No."

"Good, although I didn't think there would be. There were no photographs taken at the institute to my knowledge, and most of the information kept there would have been destroyed along with the building."

"Holm doesn't know your true identity?" It hadn't escaped Ken that he didn't either.

"No, or at least not as far as I know," Michel confirmed, "and I'd prefer it stayed that way. It is safer, not only for me but my family."

"Is it Holm focusing on Lehrer and Michel?" Ken asked. Although Holm wasn't finished with him yet, it had felt like Holm's interest in him was more personal.

"There are descriptions out there for you and your team too, Herr Lowe. However, from what I've heard, your capture is important only because you might lead him to

Lehrer, who is the priority." Max whistled. "Whatever this Lehrer has done, it's certainly got the attention of not just Holm, but others very high in the Nazi chain of command."

"All the more reason why we don't want him caught," Ken said. Michel had averted his gaze as soon as the conversation had shifted to Lehrer. "The longer Liang remains in custody…" Ken reached for his gun. "I never told you my real name." He'd introduced himself by the name on his forged papers: Oskar Raske.

"No, you didn't. It was the name my contact overheard." Max glanced at the gun, but apart from that he didn't react to it. "For all I knew, you could be double agents and infiltrating my cell. It has been tried before. I wanted to see your reaction when I used your real name." He smiled. "Given that, and Michel's reaction to the information I've given you about Lehrer, I believe you are who you say you are."

"We could be double agents," Michel pointed out. "You have no reason to trust us."

"I trust my gut, Herr Werner," Max told him. "I have good instincts."

"If they're that good, why test me by using my name?" Ken asked. Max's explanation sounded a little too simple and convenient.

Max chuckled. "Not a believer in instinct, hmm?" He seemed amused, yet there was also approval in his tone. "Instinct only goes so far. Common sense and facts are also things I hold in high regard." He smoothed out the paper he'd drawn on. "The longer your friend remains in custody, the more chance there is that Holm will discover what he needs to find Lehrer."

"Liang doesn't know where Kristopher is." Michel leaned over the plans, his brow creasing in thought.

"He knows where the safe houses are," Ken said. If

Matt was out there, he'd head back to the safe house in Freudenstadt. "So does Matt, and you told me Lehrer does too."

"I told Kit to wait at the safe house in Freudenstadt if we got separated." Michel paled. "Oh hell. If Holm…"

"Exactly my thought," Ken said grimly. "It's not only Liang I'm worried about. We need to rescue him before he tells Holm where to find it."

If it wasn't already too late.

Kristopher adjusted the blankets around Leo and watched the regular rise and fall of his chest for a few moments. "I suspect he held off taking the morphine longer than he should have."

"Probably. I'm impressed you managed to talk him into it. My guess is that he wasn't expecting to come up against someone as stubborn as he is." Matt grinned. "You've got a few more years of practice on your side."

"I am not stubborn," Kristopher protested. He sat back on the other couch, keeping his voice low, although he doubted Leo would wake. He'd already been exhausted before the drug took effect.

"Yes, you are." Matt perched on the arm of the couch. "How old do you think Leo is? I figure he's in his early twenties, if that."

"He told me he was twenty-one." Kristopher stretched and yawned. Although, only mid-afternoon, he already felt tired. Sitting around waiting for something to happen made him edgy.

"Only a kid, then." Matt shook his head. "There's far too many of them serving in this war. They're having to grow up too fast, if they even get the chance to grow up." He stood. "I'm going to make more of that so-called tea. Want some?"

"Yes, please. You're sure there isn't any coffee?"

"Sorry, I turned the place upside down and no luck." Matt pulled a face. "Still, a man's gotta do what a man's gotta do. I've never been much of a tea drinker, although I've been told it's an acquired taste."

"What's passing for tea these days is definitely an acquired taste." Kristopher laughed at Matt's expression. "It could be worse. Have you tried chicory? It's what is passing for coffee in some places." Michel had told him about it. His expression had been about the same as Matt's when he'd described it.

"I've heard of it." Matt shuddered. "That was enough for me." He disappeared into the kitchen.

Kristopher debated asking if he needed any help but decided against it. He closed his eyes. What had happened to Michel? He should have been here by now. Logically, Kristopher knew it had been just over twenty-four hours since they'd seen each other, yet it felt much longer. Given the situation they were in, so much could go seriously wrong in a very short period of time. And something *was* wrong. Kristopher could feel it, although if asked to explain the feeling and why he was so convinced, he'd be hard-pressed to find an explanation.

The rest of Matt's team should have turned up by now too. Kristopher and Matt had never discussed Matt's nightmare of the night before, but despite Matt's attempts to sound cheerful, Kristopher could tell he was worried.

An inner voice nagged that perhaps the time had come to be completely honest with Matt about his true identity. He also wished he could talk to Matt about Michel and how he felt about him. Given what Kristopher had overheard of Matt's nightmare, he suspected Matt would understand.

But unfortunately it was too risky to do either. He'd wait until he and Michel were reunited and then reassess the situation.

Surely it wouldn't be too much longer? Perhaps Isa would be able to contact someone in the Resistance who might be able to give them more information. There had to be some reason why Holm was in Stuttgart, and it wouldn't be good.

Please don't have Michel. Please don't make his capture be the reason why.

Kristopher jumped at the sharp knock at the front door. Before he could reach for his weapon, Matt was already heading for the door, gun in hand.

"Stay down, and cover me," Matt whispered. He trained his weapon on the door, watching it carefully.

Kristopher moved to the opposite side of the room, his own weapon drawn. He needed some kind of cover. If the person on the other side forced the door open, they'd most likely come through armed and prepared to shoot. They'd have to be disabled as quickly as possible. Kristopher ducked down by the piano and peered around the side, pointing his Walther P38 at the door. Leo was asleep on the couch and they didn't have time to move him. Luckily he wouldn't be seen from the door, as the back of the couch hid him from view. They'd have to draw any gunfire away from him by distracting their assailant.

Matt glanced at Kristopher, then returned his attention to the door. What the hell? Why knock and then do nothing? It couldn't be the Gestapo. A locked door wouldn't matter to them. They'd demand it be opened and then break it down if their prey didn't comply.

Should they be waking Leo and heading out the back of the house? Or would doing that be falling into whatever kind of trap this was?

Someone pushed a folded piece of paper under the door. Matt frowned and edged closer. "Keep covering me," he said.

Kristopher opened his mouth to protest, to tell Matt not to take any risks, then realised it was a waste of time. What choice did they have?

He kept his gun pointed at the door, both hands on it to keep it steady. He took a deep breath. *Focus, focus.* He could do this. He'd hit a target before, and he was good at it. But this wouldn't be an inanimate object. It would be flesh and blood, moving and returning fire.

Matt picked up the paper quickly and retreated away from the door. He unfolded and read it. "Fuck," he exclaimed. "Grab Leo and the med kit. We need to leave."

"What is it?" Kristopher asked, reholstering his gun. He grabbed the medical satchel and his coat. His fingers closed around the music manuscript in his left pocket. It was one of the coded messages he'd written to Michel.

"The Gestapo are on their way. We've been compromised." Matt shoved the note into his pocket. It wouldn't do to leave it behind as evidence they'd been warned.

"I can't rouse Leo," Kristopher told him. He shook Leo again, and this time Leo opened his eyes, although he didn't seem very alert. He muttered something under his breath, but was obviously disorientated. They didn't have time to wait until the morphine wore off.

"We'll carry him between us." Matt holstered his gun and ran over to the couch. "The front door is too obvious. We'll go out the back and hope there's no one there."

"We won't get far with him like this." Kristopher didn't

think he could carry Leo on his own. If the way ahead wasn't clear how would they get out?

"It's better than staying here. I don't know about you, but I'd prefer to take my chances out there."

"Wait! There's something I need to do first. Get Leo off the couch. I'll help you in a moment." Kristopher strode over to the piano and opened the lid.

Matt gave him a look that suggested he thought Kristopher had gone crazy. "What the hell are you doing? We haven't got time for this."

"I promised I'd leave a note." Kristopher tucked the manuscript between two pages of the book fourth down in the stack on top of the piano. If it was open, Michel would know to look for it there. A closed piano meant no note, or that one had been written under duress. Both were better options than resorting to the alternative plan. They'd agreed that leaving any kind of note in plain view would be foolish, to say the least.

Matt dragged Leo to his feet and draped his coat over him. Leo hung on to the back of the couch and looked up at them blankly. "What's happening?" he mumbled. He yawned and sat down again. "Going back to sleep, Mum. Tell the cows they can wait."

"You're not on the farm, Leo," Matt said urgently. "Think. You're in Germany with me and Paul."

"You and Paul?" Leo blinked a couple of times. He frowned and looked around. His eyes widened. "Oh shit. This isn't part of that crazy dream I was having, is it?"

"No. This is real." Matt pulled Leo upright again and helped him put on his coat. He'd need it as it was freezing outside. "I know you're drowsy, but you have to fight it. Can you try to do that?"

"I can try." Leo nodded and wrapped one arm around

Matt's waist. He put weight on his injured knee and hissed. "Fuck," he exclaimed. "That hurts!"

Kristopher put his arm around Leo's other side. The morphine would take a few more hours to wear off completely and help with the pain, although timing was problematic, given Leo's drowsiness. "We need to find some kind of transport. We can't get far with him like this."

"The bad guys are coming?" Leo asked.

"Yes. We need to get out of here before they arrive." Matt began moving them towards the back door. Kristopher took more of Leo's weight and half carried him to the door. Matt ran ahead and opened it cautiously, peering through it. "Looks clear out here," he whispered. "Come on."

Leo gritted his teeth. The pain he had to be feeling seemed to be negating some of the drowsiness the longer he was on his feet. "Where to now?" he asked once they were outside.

"Anywhere that's not here." Matt had closed the door behind them. Although it wouldn't be immediately obvious where they were, it wouldn't take their pursuers long to figure out.

They ducked out into the street behind the house. Leo's breath came in gasps. "I'm going to slow you down. Leave me and get away. I'll tell them you went in the opposite direction."

"We're not leaving you." Matt's expression darkened. "So get that idea out of your head. It's not going to happen."

"Wait," Kristopher said. "I have an idea."

"It had better be good. We're running out of time. I'm sure as hell not staying here and waiting for them for find us." Matt glanced up and down the street. "Start walking," he ordered, "and look as though you're supposed to be here." At least Leo was now wearing civilian clothes so he wouldn't stand out too much. Kristopher and Matt were still in their uniforms. As such, it was doubtful they'd get asked too many questions by members of the public.

Two German soldiers supporting an injured man between them would be something that would be noticed. Leo was right. He would slow them down.

"Leo, can you walk on your own?" Vehicles were approaching. Leo wouldn't get far on foot, and once the soldiers figured out the house was empty, they'd start looking nearby. "It doesn't matter how fast you go, and if you need to rest, rest. If you're stopped, act as though you can't speak. Better that than it being obvious you don't know the language." Kristopher had kept his voice low since they'd left the house, not only so they wouldn't be over-heard, but so they wouldn't be caught speaking English.

"I'll be going slow, don't you worry about that."

"We're not leaving him," Matt reminded Kristopher.

"We're not. At least not for long." Kristopher grinned, the plan he was formulating becoming more appealing the more he thought about it. "Matt?" he asked. "Do you know how to bypass the ignition on a car?"

CHAPTER FIFTEEN

The streets were in a worse state than Michel had realised. He hadn't noticed much the previous night, as their focus had been finding Max and getting somewhere safe.

An old woman sat on a wheelbarrow filled with what was left of her belongings. She was talking to a young boy and glanced up at Ken and Michel as they passed. Her eyes were haunted, the building behind her in ruins only one of many.

There had been more bombings during the day, and Michel suspected the quiet they were experiencing now was only a slight reprieve.

Ken let out a low whistle. "This is a real mess. I feel sorry for these people."

"Kit and I were in Feuerbach during the bombing earlier in the week." Michel couldn't help but think of Fritz when he'd seen the boy with the old woman. "The damage here is much worse. I'm guessing it is there now too."

"It's always the civilians who suffer. Most have done nothing wrong, and so many of them lose everything." Ken looked away, and a shadow fell over his face. "I'd like to see the people who give these orders go through the same thing. It might make them think twice."

"Unfortunately it doesn't seem to deter the people it needs to." Michel thought about what Ken had told him about Holm and how he'd been caught in the bombing of the institute. He wasn't the sort of man to let anything deter him from what he perceived to be his duty. It seemed the way of the world. Good men died while others survived and continued to make others' lives a misery.

"I wish we could stop and help." Ken glanced back over his shoulder at the old woman. "Anything we do that could bring this war to a close is helping, right?"

"I helped to clear rubble in Feuerbach," Michel said quietly. He shivered, remembering the sightless eyes of the woman he'd freed. "I'll never forget it. I agree with you. This needs to be over so people can start rebuilding their lives. Too many have died already." He looked up at the familiar noise in the distance. Although he couldn't see the aircraft, they weren't far away. Sirens began to wail. "More bombers? They're not letting up at all, are they?"

"I have no clue how long this is going to go on." Ken sped up his pace. "Come on, we need to get off the street before all hell breaks loose. With any luck this is the distraction we need."

"We're going ahead with it?"

"Sure, why not?" Ken smiled grimly. "According to Max, Holm and Reiniger left late this morning, and an air raid should distract whoever's left." He brushed his hand against the bag he wore across his shoulder. "I'd prefer that than having to use these explosives. Better to get in and out with a minimum of fuss."

"We're planning to break a man out of Gestapo

custody," Michel pointed out. "That's hardly going to be a minimum of fuss, whatever happens."

"I'm working on being more optimistic," Ken said.

People ran past them, heading to bunkers. Michel kept to the shadows of the buildings, not wanting to be stopped and asked why he wasn't at his post. Once most of the population was off the streets, it would make their job easier. Max's contact would do as much as he could, and then it was up to them.

Their journey to Holm's headquarters seemed to take forever, although it wasn't that long. The building appeared quiet from the outside, but that didn't mean it was. Holm wouldn't be foolish enough to leave a prisoner unguarded, and depending on what he already knew, might be expecting them to attempt some kind of rescue.

"You ready?" Ken kept his gun holstered, as did Michel. They needed to get into the building on the pretence they were supposed to be there.

"As much as I'm going to be." Michel took the lead and approached the two soldiers on guard. "Heil Hitler." He saluted and then produced his papers.

"You're early for your shift." The soldier scanned the forged documents and then put his hand out for Ken's identity papers.

"We heard the sirens," Michel said, "and wanted to be off the street." Not that it would be any safer in a building that might collapse around them than to be in the street and be caught under one, but it was as good an explanation as any.

"Report to the Oberleutnant on the ground floor, Obergefreiter Werner." The soldier saluted. "Heil Hitler." He stood to one side to let them pass. His companion glanced at both of them, saluted but kept silent.

"Heil Hitler." Ken fell into step with Michel. If the information they'd been given was correct, the Oberleutnant was Max's contact and would help in any way he could without compromising his position.

As they approached the guard post, one of the men looked up. "Heil Hitler."

Michel and Ken responded and saluted him.

"Herr Oberleutnant, we've been told to report to you for further orders," Michel said.

"Ah yes, Obergefreiter Werner, isn't it?" The Oberleutnant peered at both men. "And Gefreiter Raske. Come with me," he continued once they nodded. "You have guard duty. We have an important prisoner in custody. No matter what happens, you will not leave your post. Is that clear?"

The building rocked, but the Oberleutnant acted as though nothing had happened. He led them past a set of doors into a narrow corridor. Another set of doors stood at the end of it. "The cells are through here." Before they got to the door, he lowered his voice. "The raid will distract many of the men. With all the bombings of late, several are in fear for their lives. This building appears sturdy but is very old. Let us hope there is not too much damage." He winked then, the gesture so unexpected that Michel wondered if he'd imagined it.

He composed himself quickly. "Let us hope not," he replied.

"You are clear about your orders?" the Oberleutnant continued in a normal tone as they reached the cells. He nodded to the soldiers on duty. They stood to attention and saluted. "You are relieved a few minutes early," he told them. "Any trouble from the prisoner?"

"No, Herr Oberleutnant," one of them answered. "He's been very quiet. A little too quiet in fact." He hesitated before continuing. "I took in the water as requested, but it was refused."

"Thank you, Gefreiter. Anything else to report?"

"No, sir. Heil Hitler." He took the ring of keys from his belt and handed them over to the Oberleutnant. Both guards saluted their superior officer again and went on their way.

The building rocked again, and this time dust fell from the roof. Ken coughed but didn't speak. If they got Liang out, they still had the problem of the bombing raid to deal with.

The Oberleutnant handed Michel the ring of keys, holding out one in particular. "Keep these on your person at all times. I suggest you check on the prisoner once I have left. Try to get him to cooperate and drink some of the water. Herr Holm wishes to interrogate him further upon his return and will not be happy if he does not survive the night. Heil Hitler."

Ken watched him go. "That was interesting. I'm presuming we shouldn't take most of what he said at face value."

"Of course not. But none of what he told us could be taken as anything but a superior officer giving orders, if anyone did overhear." Michel waited a few minutes to be sure they were alone. "I didn't expect it would be this easy and we'd be given guard duty outside Liang's cell." It had to be Liang in there, especially given his was the only cell with two guards posted outside. He slid open the square metal flap at the top of the door and peered inside, but all he could see was a figure huddled in the corner facing the wall.

"The easy part won't be getting him out of the cell," Ken reminded him. "Come on, we need to get on with this while there's a building to escape from." He watched

Michel unlock the cell door. "At least this means we don't have to use the dynamite."

"Hang on to it," Michel suggested. "We might need it later."

The other exit from the building, as not commonly used, was kept locked and the door only had one key.

The cell door opened with a sharp click. Michel attached the key ring to his belt. The Oberleutnant had told him to keep the keys on him, and he intended to do just that. It was highly improbable, though not impossible, that the ring included the key they needed. Like Ken, he preferred to use the dynamite as a last resort as it tended to be noisy and somewhat messy.

The figure in the corner didn't turn around. Instead he curled into himself tightly.

"Liang?" Ken took a step into the cell and exchanged a glance with Michel. Liang had his back to them. His shirt was in tatters and smeared with blood. Angry welts covered his raw back.

"Leave me alone." Liang muttered something under his breath in a language Michel didn't know. "You can tell Holm to go fuck himself. I'm not interested."

"I wouldn't be interested in seeing that either." Ken kept a careful distance from Liang and spoke softly. "Liang, it's Ken. We've come to get you out of here."

"Why?" Liang didn't turn around. "I'm no bloody use to you, not anymore." His voice sounded hoarse, his tone flat.

"You're my friend. I'm not leaving you here. As much as I'm reluctant to admit it, I've missed your less than witty repartee." Ken sighed and turned to Michel. "We don't have time for this. Do you want to carry him, or shall I?"

"Ken?" Liang slowly edged back from the wall and struggled to stand as Ken started to talk again. His face was covered in bruises, and he gasped in pain with each jerky movement. "It is you, isn't it? Only you would come out with a comment like that." Finally facing them, he peered at Michel. "Gabriel? What are you doing here? I thought you'd be in Switzerland by now."

"That's still the plan, but it's taking longer than I thought it would." Michel took a step back towards the door as Ken moved closer to Liang. He'd heard something. He drew his gun and glanced in both directions down the empty, silent corridor. Perhaps he'd imagined it.

When he turned around, Liang had his arms around Ken in an embrace. Ken glanced up at Michel with an expression of shock and embarrassment.

"I didn't believe everything he said about you. I didn't believe him." Liang let go of Ken suddenly, pushed him away, and flushed bright red. "I didn't just do that. Did I?"

"Definitely not," Ken agreed, scooting back to join Michel at the open door. "Don't worry. We'll never speak of it again."

"Of course not." Michel had seen the effects of torture. The relief of being rescued when they'd given up all hope did strange things to people. Unfortunately, they didn't have time to allow Liang to recover his composure. "Can you walk, Liang? We need to get out of here."

"Yes, I can walk. Although my back is sore as hell, the rest of me is fine. Apart from the bruising, which I'm ignoring for now." Liang laughed shakily. "I've had more than enough of Holm's hospitality." He took a few steps forward and stumbled. "I don't suppose you can give me a few minutes?"

"No, sorry." Michel held up his hand for silence. This time he'd definitely heard something. "Stay behind me," he ordered. The building shook again. The bombers were close. He hoped this wasn't one of their targets. He edged to the door leading from the corridor and took up position to the side of it.

The door opened, and someone came through. Michel snaked one hand around whoever it was and pulled them back against him, away from where they could be seen. He shoved the door closed with his foot and dragged his captive back to the cells. He couldn't allow whoever this was to sound the alarm, although hopefully it wouldn't be someone who would be missed quickly.

"Don't make a noise," he hissed, "or I'll put a bullet in you."

"It's lovely to see you again too, Herr Schmitz." The woman addressed him by the name he'd used while undercover at the institute.

Michel nearly let her go in his surprise. He hadn't thought about who he'd grabbed, just moved on instinct. Once they were inside the cell, he turned her so he could see her. "Fräulein Huber."

Margarete Huber smiled and smoothed down her blouse. "How interesting that I'd meet you here. I would have thought you'd be with dear Kristopher, considering how ready he was to trade for you."

"Trade for me?" Michel frowned, confused by her comment at first, before he remembered what she was referring to. When Reiniger and Müller had caught him and Kit in Berlin, Kit had offered to trade his cooperation for Michel's life. It had been a bluff then, but given their relationship now, if Kit was put in that situation again, he'd do whatever it took to keep Michel safe. "He's not here, and you're not getting anywhere near him."

He also remembered what Kit had told him about

Margarete and how she'd tried to get close to him. It had made Michel's skin crawl.

To his surprise, Margarete laughed. "Friendship makes one vulnerable, don't you think, Michel? That is your name, isn't it?" She shrugged, seemingly unperturbed that she was in a cell with two armed men. "Herr Dr Lehrer is so full of surprises but at the same time so very predictable. I told Herr Holm that if he found you, he'd soon have Lehrer." She gave Ken a polite nod. "Good afternoon, Herr Lowe. It's also rather predictable that the two of you are working together. I don't suppose your other friend is here too? Matt, wasn't it? You must excuse the informality, but we were never formally introduced, although the last time we saw each other, he was using another name." Margarete sighed. "I really don't know how I'm expected to keep up with the different identities you use—"

"I've had enough of your games for one day," Liang snapped at Margarete, cutting her off before she could speak further. "You said we needed to get out of here," he told Ken. "I hope you're not intending to take her as a hostage."

"Certainly not." The more distance Michel put between himself and Margarete, the better.

"Lock her in the cell," Ken suggested.

Margarete's eyes widened. "They're bombing the town!" she exclaimed. "What happens if this building is hit? I'd be trapped in here with no way out."

"You would have been seen coming in here," Ken reminded her. "As soon as you don't return, someone will look for you." He rolled his eyes. "Don't worry, Fräulein. I'm not about to leave you to die, as tempting as the thought is right now." He kept his gun trained on her. "Take off your stockings." The next word sounded more of an afterthought. "Please."

"I beg your pardon?" Margarete stared at him as though she'd misheard. Then she smiled. "Why, Herr Lowe, I had no idea—"

Ken cut her off quickly. "No arguments. Just do it. I won't kill you, but I will shoot you." He spoke over his shoulder to Michel, not taking his eyes off Margarete. "Help Liang out of the cell. I won't be long."

"What was all that about Lehrer making a trade?" Ken asked after he joined them in the corridor.

"A bluff, nothing more," Michel said evenly. "What was all that about getting her to take her stockings off?"

"I needed something to tie her up and gag her with." Ken shrugged. "They did the job, which was all that mattered." The side of his mouth twitched. "After all, we don't want her raising the alarm, do we?"

"Of course we don't," Michel murmured. "Come on." He led the way to the door at the other end of the corridor while Ken took over supporting Liang to the exit, which wasn't far from their present location. A few metres later Liang indicated he could walk on his own.

Michel opened the door cautiously and peered out. He couldn't hear anything apart from men running in the distance, boots against concrete. They'd need to prepare in case the worst happened. Their fear of the building being hit gave Michel's team the chance to get away before Liang's or Margarete's absences were noticed.

"If we see anyone, we're transporting the prisoner to a safer location," he whispered to Ken and Liang. While not a great plan, it had a chance of working, at least long enough for them to take out one or two men. They'd worry about getting Liang's back dressed and replacing his shirt once they were clear. Trying to do it now would only draw unwanted attention and alert the guards that they weren't who they were supposed to be.

"I'm holding on to the thought that it is what you're doing," Liang muttered.

"Let's go. Until we see someone else, I suggest we run and cover as much distance as we can." Ken put out a hand to steady himself when the building shook. "That one felt closer. Much closer."

"I noticed." Michel grimaced.

Someone yelled out nearby. Their warning was followed by a loud crack, then an explosion. All three men ducked down instinctively.

"I can smell something." Liang glanced around.

"Smoke," Ken confirmed. "It doesn't always take a direct hit to bring down a building. Just something falling where it shouldn't and igniting something flammable. Come on."

They ran quickly to the other end of the corridor, Liang lagging behind. Ken slowed down to help him. Michel surveyed the area ahead. It looked clear. "Left." Michel remembered the directions on the map he'd memorised. "Another right after that and we should be at the door."

"I hope you're right." Liang grunted and stumbled. For all his bravado, he was struggling to stay upright. How long had it been since he'd eaten? Ken kept one arm wrapped around Liang's waist, ignoring his protestation, and continued to help him along.

"I can see it!" Michel exclaimed after they turned the corner. Another couple of metres and they'd be there.

"Stop!" yelled someone.

Michel picked up his pace. Out of the corner of his eye, he saw Ken do the same, half dragging Liang with him.

They had turned into another corridor, this one wider than the previous one. They had nowhere else to go. They were running towards a dead end. Michel skidded to a halt and yanked the key ring from his belt.

The first key turned partway but no more. He inserted the second. "Work, damn it," he muttered. The key had to be on here. They had no way of getting the door open otherwise. Retreating to a safe place while they waited for a dynamite fuse would only send them back in the direction of the men they were running from.

"Get away from the door!" Now he was closer, Michel recognised Müller's voice. It figured that bastard would be here. Michel had hoped he would have gone with Reiniger and Holm.

He turned and drew his gun. "Liang, keep trying the door." Michel shoved the key ring at Liang. "Ken and I will hold them off."

"Schmitz!" Müller exclaimed. "Lower your weapon and surrender."

"Not likely," muttered Ken. He took aim and fired a shot in Müller's direction. Müller ducked back around the corner, but not before returning several shots of his own.

"Standartenführer Holm wants them alive," Margarete called out. "Shoot to disable, not kill." So she'd escaped from the cell already. At least Michel wouldn't have her death on his conscience if the building was destroyed. He hoped he didn't end up regretting the sentiment.

Wait. She'd said Holm wanted them alive. Did she mean *all* of them? Michel had already seen what Holm had done to Liang. He wasn't about to let Holm get a second chance at it. He narrowed his eyes. Nor would he allow himself to be captured and used as leverage to get Kit to surrender. Holm's orders meant Müller was at a disadvantage as Michel and Ken could kill their opponents.

Another bullet whizzed past him, imbedding into the wall. Michel returned fire, then glanced around frantically for some kind of shelter. A stack of wooden crates stood by the side of the door. Luckily, with the door not being an exit in common use, someone had decided to use the area for storage.

"Pull them forward while I distract them," Ken said, obviously thinking the same thing as Michel. He fired another shot at Müller. Someone yelled out in pain. Unfortunately it wasn't Müller. "Hurry up!" Ken fired again, ducking down to avoid another bullet.

"Bloody hell," muttered Liang, "another inch and that one would have got me." He fumbled for another key and tried it in the lock. "I second that. Hurry up!"

Michel yanked at the bottom crate, edging it forward. Given its weight it wasn't empty as he'd first thought. Another few centimetres and he'd be able to get between it and the wall and get his weight behind it. Perspiration ran down his face as he struggled with it. "Get the damn door open!" he hissed.

"I'm trying!" Liang snapped.

One more shove and the crates were in front of Liang and the door. Ken dived behind them as Michel did. The bullets barely missed him. Instead they hit the top of the crate just above where he'd been standing.

"Either Müller's ignoring orders or his men are lousy shots." Ken turned and fired, then ducked down again. He'd need to reload soon. Michel glanced at Ken's gun, and Ken held up four fingers. Four bullets left.

Another shot rang out. It hit the crate a couple of centimetres from their heads. Michel returned fire, once, twice, and then slid back down to sit on the floor. He held up five fingers. Five bullets left.

They were outnumbered. While Müller's men would also need to reload at some point, there were more of them, so they wouldn't have the same issue.

"Got it!" Liang exclaimed. He pushed open the door and ran through it. Ken fired more shots in the direction of their would-be captors, then followed Liang, Michel bringing up the rear. Once they were through, Liang slammed the door closed behind them, then shoved the key back into the lock. He turned it with a sharp click. "That should slow them down a bit."

"The truck's this way! Can you run?" Ken asked Liang.

"For now, but I'm not sure for how long. This adrenaline rush is going to wear off very soon, and I'll be fit for nothing."

The door behind them rattled on its hinges but didn't open. "They're ramming it." Michel wanted to be long gone when their pursuers broke through.

Müller could be as determined to follow orders as Reiniger. He wouldn't rest until he'd found his prey. Michel had no intention of ending up in his custody. He'd seen what Müller was capable of. He was a sadistic bastard like his superior officer.

"Follow me." Ken ran to where they'd arranged for the truck to be left. If Max hadn't come through and it wasn't there, they'd be in trouble.

Liang stumbled as he ran. He picked himself up after the first fall, but the second time, Michel slid one arm around his waist and steadied him. Ken reached the truck first and had it started when Michel and Liang reached it. Michel helped Liang inside, then climbed in after him.

Aircraft roared overhead. Ken put his foot down on the

accelerator. The truck lurched forward, half skidding when a loud explosion rocked the ground beneath them.

"Oh my God." Liang glanced behind them. The building they'd escaped from was burning. Men burst through the door he'd locked, their figures dwindling in size as Ken put distance between them and the chaos that remained of Holm's headquarters.

If they hadn't rescued Liang when they had, there was a good chance he'd probably be dead by now.

CHAPTER SIXTEEN

Leo slid sideways in the seat, his head resting on Kristopher's shoulder, his breathing steady as he finally slipped into sleep. "He's done well to stay awake this long. When we reach Freiburg, I'll take another look at that graze on his leg." Kristopher placed his hand briefly on Leo's forehead. "I think he's running a slight fever. Sleeping will be good for him and give his body a chance to fight the infection."

"We'll have to make sure he keeps up with taking his medicine too." Matt took his eyes off the road for a moment to glance at Leo.

They hadn't spoken much since they'd left the safe house. Kristopher kept thinking about what he'd overheard while waiting for Matt. Matt too seemed preoccupied with his own thoughts.

"I hope Isa is all right."

All she'd tried to do was help Leo, and now she'd been caught.

"So do I," Matt agreed, "but you know as well as I do that her chances of surviving this are not great." He shook his head. "The worst thing is that it was her father who betrayed her."

"It sounded as though he thought he was trying to save her." Kristopher stared out the Kübelwagen window at the passing countryside. They'd already been driving an hour, but it seemed much longer. "I heard him begging Reiniger to honour the deal they'd made. He'd traded information to keep her safe."

"Or he thought he did." Matt frowned. "Reiniger told Dr Beckert he'd merely confirming what they already knew?"

"Yes." Kristopher hadn't heard all of the conversation, and he'd been more focused on slashing tyres at the time, but both men's voices had risen as Beckert had become more agitated. "Reiniger called her a traitor and told her father she was already in custody."

"So how did Reiniger already know?" Matt glanced over at Kristopher again. "I was careful when I met with Isa. I'm sure I wasn't followed. None of my team knew about her. You gave me her name and where to find her."

"Surely you're not thinking..." Kristopher trailed off. *Oh God. No.* Maybe that was why Michel hadn't turned up yet. He'd been caught or worse. But he wouldn't have told Reiniger anything. Kristopher was certain of that—and it terrified him.

"I'm not thinking anything. They wouldn't have to know about her. If they already knew about the safe house and she was the one who tried to warn us, they would have caught her at the scene. You didn't see her, did you?"

"No, but I was trying to keep out of sight, so I didn't see much of anything." Kristopher had also acted as lookout while Matt bypassed the ignition on the Kübelwagen. Slashing the tyres of the other Gestapo vehicles had been an afterthought, something he could do while keeping an eye on Reiniger and his men. "I heard more than I saw, but that was enough to piece together what was going on."

"Great idea, slashing the tyres, by the way." Matt grinned. "But it was an even better one stealing this car. I bet it made Reiniger's day having his precious Kübelwagen stolen twice. He's going to be angry as hell."

"He's already angry as hell." Kristopher bit his lip. "Do you think Reiniger was telling the truth when he told Beckert he already knew about the safe house?"

"Honestly?" Matt shrugged. "I don't know. He's like Holm and likes to play mind games, although from my experience, he's not as good at it as Holm. But if he did know about the safe house, how did he find out? None of my team has turned up, and you were supposed to meet with your friend."

"Perhaps they haven't managed to get there yet?" As much as Kristopher wanted to believe he spoke the truth, it was getting harder to hang on to the hope that Michel and the rest of Matt's team were safe.

"Let's stick to that theory until we know otherwise," Matt suggested. He grimaced. "I don't know about you, but I don't want to think about alternatives. We can't go back there. It's suicide. Reiniger's going to be turning the area upside down now he's had it confirmed we're in the vicinity."

"I left a note," Kristopher said slowly. "Don't worry. I doubt they'll be able to decipher it, but it's why I made sure we were heading to Freiburg." They'd discussed their destination before he'd written the note. He didn't see the point telling Michel they were heading in one direction when they were going in another, and only he would be able to read the musical code. "Do you think Reiniger's keeping an eye on the safe house?"

"That depends on who exactly he's trying to catch. If it's one of us, he knows we're long gone from the area, and he'll be widening his search. He might leave a couple of men posted there in case we're stupid enough to double back or in the hope that whoever he is after knows about the safe house but not that it's compromised." Matt pulled off the road and studied Kristopher intently. "This situation is escalating. It's time to put all our cards on the table. You're not just some concerned German citizen who's decided to work with the local Resistance."

"No, I'm not," Kristopher admitted. He swallowed. He'd seen enough of Matt over the past few days to come to the conclusion he was a good man, and his gut feeling was that he could be trusted. They'd worked together to escape Reiniger, and they'd need to again if they wanted any chance of completing this mission. But could he tell Matt who he really was? Did he trust him that much? What if he was wrong about Matt's identity?

"Not ready to tell me yet, huh?" Matt sighed. "I guess in your situation I wouldn't be either. I'll start with the introductions, and perhaps that will help. My real name is Matthew Bryant, and as I've already told you, my friends call me Matt. I'm a sergeant in the US Army, and I'm in Germany on a mission that could make all the difference to who wins this war."

Kristopher took a deep breath. He'd been right about who Matt was. Michel had told him Matt could be trusted but to also trust his own instincts and be careful. "I'd already guessed who you were. A friend told me about you. He met you in Berlin."

"Gabriel," Matt said softly.

"Michel," Kristopher corrected. "His name is Michel. Gabriel is his code name." He didn't see the harm in giving the information, as it merely confirmed what Matt already apparently knew. After nearly catching them in Feuerbach, Holm would also be aware of the identities Kristopher and Michel were currently using. Kristopher had also introduced himself as Paul Reichel to Isa. It wouldn't be long before Holm knew he'd been at the safe house too.

"He's the friend you left the note for?" Matt didn't seem as surprised as Kristopher thought he'd be. "I'm on your side, Paul, although if I've guessed right, that's not your real name."

"I told you it wasn't when we first met."

He had nowhere to go, nowhere to run. The road was deserted, and it would be dark in a few hours. Matt had the keys, and they were already heading in the direction of the next safe house. Kristopher had recognised some of the place names and checked the distances between them matched the map he'd memorised.

"You can trust me. I promise."

"I'm going to. Not because I have no choice but because I want to. You've been a good friend these last few days and..." Kristopher inclined his head in a greeting that was probably completely out of place, given the situation and what they'd already been through. "My name is Dr Kristopher Lehrer, and I have what you need to complete your mission."

"There's no one here." Ken stood in the middle of the living room and looked around. "It's one hell of a mess, though. Someone's been here looking for something or someone."

Both couches were upended and books pulled from the case at the end of the room. Michel absently righted a chair. On the wall opposite the bookcase stood a piano with its lid open. Michel walked over to it. A pile of sheet music sat on top. It too had been rifled through, but unlike the books been dumped back on the piano.

"The kitchen is too." Liang came back into the living room. Michel had filled him in on the situation once they'd had the chance to talk. "If Lehrer or Matt were here, they're long gone. At least if they had any sense they'd be long gone. I'm guessing if the Gestapo found them, they wouldn't have had to tear the place apart." He picked up a couple of books and put them back on the shelf. "Good luck to them with that. I doubt Matt would have been foolish enough to leave a note telling the world where they've gone."

"It's strange no one was posted outside." Michel began to look through the pile of sheet music, lifting several books and shaking them in the hope something loose might fall out.

"You're not going to find anything in there." Ken glanced at the door, then back at Michel. "If they left any clues, Reiniger and his men would have found them. I agree with Liang. Matt wouldn't have taken the risk."

"Kristopher promised to leave me a note if he could, so I'm going to look for it in case he did. Given the code we worked out, I doubt Reiniger would recognise it for what it is, if he did find it." Michel shook the next pile of books. A loose sheet of manuscript fell out. He caught it before it hit the floor. His hand shook.

Please, let it be from Kit.

He needed some sign that Kit was alive and free. A message would give him hope that he still might be. Michel hummed the notes, recognising the tune immediately. Kit had taught him the Brahms lullaby while they were hiding at the convent, but it had been transposed into a minor key and arranged as a duet. A duet that could be easily played by a violin and flute.

"You've found it?" Liang walked over to see what Michel was looking at. Liang had been quiet since they'd left Feuerbach. Dr Osterhagen had treated his physical wounds but had told them his emotional and mental trauma would take longer to heal.

It had been a relief to find Dr Osterhagen was unharmed, apart from a few bruises. Michel would be able to put Kit's mind at ease when they were reunited, as he was concerned Reiniger might take his frustrations out on the old man if he suspected Osterhagen had done what he could to help Kit escape. Michel had taken the opportunity to ask about Fritz in the hope Osterhagen might have some news about the boy. His mother and baby sister had not been located, but he'd been taken in by a local family who would look after him for as long as it was needed. Although Michel had been tempted to go see for himself, it wouldn't have been a good idea. Fritz needed to get on with trying to make a new life for himself, and besides, Michel didn't want to take the risk he'd be noticed. Reiniger didn't appear to know Fritz was the boy Kit and Michel had been seen with, and it needed to stay that way.

"Yes." Michel pocketed the note before Liang could read it, wanting to keep it close. If Kit were caught, the note could be the only thing Michel had of him, apart from the memories of their short time together. "Kristopher was here. He's heading for the safe house in Freiburg."

"Any clue as to whether he's alone?" Ken asked, somewhat sharply.

"I'm sorry. No, there isn't," Michel told him. "We haven't heard anything about Matt being in custody, and we know Reiniger didn't have him, so we have to believe he's out there somewhere. He was in the same area of the Black Forest as Kristopher when I left him, so there's a good chance they did meet up."

"Someone knew they were here," Liang said. "Otherwise why pull the place apart?" They hadn't checked upstairs, but there hadn't seemed much point. It would only be in the same state as the rest of the house.

"You still don't remember if you told Reiniger about the safe house?" Ken asked.

"No, I don't," Liang replied, somewhat irritably. "Do you honestly think I would have come here if I thought I had?" He shuddered. "I have no intention of coming anywhere near that bastard ever again."

"He has to have found out from somewhere." Michel shook his head. "There's no point worrying about his source of information now. It could have been anyone, even a concerned citizen giving the authorities an anonymous tip."

"Let's hope they didn't find out about the safe house in Freiburg too." Ken pursed his lips. "I don't like the fact there's no one on guard here. This has trap written all over it. We'll have to make sure we're not followed."

"You think he'd do that?" Liang asked. "Holm, I mean? He's the one running this investigation, isn't he?"

"Of course he'd do that." Ken shrugged. "Why waste time trying to hunt your prey when you can get someone else to lead you right to them?"

"But if he already knows about Freiburg, he doesn't need us to lead him to them," Liang pointed out. "If you're right, we're between a rock and a hard place. We can't stay here, and we can't risk leading Holm and his men to the rest of our team either."

"I don't think we have a choice." Ken spoke slowly, his words measured. "If we're careful, we can make sure we're not followed, and if he already knows, it's too late to worry about it."

"I don't know about you, but I'm going to Freiburg." Now he had a clear trail to follow, Michel didn't want to waste time. "If Kit's there, he needs to be warned. At least this way we're doing something."

"If Matt's with him and they'd been followed, he would have noticed. I'm sure of it." Ken sounded confident, yet doubt reflected in his eyes.

"I hope you're right." Michel had already started towards the back door. They'd parked several streets over, not wanting to take any chances if the safe house had been compromised. He hoped the luck on their side was on Kit's too, and that he'd managed to find Matt.

Even without the additional training Matt had received since he'd enlisted, he sounded more than capable of looking after himself. Kit might be a brilliant man, but he was out of his depth in this kind of situation. Given the fact he'd also refuse to leave an injured man behind, Michel hoped like hell they weren't already too late.

Karl eyed the man in front of him with a mix of amusement and annoyance, although he hid the former. "So, not only did you allow Lehrer to escape again, but he stole your Kübelwagen." He paused, knowing doing so would make Reiniger squirm a little more. "This is not the first time your Kübelwagen has been stolen, is it? And by Lehrer?"

For a trained soldier, Reiniger's incompetence was unbelievable. Lehrer, a scientist who had spent a good deal of his time behind a desk, had repeatedly got the better of him.

"Yes, Herr Standartenführer." Reiniger lowered his head.

"It does rather sound as though he had help, Herr Holm." Margarete sat in the corner of the room, only there under protest and with the understanding she would not interfere.

She obviously needed to be reminded of that fact.

But before Karl could do so, Reiniger took the opportunity to answer her. "Indeed he did, Fräulein. I suspect the man we know as 'the priest' was probably the one who stole my Kübelwagen."

Karl consulted the interrogation notes Reiniger had given him, although he already knew their contents. "Ah yes, continuing to use the name 'Matt,' I see." Lowe had called him that at the institute. At least Lehrer had had the foresight to use a false name, although the name he'd chosen was his late father's. "And they appear to be travelling with the RAF pilot who was shot down in the Black Forest area."

"He's injured, so that should slow them down... sir." Reiniger still sounded confident he could resolve the matter. "From the information I was able to get, it appears he does not speak much German. That will also be to our advantage."

"Schmitz is still on the loose too." Karl added the notes to his folder and closed it. "You're really not having much luck in locating any of them, are you?" Not only had Schmitz not been caught, but he'd broken Zhou out and was now working with Lowe.

None of their bodies had been recovered from the

rubble, so at least Karl presumed they had escaped the direct hit on his temporary headquarters in Stuttgart. Shame he'd lost many good men in that raid, including Müller. He'd been a good man and one who could be relied upon to complete any task given to him, no matter what obstacles were put in his way.

Margarete's good luck had continued. While she'd escaped the bombing of the institute with an injured arm, somehow this time she only had a few cuts and bruises to show for her experience. One day that luck would run out, especially if she kept insisting on placing herself in dangerous situations. But that was not Karl's problem. He'd told her often enough that her presence was not welcome but merely tolerated. Perhaps this unreasonable obsession with Lehrer would prove to be her undoing.

While part of him hoped so, he didn't particularly want to be the one to report her fate to her grandfather. After all, Herr Bauer did supply a good deal of funding for the project and had connections in the Nazi Party that might be useful at a later date.

Karl steepled his fingers. At least now they only had two groups of men to catch, not several individuals. It should make their task a little easier. Lehrer was the priority, despite Karl's desire to renew his acquaintance with Lowe.

"When you locate Schmitz, he will lead you to Lehrer," Margarete said. "Or if you ensure Lehrer finds out you have Schmitz in custody, I suspect it will not be long before he gives himself up." She glanced at Reiniger. "What does surprise me is that Lehrer did not leave some kind of note for Schmitz. Given my brief meeting with Schmitz, I got the impression he knew where Lehrer was and they'd arranged to meet. Now their so-called safe house has been compromised, they would have had to alter that arrangement."

"There was no note, Fräulein," Reiniger told her. "My men were very thorough."

"Oh, I'm sure they were, Herr Reiniger." Margarete smiled, although her expression was more a grimace that highlighted the coldness in her eyes.

When had the conversation shifted so she was asking the questions? Karl squeezed the bridge of his nose. As long as she achieved results, he supposed this once it couldn't hurt. After they'd extracted the information they needed from Lehrer, the project could continue as planned, and Herr Bauer could find some task to distract her.

"But?" Karl ventured when the unspoken question he was certain Margarete was leading into wasn't forthcoming.

Margarete looked smug. "Oh, so you don't mind if I ask a question, Herr Holm?"

"Yes, but it's not going to stop you, is it?" Karl muttered under his breath, not really caring if she heard him or not. He plastered on a smile. "Isn't that the reason you wanted to be here, Fräulein? To ask questions?"

"Why yes, it was. Thank you." Margarete appeared thoughtful, although Holm suspected she already knew what she wanted to ask. The damn woman was playing one of her games, and this was merely one facet of it.

He had a good mind to allow her to be present at Lehrer's interrogation to see his reaction. From the little he'd seen, Lehrer didn't like her. At least he'd shown some common sense in one part of his life. Karl was curious to know what exactly had persuaded Lehrer to become a traitor and sell out his country and his colleagues. If he'd had doubts about the project before he'd left the institute, he'd certainly hidden them well.

"Your question, Fräulein?" Karl asked.

"Not so much a question, Herr Holm, but more that I'm

curious." Margarete turned her attention to Reiniger. To his credit, he met her gaze squarely and didn't flinch. "Describe the house to me in detail, Herr Reiniger."

"Yes, Fräulein." Reiniger grew quiet, obviously collecting his thoughts. "There was nothing about the house that would draw attention to it. The furniture was old and well worn. The living room had two couches, a large bookshelf, a piano, and—"

"A piano?" Margarete asked. That bit of information seemed to have piqued her interest.

"Yes, Fräulein."

"Was the lid open or closed?"

"Open, Fräulein."

"Was the keyboard dusty, Herr Reiniger?"

Reiniger frowned, as though he couldn't make sense of what she was asking. "Dusty?" he asked.

"Humour me. Can you remember whether it was dusty?"

"There was no dust, Fräulein," Reiniger admitted finally.

"You checked the keyboard for dust, Reiniger?" Karl asked, raising one eyebrow.

"I remember thinking it odd that the lid was raised, sir."

Karl ignored the twinge of a headache. "You thought it odd, yet you never mentioned it in your report?"

"I didn't think it was important, Herr Holm." This time Reiniger did flinch.

"Of course you didn't." Karl sighed. "Fräulein Huber, are you going to tell Herr Reiniger why he should have included it in his report?" For all his mistrust and dislike of Margarete, it appeared they had come to the same conclusion. Before entering the field of science, Lehrer had been a very good amateur musician.

"There is no point in leaving a note where it might be found and deciphered by an enemy. That is why both sides in this war use code. Kristopher Lehrer is no fool. He also has the tendency to listen to music when he's working through a problem, and often scribbles notation when he's doing so. If he was going to leave a coded note, what better way to do it than use musical notation?"

Karl hadn't known that about Lehrer. He filed the information away for future use. "But for the plan to work, it would have had to be some code he and Schmitz had worked out together," he surmised.

"We don't know where either of them was before they were spotted in Feuerbach. If they fled Berlin together, as our information suggests, that gives them a couple of months to work out something." Margarete shrugged. "Of course, I might be wrong, but I know Kristopher well enough to think I'm not. I've observed the way his mind works. He's clever, but even clever men resort to old habits when under stress. Why should he be any different?"

Reiniger paled. "When one of my men checked through the pile of music books on the piano, a handwritten sheet of music fell out. I thought nothing of it at the time."

"The note!" Margarete exclaimed. "You see, Herr Holm, I was right."

"We don't know that for certain, Fräulein." Although prepared to admit she might be right, Karl wouldn't without proof. "Reiniger, return to the safe house and find that sheet of music." It might be merely a piece of manuscript and nothing to do with Lehrer, but Karl couldn't afford to dismiss it. As much as it pained him to admit it, his gut feeling told him that in this case Margarete could be on to something.

"Very well, sir." Reiniger sounded relieved, and well he

should, having dismissed the very clue that might lead them to Lehrer. He saluted and turned to leave.

"Wait." Karl had a thought. Retrieving the note before Schmitz had read it might not be the wisest decision, as its absence might forewarn him that Karl was closing in. "Leave the note where it is, Reiniger, and tell the men you left on duty to move away from the house. They are to keep it under observation, but from a distance." He smiled. Yes, this would work so much better. "We already know where Lehrer is headed. This way, instead of splitting our manpower and risking alarming our prey and them slipping through our fingers once again—"

Margarete interrupted him by clapping her hands. "It's brilliant, Herr Holm. A very sensible plan indeed."

Reiniger looked puzzled. "I don't understand."

"It's simple, Herr Reiniger." Margarete leaned forward in her chair. "As Herr Holm has pointed out, we already know where Lehrer is heading. It stands to reason that if Schmitz has it confirmed when he reads the note, he'll go after him as quickly as possible. If he does, we'll wait until they're all together, and then we can catch them all at once."

"We?" Karl put a stop to that line of thought immediately. "Fräulein, I thank you for your assistance, but this is a military operation, and you are to retreat." Of course, there was always the risk that Lowe's team already knew Karl was privy to the information he'd been given, but so far they showed no sign of it. If that changed, he'd have to move more quickly and with force.

"Of course, Herr Holm." Margarete's tone suggested that doing anything else had never occurred to her. She smiled, this time a genuine one. "You will let me know when you have Lehrer, though, won't you? I'm growing impatient."

"Of course." After all, it wouldn't be long now before Karl was able to close the net once and for all. He was looking forward to it. All his prey together, trapped like rats with no way out.

CHAPTER SEVENTEEN

Michel was happy to be out of the city, and not only because they'd left the bombings behind. He only half listened to the conversation between Ken and Liang and instead found his thoughts wandering the closer they got to Freiburg. The houses, for the most part, had given way to farmland, and although it was winter, he could easily imagine what the vineyards would look like in the harvest season, branches heavy with fruit.

It reminded him of home and how badly he missed it. Although his family were wheat farmers, there were also several vineyards in the Seine-et-Marne area, and working the land was very much a part of who he was. Who he'd been before this war. Their farm had passed down from father to son through many generations, and one day it would be Michel's. If he closed his eyes, he could imagine watching a sunset with Kit while lying on their backs among fields of wheat, the gold of the fading sun reflecting the colour of Kit's hair.

"What exactly are we looking for again?" Liang peered

past Michel out the window on the right side of the truck. "There's nothing out here."

"There's supposed to be some kind of cottage." Ken didn't take his eyes off the road. "It's not much farther." Liang turned to look at him, eyebrow raised. "We're heading in the right direction," Ken explained, "and given the time I've been driving and the distance we needed to cover, we should see the road we need to turn down in the next few minutes and then another off that soon afterwards."

Michel couldn't help but chuckle at Ken's matter-of-fact tone. "My guess from the description and location is that it's a cottage used by seasonal workers. This area will look completely different in September when it's time for harvesting the grapes. It will be far from deserted."

"You both sound very sure of yourselves." Liang rolled his eyes.

"Logic and simple mathematics," Ken said. "Isn't that supposed to be your strong point, Liang?"

Liang shifted uncomfortably in his seat. "My back hurts," he complained. "It's distracting. Every time you go over a pothole, this excuse for a truck jars my whole body."

"You've never worked on a farm?" Michel asked, partly to distract Laing and because he was curious. Like Michel, Liang hadn't been very forthcoming with information. Once they completed their mission, he doubted any of them would see each other again.

"I've always lived in a city. I grew up in London and stayed there. I'm busy with my work, and going for a holiday in the country never appealed to me." Liang grimaced. "Cow pats and the smell that goes with them. I can't think of anything worse."

"There's a lot more to it than that, and some of the smells are quite pleasant." Michel grinned when Liang shot him a look of total disbelief. "You sound like Kit when you talk about work." Although Kit had spoken of wanting to see more of Germany, Michel doubted he would have ever taken the time away from his work to do so under normal circumstances. "When was the last time you had time off?"

"Two days in February last year," Liang said without hesitation.

"And you didn't take work home with you?" Michel asked.

"Of course not." Liang sounded indignant. "My grandparents' fiftieth wedding anniversary and my grandmother's seventieth birthday both fall in that month. If my grandmother suspected I was not properly celebrating either of them, I would have never heard the end of it." He sobered suddenly. "I wish I had a way to send word to them."

"Once the snow is gone enough so we can make our way safely to Switzerland, we will be able to organise getting home. You'll be able to see them again soon." Ken glanced at Michel. "Will you come back with us or go on to France?"

"I need to go home." Michel turned away and looked out the window again. And Kit would travel with Ken and the others to London and most likely on to America. Whatever his final destination, it would not be safe for him to stay in Europe until this war was over. Holm and his men would never give up looking for him.

"Home is not always exactly where you want to be." Liang smiled, and his gaze unfocused.

Michel shrugged but didn't reply. Ken had let something slip during their journey to Stuttgart that hinted Liang had fallen for a German girl. No names had been mentioned, and it was none of his business, so Michel hadn't asked, and he doubted Ken realised what he'd done.

Ken took a left turn onto a narrow road once they'd

passed the outbuildings of the winery. "Sometimes you have to grab tightly on to what you have because the alternative is unthinkable. Life doesn't always give the choices you think it's going to, and it doesn't take much to rip everything from under you."

"Very philosophical." Liang tilted his head to one side and studied Ken. "You surprise me at times with these bursts of insight."

"It sounded more like the voice of experience to me." Michel didn't want to think of the alternative either. "Which is it?"

"Something you need to figure out for yourself." Ken took another left turn, and they found themselves in front of a medium-sized cottage. It looked old but sturdy. Faded curtains hung from the shuttered windows. Behind it, rows of vines stretched up the hill into the distance. Under different circumstances the cottage might be thought of as homely. Or it would be, once someone like Michel's mother got hold of it. "This is it," Ken pulled in close to the side of the building. "Although it takes a while to get here, the cottage itself is very exposed. There's no way out if Holm and his men find it unless we head into the hills."

"I agree." Michel jumped out of the truck before Ken had turned off the engine. He sprinted to the front door. No noise came from inside, and although he hadn't seen anyone at the window, its inhabitants would be too wary of a trap to show themselves.

What if he'd arrived too late?

If Kit and the others had been discovered, their captors wouldn't have wasted time closing the front door. Michel hesitated. The safe house in Freudenstadt had appeared undisturbed until they'd made their way inside. Then it had told a different story.

Ken strode past him and knocked sharply on the front door. He then whistled a tune very loudly. It wasn't one Michel recognised.

An answering whistle came from inside, and then the door swung open. "Still swinging to Glenn Miller?" Matt grinned. "Ken. It's very good to see you again."

Michel pushed past Ken. "Kit..." He remembered too late the code name Kristopher was using. He wouldn't have told Matt his real identity. "Is Paul here? Is he safe?"

"Michel." Kit stood behind Matt. He'd been out of sight of the door. He took a step towards Michel, then stopped. "You're all right?" His voice was strained and shaking. "You're all right."

"I'm all right." There was so much Michel wanted to say, and he badly needed to take Kit in his arms and hold him tightly. He forced himself to appear calm. "You?"

"Fine." Kit smiled, his face lit up. He had a day's growth of beard, although the blond whiskers were barely noticeable and in stark contrast to the dark colour of his dyed hair. His eyes were bleary, as though he'd just woken up from sleep.

Michel walked into the main room, getting out of the way so Liang and Ken could enter. The movement brought him closer to Kit, who lightly brushed his arm against Michel's. The familiar warmth of close contact made him smile before he could stop himself.

"The cottage isn't very big, but it's somewhere to hide for a few days." Matt glanced outside, then shut the door behind them. "Although I don't think we were followed, I don't want to stay here too long. There's a hidden tunnel out through the cellar. I'm hoping we don't need to use it as it looks narrow, and we'd have to crawl through."

"I was careful not to be followed either, but I think

moving on is sensible, especially as the last safe house was compromised." Ken yawned. "It was a long drive, and we didn't get much sleep last night. I'd like to get some before we work out our next move."

Liang sat on one of the two couches in the room. Michel recognised the man lying on the other one with his leg propped up. Leo. He looked tired and pale.

"What about some introductions before we go further? Now we've established everyone is fine, that is." Liang stretched and grimaced. "Or rather that some of us are fine. I, for one, am bloody sore and looking forward to not sitting in that truck again for some considerable time." He looked up at Kit. "You're Lehrer. I recognise you from your picture."

"Yes, I am." Kit walked over to Liang and held out his hand. "Dr Kristopher Lehrer. I know Michel, but I haven't met you or Herr Lowe. Matt's told me about you, though, and your role on the team."

"Dr Zhou Liang. Liang. I don't see the point in formality, given the situation. You're not an easy man to find. We need to make some time to talk, and soon."

"You need to know whether the information I have is genuine." Kit nodded his understanding. "That's fair enough. I would do the same in your situation. I will answer your questions as best I can."

Leo looked from one man to the other. "I still have no idea what's really going on. It's one of those top secret hush-hush things I'm probably not cleared for, isn't it? I guessed that much when I found out Kristopher was using an assumed name. I'm Leo, by the way. Michel and I have already met."

"Ken Lowe. Michel has told me about your meeting. Dr Lehrer..." Matt coughed loudly. "Kristopher," Ken amended, shifting his attention to Kit. "I was beginning to think this was a wild goose chase." He looked him up and down. "Despite knowing you were Fräulein Lehrer's younger brother, I expected someone older, given your reputation."

"Have you heard anything of Clara?" Kristopher asked.

Michel shook his head. "I'm sorry. Nothing new." So many people had been arrested, and it was difficult to find information about what had happened to them.

"There's two bunk rooms. Why don't Ken and I take one, and I can brief him on what's happened since we got separated." Matt frowned when Liang shifted uncomfortably. "Was it you who was captured? You're moving like you're injured."

"Reiniger had him in custody," Ken said quickly before Liang could answer. Matt glanced at Liang, and his expression darkened, but he didn't say anything. Matt had dark circles under his eyes, as though he hadn't slept well for several days. "I'll debrief you in the bunk room," Ken continued. "Liang needs rest, and he's not the only one." He took off the bag he carried and hung it over the coat hook by the door, hiding it under his coat once he'd removed it.

"Good idea. You all need to get some rest while you can. I don't know how long it's going to be before all hell breaks loose. Kristopher, show Michel the other bunk room. He could probably do with some sleep, and this debrief with Ken is going to take some time." Matt nodded towards Liang. "The couch's more comfortable than the bunk beds. Have you got pain medication for your back?"

Liang nodded. "I have some, and I'll take more soon. In the meantime, Leo and I can get acquainted." Neither Ken nor Liang had mentioned where Liang's injuries were. Matt must have worked out what had happened.

"I think Matt's idea is a good one." Michel wasn't about to turn down the opportunity to speak to Kit alone. Ken and Matt had wasted no time in leaving the room following Liang's reply, and Michel wasn't going to either. "There is much Kit and I need to talk about too."

"If you need anything call out," Kit told Leo. "Try and get some rest." He sounded worried. Whatever was going on with Leo couldn't be good.

Kit led Michel through the other door into the other bunk room. "You called me Kit." He shut the door behind them. "I've missed that... missed you so much."

"Kit," Michel whispered. "Mon cher... I..." His words were swallowed by Kit kissing him, hard and desperate. He leaned into it, running his hands over Kit's body, touching him anywhere he could reach.

When they broke the kiss, they were both breathing heavily. "I thought I'd never see you again. I was scared I'd lost you." Kit looked around the room, grabbed a chair, and shoved it under the door handle.

"Kit?" Michel could see the hunger in Kit's eyes. Hunger, desire, and need. Michel yanked off his gun holster and the rest of his gear, but his fingers fumbled on his coat buttons. Kit helped him undo them. The coat fell to the floor.

Kit pushed Michel back against the wall. He kissed him again, already reaching for Michel's fly, stroking him through his trousers. "I want you. So badly. I need to know you're real. That this is real. I..." Kit choked on his words. "I... Please. In case there is no next time. In case this is all that's left of our future. I want it. I want you now."

"Mon cher." Michel pulled Kit's shirt from his trousers. He kept his voice low, like Kit, so they wouldn't be overheard. "Ich liebe dich, Kit. I want you too, but we need to be quiet." As much as he wanted this, wanted Kit, he didn't trust the others enough for them to find out about this, about Kit and him and what they truly felt for each other.

"Quiet," whispered Kit. "Je t'aime, Michel." He undid Michel's belt and the top button of his fly and slipped his hand inside. "Touch me. I want to feel you. I'm yours."

Michel backed them across the room to one of the bottom bunks. He lowered Kit onto it and climbed on top of him, kissed him hard, their tongues sliding against each other, tasting, touching. This was real, not a dream. Real. Like Kit wanted it to be. Like he *needed* it to be. Michel lifted Kit's hips, dragging down his trousers as he felt his own being yanked off. Bare skin against bare skin. Heat started to build. He groaned. Kit kissed him again, silencing him.

"Quiet," Kit whispered. He unbuttoned Michel's shirt, nipped Michel's collarbone and dragged his teeth over it. "You taste so good."

Michel helped Kit out of his shirt and wrapped his arms around Kit, their bodies tangling together, moving against each other.

They had no lubrication to aid their joining. At this rate it wouldn't be necessary. Neither of them would last that long. Michel didn't want to. He wanted Kit.

"I love you. You're mine." Michel buried his head in Kit's shoulder. Their movements sped up.

"Yours," Kit gasped. He ran his hands up and down Michel's bare back. "Oh... oh."

Faster. Frantic. Michel bit his lip to stop crying out. Heat pooled in his groin, spread out. He linked his fingers with Kit's as they came together, held him tightly and shuddered, trying to catch his breath.

"I thought I'd lost you," he whispered, his voice cracked.

"Oh, Kit. I thought I'd lost you. I knew someone had been caught. I thought it was you."

"I know." Kit sobbed, shivering. He curled around Michel. "I was so scared it was you. I kept... Michel. I don't want anyone to hurt you. I don't want you to die."

Michel ran his fingers through Kit's hair. Kissed his forehead. "I've got you now. I'm here. I've got you." He held Kit close. The few nights they'd spent apart, Michel had fooled himself into thinking that although it would be difficult, he could let Kit go. He was wrong. He wanted this, wanted him. They'd hide their relationship in public, they'd have to, but he couldn't give up their time together in private.

To hell with this war. Why couldn't it end and leave them alone to live out their lives together in peace?

"Stay with me," Michel whispered. "Just for a while? I need to know this is real too."

"It's real," Kit said, "and I'll stay. For as long as I can, I'll stay."

It was such a relief to be finally out of the truck. Liang swore his bruises now had bruises. The ointment Dr Osterhagen had used on his back was simply wonderful, but it wasn't a miracle cure by a long shot. Leo had been watching him since the rest of the team had deserted them. However, he hadn't ventured forth with anything resembling conversation yet.

Liang sighed. He supposed he should do the right thing and get the ball rolling on that one. It would be a welcome distraction from his own thoughts. "So... Leo, isn't it? Do you have a girlfriend at home?"

"Yes, I do." Leo looked surprised by the question. Why hadn't Matt or Kristopher thought to ask him during the time they'd spent together? "Her name is Mary. We've been friends since school, but I finally got the nerve up to ask her out a week before I had to leave." He smiled when he spoke of her. Despite his downplaying of their date, Liang suspected Leo was in love with the girl. His face lit up as soon as he mentioned her name.

"It's often good to get to know someone first before you ask them out." Liang's parents had been friends before they'd admitted their love for each other. It hadn't been easy for a white woman and a Chinese man together, and it had taken a while for both families to come around to the idea. How would his grandparents react when he told them about Juliane?

"Do you have a girlfriend at home too?" Leo took a long drink of water. His skin was flushed, and he didn't look at all well.

"No," Liang said, "although..." Was Juliane his girlfriend? They hadn't dated, hadn't had the chance to given the circumstances, but he loved her, and if they both survived this war and found each other again, he fully intended to ask her to marry him if she'd have him. "There is someone," he admitted. "This war has changed so much. Relationships are more complicated than they used to be."

Why was he telling Leo about her? They'd only just met. This war was complicating far more than relationships. Traditional social etiquette seemed rather a waste of time under the circumstances. For all either of them knew, this might be the first and last time they had the opportunity to talk. He'd made friends over the past few months who he never would have met otherwise and he'd probably never see or hear from again once this was over. Their group was a diverse one, given their nationalities and backgrounds.

"You don't have to talk about her if you don't want to." Leo leaned back on the sofa, wincing when he moved his leg. "You don't have to listen to me talk about Mary either. I guess I wanted to talk about her so someone else knows she exists. It's so easy to think she's not real. I close my eyes, and it's getting harder to picture her face."

"You could have talked to someone else about her."

"Matt and Paul—Kristopher—have got a lot on their minds. They've been really worried about their friends, although both of them have tried to hide it." Leo glanced in the direction of the bunk rooms. "I'm glad they got to spend some time together before..." He bit his lip.

Liang hadn't thought he'd hear that turn of phrase from Leo. While he'd recognised something of his own feelings for Juliane in the way Ken and Michel spoke of Matt and Kristopher, he'd doubted anyone else had.

Noticing something familiar made it easier to spot.

Or perhaps Liang had read too much into Leo's last comment because of his own observations?

"It's important to spend time with those you—" Not about to voice his suspicions aloud, Liang chose his words carefully. The past few months had shattered his ideas about what he considered acceptable and not. "—care about." To hell with it. They could all be dead tomorrow. People deserved to grab happiness wherever and with whomever they could.

"I've written a letter to Mary. Could you make sure she gets it?" Leo fingered something under his shirt, around his neck. "I also have a dog tag that belonged to a friend. Mary knows Alec's wife. She'd make sure she gets it."

"You could give it to her yourself," Liang suggested.

Leo made a half-strangled noise somewhere between a laugh and a sob. "You're more likely to get out of this alive than I am." He pointed to his leg. "I've seen the worry in Kristopher's eyes. I know how I'm feeling, and enough to know the sulphanilamide isn't working. My leg's infected, I can barely walk, and I feel like hell. If we're surrounded, I'll only slow you down. I'd surrender to the Germans first." He looked away. "I'm not going home without a leg. Mary doesn't deserve that."

"She won't care if she loves you." How the hell had Liang ended up having this conversation with someone he barely knew? Matt was better at this kind of thing. "Matt won't let you be left behind. We don't do that."

He cringed inwardly. They'd already lost two of their own. Walker had died in the aftermath of the institute bombing. Palmer was in custody and in some POW camp somewhere.

"If she doesn't care, I will." Leo shrugged. "I appreciate the sentiment, although you might not have a choice. Isn't it better that you escape rather than we're all captured because of me? I don't know what's going on with this mission of yours and why the Gestapo are after Kristopher, but it's important to the war effort, right?"

"Yes, it's important to the war effort." Liang didn't want to tell Leo any more than that. The information being classified aside, it would only probably make him more determined to play the hero.

A cough from the doorway made him turn. Kristopher stood there, paper and pencils in hand. He was flushed, and he had a sad look in his eyes. How much had he overheard?

"Excuse me for interrupting," he said, "but you and I need to talk, Liang."

"Do you mind?" Liang asked Leo. "We'll go somewhere else. Don't move."

"You mean I can't go outside and do a few laps?" Leo grinned as though their conversation had never happened. He was putting on a brave face, but Liang doubted Kristopher was fooled by it either.

"I don't think that would be a good idea." Kristopher gestured to Liang. "We can talk in the kitchen. There's a table we can use too, and a stove. Is there anything you need, Leo?"

"A new leg?" Leo shook his head. "Sorry, that was probably in bad taste, but if I don't joke about this, I'm going to..."

"I know. I'm sorry. I won't be long. I promise." Kristopher walked past Leo, pausing to place a hand on his shoulder for a brief moment before continuing on to the kitchen. Liang followed.

"The poor blighter knows his leg isn't going to get better." Liang lowered his voice. "You're not doing him any favours by not telling him the truth."

Kristopher sat down heavily on one of the kitchen chairs. "I know that. Clara always knew what to say to her patients and how to say it. I'm no doctor. Hell, I'm not even the medic I've pretended to be, but every time I change his bandages I can see it's worse." He grimaced. "It smells, the area around it is red and feels very hot, and there's yellow pus coming out of it. I don't know what else to do. He's taking the medicine we were given for him, and it's not doing anything. I've tried to clean it out. Matt even cauterised it."

"He'll probably lose the leg." Liang doubted any of them would get out of this without some sort of trauma. If only he could remember the details of what had happened to him. Despite it being important, every time he tried, he felt sick to his stomach and had the overwhelming urge to run as fast as he could in the opposite direction.

"He needs a doctor before the infection spreads and kills him. How are we supposed to get a doctor out here? Michel thinks it's only a matter of time before Holm's men find us."

"None of this is your fault. We do what we can under the circumstances, and that's all any of us can do." Liang pulled up another of the chairs and sat down next to Kristopher.

"I suppose." Kristopher looked up at Liang after a few moments' silence. "I've tried to explain to Michel and Matt about the project we were working on at the institute. They understand what it's capable of but not how it works or if it's capable of working. Matt told me it sounds like something out of an H.G. Wells story."

"They're not physicists." Liang took a deep breath. "I haven't seen any sign of the plans yet. Michel said they were in your head and that you have a very good memory. I need more than that."

"That's what the paper is for." Kristopher laid out several sheets on the table. "I found it and the pencils stuffed in one of the drawers in the bunk room shortly after we arrived." He began to sketch. "I do have the plans and the formulae in my head, as Michel said."

"All of it?"

"All of it," Kristopher confirmed. "I have an eidetic memory. Sometimes I think it's a blessing, other times a curse."

"I've never met anyone with one of those before. You remember everything?"

"Not everything, but mostly everything." Kristopher

continued sketching and scribbled a couple of formulae over the diagram he'd drawn. "It's easier to remember what I've seen than what I've heard. That's how it works for me, anyway."

"Does Holm know about your memory?" Liang leaned in to examine Kristopher's drawing. He let out a sharp breath and quickly scanned the rest of the page. "Bloody hell," he said. "This could very well be the real thing."

"It is the real thing." Kristopher paused, pencil in hand. "I don't know about Holm. Dr Kluge knew, and he could have told him."

"No wonder the Nazis are so determined to get their hands on you."

Liang read over the formulae, doing calculations in his mind. He'd had his reservations when he'd been briefed about this weapon and its potential. He hadn't wanted to believe it, yet what Kristopher had drawn—it was real. Oh God, this was real. He'd seen something similar to this, although not as advanced. The plans Liang was looking at appeared to be for a device that had the potential to channel atomic energy into something that could benefit mankind, but it wouldn't be used for that. Not during a war, with each side desperate for a way to end it. He picked up one of the pencils Kristopher had left on the table and added something to the plans. A slight alteration to the blueprint itself and a formula he'd been shown during a long discussion with one of the scientists brought in to prove that Liang did in fact know enough to be worth the risk of sending a Chinese man into Nazi Germany. On its own it meant nothing, but Kristopher would understand the implication of what Liang had written. Of that Liang was certain.

"What you've written is what we originally had." Kristopher crossed one symbol out and added another. A few more strokes of his pencil and the look of the device he'd drawn began to change into something much more deadly. Kristopher stood back for a moment, surveying what he'd done instead of finishing what he'd very obviously set out to complete. It didn't matter. He'd already demonstrated very clearly what his ideas would most likely be used for. "The answer puzzled both of us for weeks, but then I figured out what we were missing just before Kluge died."

"So no one knows but you?"

Kristopher shook his head. "And now you." He ran one hand through his hair, his shoulders sagging a little as though he had the weight of the world on them. "I've been carrying this around for months with no one to talk to about it. I think the answer I have solves the problem, don't you?"

"I think it could, yes," Liang said, "but I can't be sure." While he recognised what he was looking at, he was in the company of a man way out of his league. "You're a brilliant man, Dr Lehrer."

"I don't feel particularly brilliant." Kristopher snorted. "If I was, I wouldn't be here now with the plans to a weapon that should never be built and which I helped design. I think idiot is more accurate, don't you? The more I've seen of this war, the more convinced I am that this is not a weapon either side should have access to." He indicated the paper. "Have you seen enough? It makes me nervous having it in plain sight like this."

"I've seen enough."

Kristopher folded up the papers and then walked over to the stove. He lifted the lid to the fire beneath it and began to rip the plans he'd drawn into small pieces, which he fed into the stove. Scientific history in the making that could well have been destroyed forever. Liang wasn't sure whether to be awed by the potential of this weapon or be scared shitless by it.

"You're serious, aren't you? About *neither* side having access to it?"

"Yes, I am." Kristopher used a small poker to destroy any evidence, flames turning white paper to black ashes. "I haven't made a final decision yet, though."

"If you have, it wouldn't be wise to say so," Liang said. "After all, I doubt London would be as willing to arrange your escape from Germany if they thought you weren't going to cooperate once you got to England." He rubbed at his itchy, heavy eyes. He swallowed a yawn. "Either side could still work out the information they're missing, even if you aren't the one to tell them. They could build this bomb."

"That's what scares me, but I keep telling myself that if they do, at least they haven't got it from me." Kristopher filled the kettle with water and put it on the stove to heat. "I was in Feuerbach when the bombs fell. I saw the damage they did. This would make that look like nothing." He brought three mugs over to the table, his expression eerily calm. Whatever he was feeling, he kept hidden. "Michel," he explained when Liang raised an eyebrow. "He was giving me time to talk to you. I promised him some tea when we were done."

As though on cue, Michel appeared in the doorway. How much of the conversation had he heard?

"And you always keep your promises. Sit down, Kit. I'll make the tea."

"He's told you about the weapon?" Liang remembered too late that Kristopher had already said he had.

"Yes." Michel was watching Kristopher and frowning. "Do you want to sleep after this? You're tired."

Kristopher shook his head. "No." His gaze kept flitting back to Michel, as though trying to convince himself Michel was still there. "I have nightmares about this weapon and what it will do."

Liang got the impression the comment was made to him, although Kristopher looked at Michel when he spoke. "Nightmares are not reality," Liang reminded him firmly. "They're often our subconscious prompting us not to take the paths in life we are tempted to. Make your decision. Perhaps it will help." He massaged his temples, feeling the beginnings of a headache.

"Perhaps it is you who needs to sleep?" Kristopher suggested. "Michel told me what happened to you. I'm sorry."

"I hope you won't be." Liang grimaced.

"What do you mean by that?" Michel took the kettle from the stove when it began to boil. "You told us you couldn't remember most of what had happened."

"That is what worries me," Liang admitted. He looked up at both men, not missing the way Michel moved closer to Kristopher. Now he'd seen them interacting, Liang was more convinced his suspicion about their friendship was correct. "Reiniger found out about the location of the safe house somehow."

"You think it might have been from you?" Michel asked. Kristopher had gone quiet and very pale.

"I don't know! I just don't know." Why couldn't he remember? Liang remembered the rest of it with such clarity, to the point where he could almost feel the edge of the whip burning against his skin. But after he'd screamed "no more" it was as though someone or something had pulled a curtain down between him and his memories until he'd woken again in his cell.

"What else are you thinking?" Michel glanced at Kristopher. "I know there's more. I can hear it in your voice."

"What if it wasn't only that safe house he knows about?" Liang whispered, no longer able to ignore the growing feeling of dread he'd pushed aside since they'd arrived. "What if that's why Ken didn't think he was followed? After all, there's no need to follow someone if you already know where they're going, is there?"

CHAPTER EIGHTEEN

Leo stumbled into the kitchen. "There's someone outside! I thought I heard voices."

"Keep out of sight and stay here," Michel ordered. "I'll go take a look. If there is someone out there, we don't want to alert them that we know."

Kristopher opened his mouth to tell Michel he'd come with him but stopped when he saw the worried look on Michel's face. "I'll stay here."

It only took a few minutes before Michel returned, Matt and Ken close behind him. Michel handed Kristopher his gun and coat. "Not a good idea to let that out of your sight, and you'll need your coat for later too."

"If we're surrounded, I doubt one gun is going to make much of a difference." Kristopher took it anyway. "Are we surrounded?"

Matt nodded grimly. "On all sides. Ken spotted our mutual friend Reiniger outside. He has several men with him."

"Kristopher's right," Ken said. "Shooting our way out is not an option. We're going to have to make a run for it."

Leo paled. "Through that tunnel in the cellar?" He shook his head. "You told me it's not much more than a crawl space. I'd hoped it wouldn't come to that. I'll never make it."

"What about some kind of stretcher to drag you through?" Kristopher suggested.

"We don't have time for it." Ken glanced at Matt. "If we're going to run, we need to do it now."

"What about supplies?" Liang helped Matt to push back the table and open the trapdoor that led to the cellar.

"There isn't enough room for them," Matt said. "If we don't get out of here, supplies are going to be the least of our problems."

"If there's not enough room for that, a stretcher wouldn't work either. We can't leave Leo behind!" Kristopher caught Michel by the arm. "We can't leave him behind. There must be some other way."

"Sometimes there isn't a choice, Kit." Michel glanced at Leo. He wouldn't look Kristopher in the eye.

Kristopher nodded unhappily.

Ken had already climbed down the ladder into the cellar. "There's another trapdoor down here, with a ladder leading down several feet into a tunnel that narrows into a crawl space a couple of feet in," he called up into the kitchen. "I'll lead and Michel will bring up the rear. There are a couple of flashlights down here. I'll take one. Matt, you take the other."

"Leo?" Kristopher asked again.

Leo took a step forward. He gasped in pain. "I can't do this," he whispered. "I can't. I won't die in some hole in the ground. I... I can't."

"Get going, Liang." Matt shoved Liang towards the cellar. "Kristopher, you're next." He glanced at Michel when Kristopher hesitated. "We don't have time to argue about this."

"Give me your gun." Leo held out his hand to Kristopher. "I'm not going with you, but I want to be armed. If I can hold them off and make them believe you're all here, it could buy you some time. Quickly now. Move!"

"They'll kill you!" Kristopher gave Leo his gun reluctantly.

"If I go with you, there's a good chance we'll all die." Leo took the gun and smiled grimly. Despite the determined set of his jaw, he looked so very young. Too young to have his life snuffed out before it had really begun. "I'll surrender before they get the chance to kill me," he said softly when Kristopher gave him a brief hug. "Get whatever information you have to the Allies. Make a difference to this bloody war. Finish it."

Kristopher nodded. He turned his back and climbed down into the cellar. Matt and Michel exchanged words with Leo, all three men speaking too low to be understood. Ken already had the trapdoor in the cellar open and was halfway down the ladder leading into the tunnel, Liang behind him. Kristopher followed Liang quickly. When the ladder moved above him, he dropped to the ground to give Matt room to follow.

Matt landed with a light thud on the dirt floor of the tunnel, not bothering to climb the last few rungs of the ladder. Michel followed him down the ladder a few seconds later. The trapdoor closed behind him, plunging them into darkness apart from the light from Ken's flashlight ahead.

"Get going!" Michel hissed.

A sharp click sounded above. Leo had locked the cellar door behind them. There was no way to go now but further into the darkness.

Kristopher edged forward, using his elbows to pull himself along when the tunnel narrowed. The ground was damp and cold, with barely enough room to move. Ken had been right. How long did it go on like this?

The sound of breathing filled the silence, each of his friends probably focused on moving forward and getting to the end of this nightmare. Kristopher gritted his teeth. He raised his head and knocked it against the ceiling.

Up ahead, Liang grunted in pain.

"Quiet," whispered Ken.

Kristopher heard laboured breathing behind him. "Are you all right?" He stopped crawling.

"Keep moving," Michel said.

"I can't." Matt sounded panicked. "I can't see. There's nothing here. There's no way out." He made a scrambling noise. "I've got to get out."

"You dropped your flashlight." Michel's calm tone did nothing to reassure Matt, whose breathing sped up. "Here it is." Kristopher glanced back and saw the dim glow of light.

The flashlight dropped to the ground. "Put it out. Put it out." Matt's voice rose with his panic. "You'll start a fire."

Kristopher edged backwards. "Matt," he whispered, remembering Matt's nightmare. "It's not a candle. It's a flashlight. It's safe. I promise you it's safe." He felt around in the darkness until he found it and shone it back towards Matt. "You're all right. We're all fine."

"What's going on back there?" Ken shone the flashlight in their direction. "Matt?"

"Ken?" Matt sounded confused. His voice shook. "You need to get out of here. God, please. You need to get out."

Ken swore under his breath, but his next words were slow and measured. "Listen to me, Matt. You can hear me, right?"

"I... I can hear you." Matt said hoarsely. He was breathing heavily. "I... I can't do this. I can hear you, but you're not here. I can't do this."

"I *am* here. I'm fine, but I need you to crawl toward me. I need you to be safe too." Ken's voice hitched. "Please, Matt. I'll look after you. I promise you. Can you promise me too?"

"I can... try."

The ceiling shook above them. Dirt rained down. Kristopher coughed. "It's fine. Ken's right. You need to crawl, and now."

"I'm crawling." Matt spoke barely above a whisper. "I'm crawling." He repeated the words over and over through gritted teeth.

"Crawl, Kit," Michel called. "The tunnel..." He didn't need to finish his warning. The tunnel was unstable. They needed to get out of it, and quickly. "Keep the light shining. Matt needs to see the light."

Crawl? Crawling would be a luxury. Kristopher's elbows hurt. He focused on dragging himself forward. One arm, then the next, one arm, then the next, holding on to the torch in one hand as though his life depended on it.

"The tunnel's widening," Ken told them after what felt like forever. How long was this hellish tunnel?

"Can you stand?" Matt asked. "Tell me you can stand."

"I will be able to soon." Ken swung the flashlight around. He made a frustrated noise and swore again.

"What's wrong?" Liang asked. "Something's wrong, isn't it? Hold the light steady so I can see."

"Nothing's wrong." Ken stopped moving. The light he carried reflected higher than a few moments before. That was a good sign, wasn't it?

They'd be out of there soon. It couldn't go on forever.

The ceiling didn't feel as close as it had, although the floor had developed a slight slope. Had they been crawling upwards? Kristopher gingerly got up on his knees. His head didn't connect with the ceiling anymore. He spread one arm out, judging the distance between the walls. The tunnel was definitely widening out. "Thank God," he murmured.

Another few metres and he could finally stand. His muscles protested when he pulled himself upright. Ken and Liang waited just ahead. Why weren't they moving forward?

"What's wrong?" Kristopher asked.

Matt caught up to them. Kristopher handed him the flashlight, and he shone it in Ken's direction. "A dead end. I don't fucking believe it!" Matt looked around, his earlier panic showing on his face. "There has to be a way out. There has to be." He beat his hands against the wall. All it did was bring loose dirt down on him. He began to cough.

"Stop it," Ken said sharply. "There's an exit," he continued softly. "Don't worry, there's an exit. We'll get out of here." He pulled Matt away from the wall and whispered something to him.

"I know. I'm sorry." Matt pushed back against the wall and hugged himself. "I'm sorry."

"It's all right. We all have nightmares. It's nearly over now. We'll be out of here soon." Kristopher wished he believed that.

"They wouldn't build a tunnel without an escape route at the other end." Michel brushed his hand against Kristopher's back, a gentle reminder he wasn't alone.

"Up there!" Ken shone light onto a ladder attached partway up on the opposite wall. It looked identical to the one they'd entered the tunnel by. He swung up onto it and began to climb.

Matt strode over to the bottom of the ladder and shone his flashlight upwards. "I can see it!" He didn't take his eyes off Ken.

"Let's hope the trapdoor at the top isn't locked," Liang said dryly.

"Are you always this pessimistic?" Michel asked.

"I prefer the word *practical*." Liang shrugged, a shadowy movement in the dim light. "If we can't get it open, perhaps we could throw you at it?"

"Keep the noise down." Matt sounded more like himself now they'd found a way out, although he hadn't lost the shake in his voice. He peered up at Ken, who had wound both legs around a rung of the ladder to anchor himself and was giving the trapdoor a shove. "Any luck?"

"It's stiff, but it's opening." Ken put his shoulder behind it, gave one last heave, and opened it a fraction. He peered through cautiously before opening it completely, filling the tunnel with light. He climbed the rest of the way and pulled himself over the edge. "It's all clear. Matt you're next, then Liang and Kristopher."

Kristopher blinked against the light when he was finally topside. It took him a few moments to get his bearings. Ken closed the trapdoor once they were out. Vines stood on either side of them. The cottage they'd fled was in the distance into the valley. They were now halfway up the hill overlooking it. Michel ducked down below the top of the vines, motioning the others to follow his lead.

Soldiers milled around the cottage. One shot sounded, then another. They seemed to be coming from inside. Leo. Shots were returned in quick succession. Someone yelled an order, probably Reiniger, but Kristopher was too far away for the words to be understood.

"Leo told me he'd surrender," Kristopher said. They

were safe now, although Leo had no way of knowing. "If he doesn't give himself up soon, it will be too late."

"He did?" Liang spoke sharply, blood draining from his face. "He told me… Bloody hell, Leo." He turned to Kristopher. "You didn't actually believe him, did you?"

"What did he say to you?" asked Matt.

"He told me—"

An explosion cut off whatever Liang was about to say. The ground rocked beneath them. Michel caught Kristopher's arm, steadying him before he could lose his balance.

"What the hell was that?" Liang asked.

"Fuck!" Ken shoved his hands into his pockets. His face was ashen. "Leo found the dynamite. He must have." He stood long enough to peer into the distance. "Half the cottage is gone."

"Reiniger knew. He knew about this safe house." Liang sat down with a soft thud. "I must have told him. I must have told him. This is my fault, isn't it?"

"It's no one's fault. If you did, you did. You were tortured, and badly." Matt sounded more thoughtful than anything else. "We can't go near any of the safe houses we'd already discussed. We'll have to presume Reiniger and Holm know we're heading for Switzerland and where we're planning to cross over."

"There's more than one way out of Germany," Michel reminded them. "I have contacts in the French Resistance."

"Cross the border into France and then head for the Channel?" Ken didn't look convinced. "It's a huge risk."

"Switzerland is more of one," Michel said. "They could be waiting for us at any point of our journey. It makes sense to do something they won't expect and we'd never talked about."

Kristopher looked around the group of men he now

dared to call his friends. They'd made it this far with the odds stacked against them. Although he'd told Michel he'd stay with him as long as he could, he could already see their future slipping through his fingers. "Leo made a choice. I agree with Matt that we should honour it, and how better to do that than making one too?" Kristopher glanced at Michel. "Michel's suggestion is a good one."

"If you're heading to France, then so are we." Matt made the decision for his team. "We lost you once before. I'm not doing it again. We've got a mission to complete, right?"

"Right." Ken echoed the sentiment. "France it is, then."

"I'm not getting left behind," Liang said.

"It's settled, then." Matt glanced at what was left of the cottage. "But for now, let's get away from here and find somewhere to shelter before nightfall. We've got a long journey ahead."

Karl leaned back in his chair and studied the man standing in front of him. He was quickly losing patience with Reiniger, who had done nothing to redeem himself since returning to active duty. Several weeks had passed since the incident at Freiburg, and they were no closer to finding Lowe and his team.

"I hope you have good news for me, Obersturmführer Reiniger."

Reiniger raised his head and met Karl's gaze directly. The patch only partially covered the scarred skin over his missing right eye. This mission to find their prey and the plans Lehrer possessed had become somewhat of a personal vendetta for him. His mindset was not necessarily a bad thing as it would provide him with the focus he'd so obviously been lacking in the past.

"There was definitely only one body discovered in the remains of the cottage, Herr Standartenführer. The tunnel beneath it has not provided any further clues."

"Tell me something I don't already know, Obersturmführer." Karl grew tired of Reiniger's report. Why was he wasting time repeating information? "Did the list of safe houses provide anything further?"

"No, sir. There have been no sightings of the fugitives anywhere, and I have men posted at all the locations we were given." Reiniger frowned. He had a distinct twitch over his eye that hadn't been there before his injury. "Is it possible that the prisoner gave false information?"

"Possible, but I doubt it. It's more likely that they realised we discovered their original plans and have decided to change them because of it. Well," Karl said thoughtfully, "there is really only one response to such a move." He had always enjoyed a decent game of chess, especially against a player who provided rather more of a challenge. "If they have changed their strategy, so should we." He steepled his fingers, glanced at the report on his desk, and smiled.

ABOUT THE AUTHOR

CONNECT WITH ANNE

Contact me at:
annebarwell.wordpress.com
darthanne@gmail.com

Anne Barwell lives in Wellington, New Zealand. She shares her home with Kaylee: a cat with "tortitude" who is convinced that the house is run to suit her; this is an ongoing "discussion," and to date, it appears as though Kaylee may be winning.

In 2008, Anne completed her conjoint BA in English Literature and Music/Bachelor of Teaching. She has worked as a music teacher, a primary school teacher, and now works in a library. She is a member of the Upper Hutt Science Fiction Club and plays violin for Hutt Valley Orchestra.

She is an avid reader across a wide range of genres and a watcher of far too many TV series and movies, although it can be argued that there is no such thing as "too many." These, of course, are best enjoyed with a decent cup of tea and further the continuing argument that the concept of "spare time" is really just a myth. She also hosts and reviews for other authors, and writes monthly blog posts for Love

Bytes. She is the co-founder of the New Zealand Rainbow Romance writers, and a member of RWNZ.

Anne's books have received honourable mentions five times, reached the finals four times—one of which was for best gay book—and been a runner up in the Rainbow Awards. She has also been nominated three times in the Goodreads M/M Romance Reader's Choice Awards—twice for Best Fantasy, once for Best Historical, and once for All-Time Favourite M/M Author.

Shadowboxing

Complete their mission or lose everything.

Berlin, 1943

An encounter with an old friend leaves German physicist Dr Kristopher Lehrer with doubts about his work. But when he confronts his superior, everything goes horribly wrong. Suddenly Kristopher and Michel, a member of the Resistance, are on the run, hunted for treason and a murder they did not commit. If they're caught, Kristopher's knowledge could be used to build a terrible weapon that could win the war.

For the team sent by the Allies—led by Captain Bryant, Sergeant Lowe, and Dr Zhou—a simple mission escalates into a deadly game against the Gestapo, with Dr Lehrer as the ultimate prize. But in enemy territory, surviving and completing their mission will test their strengths and loyalties and prove more complex than they ever imagined.

ECHOES RISING BOOK 3

Comes a Horseman

What if those who stand by you are the ones who betray you?

France, 1944

Sometimes the most desperate struggles take place far from the battlefield, and what happens in secret can change the course of history.

Victory is close at hand, but freedom remains frustratingly just beyond the grasp of German physicist Dr Kristopher Lehrer, Resistance fighter Michel, and the remaining members of the team sent by the Allies—Captain Matt Bryant, Sergeant Ken Lowe, and Dr Zhou Liang—as they fight to keep the atomic plans from the Nazis. The team reaches France and connects with members of Michel's French Resistance cell in Normandy. Allied troops are poised to liberate France, and rescue is supposedly at hand. However, Kristopher is no longer sure the information he carries in his memory is safe with either side.

When Standartenführer Holm and his men finally catch up with their prey, the team is left with few options as they fight to keep atomic plans from the Nazis. With a traitor in their midst, who can they trust? Kristopher must become something he is not in order to save the man he loves. Death is biding his time, and sacrifices must be made for any of them to have the futures they want.

www.ingramcontent.com/pod-product-compliance
Lightning Source LLC
Chambersburg PA
CBHW072256130726
47910CB00012B/2026